JADED SPRING

ALSO BY KRISTEN MARTIN

THE BESTSELLING SHADOW CROWN SERIES

Shadow Crown

Renegade Cruex

THE BESTSELLING ALPHA DRIVE SERIES

The Alpha Drive

The Order of Omega

Restitution

JADED
SPRING

BOOK THREE

KRISTEN MARTIN

BLACK FALCON PRESS

For my readers – without you, my stories would never see the light of day. Thank you for supporting me and loving my characters as fiercely as I do.

PRONUNCIATION GUIDE

CHARACTERS

Arden: Ar-den

Rydan: Ry-den

Darius: Dare-ee-us

Aldreda: Al-dray-duh

Cerylia: Sur-lee-uh

Braxton: Brax-ten

Xerin: Zer-in

PLACES

Trendalath: Tren-duh-loth

Sardoria: Sar-door-ee-uh

Vaekith: Vy-kith

Orihia: Or-eye-uh

Ipcea: Ip-see

Chialka: Key-all-kuh

Miraenia: Mur-ay-nee-uh

Lonia: Lone-ee-uh

Lirath: Leer-ath

Eadrios: Ay-dree-os

OTHER

illusié: ill-oo-see-ayy

magick: ma-jik (magic)

Caldari: Kal-darr-ee

Cruex: Crew

Vaekith
Mountains

Drakken
Isle

Rovie

Volkharn

Miraeni

Trendalath

Dectorach

Crostan Islands

Ipcea

THE LAND

Athia

AERID

Sunngate

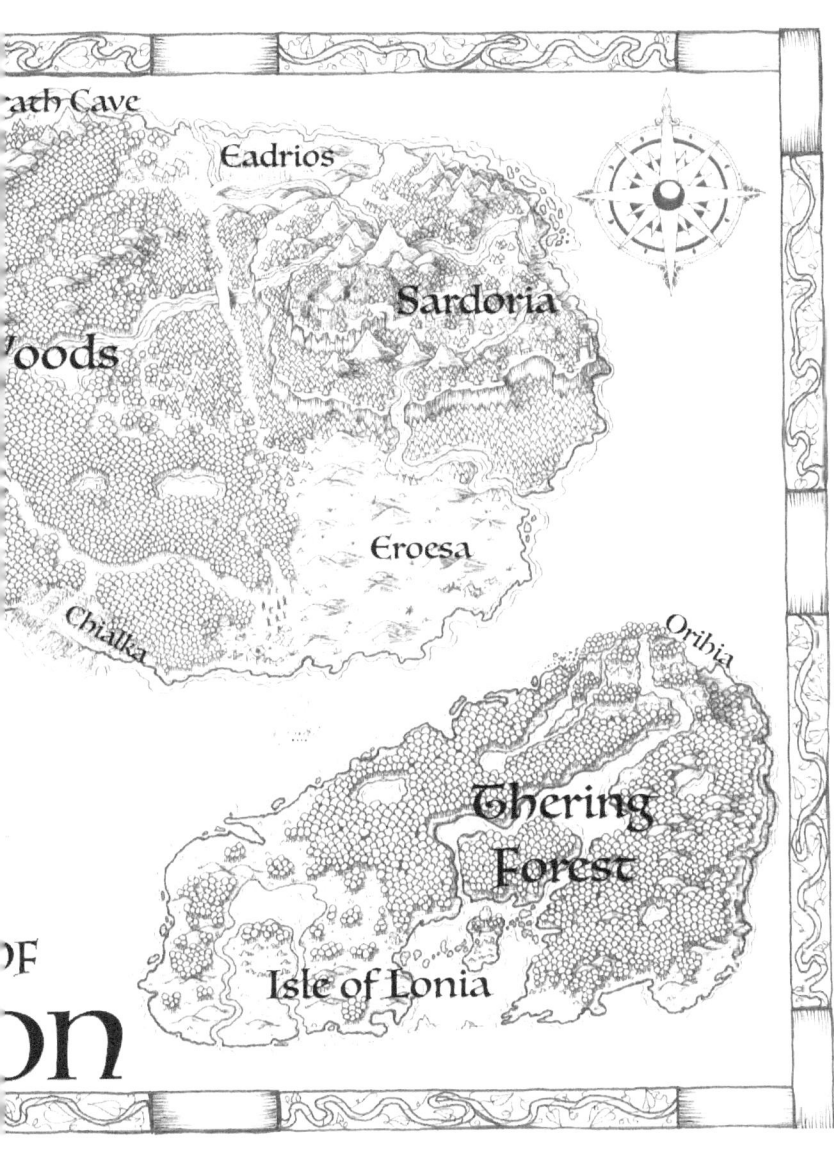

ath Cave

Eadrios

Sardoria

Woods

Eroesa

Chialka

Oribia

Thering
Forest

OF

Isle of Lonia

on

JADED
SPRING

ARDEN ELIRI

I'VE GROWN TO like it here.

Above me, the sunlight shines through the canopy of trees, warming my face. I lay on my back with my eyes closed, absorbing the peace and quiet—sans the sound of rippling water from a nearby stream. That I don't mind one bit.

A much earlier spring is approaching, thank the lords, and the signs are all around me—in the minimal snowfall remaining on the ground; the green leaves breaking free from winter's cruel captivity; the warmer, but still slightly chilly temperatures; the birds chirping their cheerful melodies in the mornings.

Winter has almost reached its end.

A cloud rolls over the rays of warmth, casting a cool shadow across my face. As I figured it would, it takes my peace along with it. My eyes shoot open as images of Aldreda's pallid face and lifeless body flood my mind. My hands hovering over her abdomen. The dark mist. The white light . . .

Darkness had prevailed.

A chill lodges in my chest. I *know* what I'd felt in that room with her. I'd called forth my light—my healing ability. I'd witnessed it take shape with my very own eyes. I'd breathed life back into her—her lips had parted, her chest had risen, her eyelids had fluttered—so how had this happened? How had the Queen of Trendalath died at my own two hands?

As jarring as the thought is, I find myself distracted by two small paws pressing against my thigh. I raise my head to find Juniper aggressively seeking my attention. She pushes on my thigh again before pouncing directly onto my lap. I sit upright before cradling her in my arms.

After Haskell had, well, *rescued* me from the horrors of that day, he'd offered to go to Orihia to look for Juniper and bring her back to Lirath Cave. I'd been going on and on about her and how I'd hoped she was all right. At the time, I'd been too weak to transport with him, so I'd waited impatiently—like a shell of a parent—until he'd returned safely with my sweet Juni in his arms. It'd only taken him a few hours. He'd even managed to pick some

2

juniper berries before returning—a good call since they're her favorite and don't grow in the northern regions of Aeridon.

After coddling Juniper for a few minutes too long—the incessant squirming is her "tell"—I finally release her from my arms, to which she happily prances off into the brush, chasing after a mouse. I watch her in amusement until I notice someone approaching in the distance. I can tell from the burly figure that it's Haskell.

My *brother.*

For seventeen (almost eighteen) years, I've been an orphan, one who'd been taken under Tymond's wing and trained to become a merciless assassin for the Cruex. I've never known what had become of my family—if I'd even had one at all—so I've been under the impression that they're no longer living. The Cruex had become my family. I'd never thought to question that.

But seeing that flash of green light in the healing ward in Trendalath castle, those piercing eyes the same shade as mine . . . I'd known. I'd known that whoever had come to save me was family.

My *real* family.

Haskell approaches with a rather cheery grin on his face, which is discomfiting given his usual rigid demeanor. We've only been here, together, for a few weeks, but in that short time, I feel as though I've really gotten to know him. I've caught on pretty quickly to a few nuances: to keep my distance whenever he's preparing a meal; to never wake him before the sun comes up; and to avoid asking questions about that day in Trendalath. That last one has been a challenge. Not surprisingly, it's the only thing I want to talk about.

When he finally reaches where I'm sitting, I notice that his hands are behind his back. I push myself up from the ground, brushing off the leaves and twigs from the back of my trousers. I give him a coy smile before greeting him. "To what do I owe the pleasure?"

He angles his head, eyes twinkling, but keeps his arms locked behind him. "I've got a little something for you."

"Oh, do you now?" I proceed to whistle to call Juniper back over from whatever adventure she's taken herself on.

"I know it's a day early, but," he says as he brings his arms in front of him, "happy early birthday, Arden."

A burlap-wrapped sack falls into my outstretched arms. My heart flutters at the sight. I can tell immediately what it is by the weight and the shape of the packaging. I lay it carefully on the ground and unroll the gift to reveal exactly what I hoped it'd be.

My chakrams.

My hands fly to my mouth as a squeal of delight escapes. I gingerly pick each blade up and secure them back into my holsters—back to their rightful place. My eyes meet my brother's. "But how did you . . . ?"

4

He remains silent, and I realize what he's done for me. What he's *risked* for me. He went back there—back to Trendalath—to retrieve my weapons. "Haskell, I don't even know what to say. Thank you. I know how dangerous that must have been. Just"—I choke on the words—"thank you."

He gives me a reassuring nod. "For family, any risk is worth taking."

A faint warmth blooms in my neck, traveling upward to my cheeks. "How was it? Being back there?" I clamp down on my tongue to keep from asking what I really want to know—how things are in Trendalath, in the castle, after everything that's transpired . . .

Haskell shakes his head as if to silence me. "Perhaps another time. Things are as you'd expect, but it's none of your concern."

I almost stumble backward from shock. *Not my concern? How can he say that?* "I'm the reason—"

"I'm going to stop you right there," he interrupts. He grabs hold of my forearm and tugs me forward. "It's time to head back. You've been out here for hours and you've hardly eaten anything all day." He sneaks a look at Juniper. "Unless you've been sharing berries."

His attempt at humor is admirable, but futile. I'm really not in the mood. I shrug off his grip and start for the cave, making sure to stay a few steps in front of him, with Juniper a step or so ahead of me.

Without warning, a bird's shadow sweeps by. For a moment, I swear my heart falters. I stop in my tracks and gaze at the sky, half expecting to see a black falcon.

Expecting . . . or hoping?

But it's just a hawk.

It isn't Xerin.

Haskell lightly knocks into my shoulder and passes me, murmuring something about the cave being close, but I'm entirely distracted by my thoughts. I look to the sky again, hoping that perhaps, somehow, Xerin will hear my thoughts and come swooping in. But the expanse above me remains empty, save for the few pockets of clouds.

My mind flits to the fellow Caldari I've left behind. Estelle, Felix, Opal . . . Braxton. After what he'd confided in me, showing me that letter—and to think, I'd killed his estranged mother. It'd been an accident, but still. I'm to blame.

And Queen Jareth. What does she think of me now? Does she even know I'd been taken to Trendalath? Do any of them know? Do they think I've conspired against them this entire time? That my loyalty lies with King Tymond?

The thought is almost too much to bear. I can feel my chest tighten as panic settles in. I grow lightheaded, scanning the area around me as quickly as I can to find somewhere to sit. A giant boulder comes into my fuzzy, dot-filled view and, even though I'm stumbling, I manage to make it over, taking a seat before my legs decide to give out, too.

I struggle to take a deep breath as more thoughts plague my mind. I never would have fled Sardoria had I known the outcome, had Cyrus not . . .

Cyrus.

His name is like a punch to the gut. Why had he brought me there? And against my will? How could he betray me like that, especially after what he'd told me about my *father*?

I look ahead to see that Haskell has already disappeared. If I had to guess, he's likely more than a hundred paces in front of me, probably wondering what in the world is taking me so long. Does he know about our father? Does he *want* to know?

No questions about family-related issues. Haskell's voice rings in my head.

Another day, then.

Juniper circles my feet, brushing against my calves. I wait until my vision is less hazy before rising from my spot on the boulder. I look ahead with steadfast determination, recognizing this particular path of trees. The cave is just around the corner.

I'd fled Sardoria to keep from hurting anyone even more than I already had, *and* to learn what the hooded figure *was*—what it wanted from me. What it *still* wants from me.

And yet, I remain completely in the dark. I'd left looking for answers only to return with even *more* burning questions than before. My life has become nothing more than a tangled web of deceit, lies, and betrayal.

Who *is* Arden Eliri? I sure as hell don't know.

Not anymore.

As I round the final corner, the cave comes into view. Haskell's bulky shadow highlights the entrance. I raise my face to the sky one final time, hoping that my fellow Caldari will somehow sense my thoughts.

That they'll come looking for me.

That they still care enough to do so.

That, eventually, they'll be able to forgive me.

I have a sinking feeling that they won't—and there's no one to blame but myself.

DARIUS TYMOND

DARIUS STANDS AT the water's edge,
alone. Thousands of stars glisten in the glassy reflection,
making the horizon nearly indiscernible. A soft breeze
ripples through the trees on the coastline, but refuses to
touch the water. It's a calm evening, unlike so many
nights before where the waves would crash violently
against the shore. It's almost as if Aldreda herself has
calmed the rising tides just to spite him. His jaw clerches
at the thought.

An opulent moon emerges from behind a haze of
white and silver clouds, casting a rather luminous glow
over the kingdom of Trendalath. He glances over his

shoulder before fully turning around to take in the sight—the four massive turrets bordering the castle; the slate-gray mortar and stone holding the monstrosity together; and the once lively garden that used to house tulips, lilies, and a multitude of herbs—but being outside the castle walls, it's not surprising it hasn't been tended to. Especially after . . .

A pit forms in his stomach at the unexpected memory. The moon falls behind another set of clouds, these darker than the last, as if encouraging him to tumble deeper into the darkness—but the memory doesn't even have the chance to play out in his head, let alone form in full. He brings his attention to his hands, twisting the amethyst ring round his finger, before beginning his trek back to the castle grounds. Another breeze. He can feel Aldreda in the strong current that's sweeping through his gray peppered hair, tugging at his robes, rattling his dragon brooch, stirring his mind— trying, in vain, to pull him back toward the sea.

He presses onward.

The day after Aldreda had passed, he'd ordered Cyrus to locate a handcrafted canoe from one of the Trendalath merchants. He'd arranged for her body to be laid to rest at sea—mostly because she'd always wished to be buried inside the castle, as most royalty would. That, and because she'd despised the ocean.

The salt never failed to gather in her elaborately coiffed hair, sting her eyes, weigh down her robes—the complaints had been endless. She'd preferred to stay inside the castle where it was safe, clean, and dry. Much unlike her sister. Her sister had loved the sea—*lived* for it, even.

Darius places one hand at the side entrance of the castle before closing his eyes and pressing his forehead against the wooden door. He pushes harder and harder until he can feel an indentation forming just below his hairline. Keeping these memories suppressed for so many years has left a lifetime of unknowns stretched before him. He crumples against the door.

After what his wife had done . . . she'd deserved what she'd gotten. The infidelity. The betrayal. The loss of an heir—or the idea of one, at least. A brutal and justifiable end to a life brimming with treachery and deceit—to which Arden had been the perfect scapegoat. No one would ever suspect that the *king* would have anything to do with the queen's untimely death.

But he'd had everything to do with it.

And for very, *very* good reason.

RYDAN HELSTROM

XERIN HASN'T RETURNED in days, which doesn't do much to ease Rydan's growing nerves. Every morning since they'd last received news of Arden, Rydan would wake before dawn, rush to the window, then fling the door open—hoping and praying that he'd spot a falcon soaring overhead. He'd been disappointed for twenty-three consecutive days.

Today isn't any different.

Not even a cheerful sky sprinkled with wisps of clouds can improve his steadily darkening mood. With a sigh, he slams the door shut, cringing slightly as the dwelling's weak structure rattles and shakes. Vira still isn't up yet, but after the ruckus he's just made, she might as well be.

Rydan pulls a stool from underneath the kitchen counter and plops down on it. He rakes a hand through his unkempt hair a few times before rubbing the sides of his temples. With each day that passes, his guilt only grows. How selfish he's been—for fleeing Sardoria and abandoning the people who had saved him from an unwarranted fate; for taking Vira with him when she'd just reunited with her brother; for trying to derail her plans to tell Arden what they'd discovered about her family. He's only been thinking about himself.

He's only *ever* thought about himself.

The clearing of a throat catches his attention. He turns over his shoulder to see Vira in her nightgown with a blanket draped over her shoulders, leaning against the wall of the living room. Her disheveled hair and soft expression tell Rydan that she's just awoken.

"Another early morning?"

It's not so much a question as it is an observation. Rydan just nods before turning back in his seat.

Vira goes to the pantry, scanning the limited options. She holds up a bag of oats and a crisp red apple. "Have you eaten?"

He considers lying to her, then thinks better of it. There's no need to answer, though, because she already knows.

"Here's what's going to happen," she says, readying a pot of water to boil. "We're going to have a nice breakfast. You're going to eat every last bite. And then we're going to go into town for the afternoon. Get our minds off of all of this."

Rydan watches intently as she begins slicing the apple. He can only imagine what Tymond's done to Arden, how much pain she's probably in.

As if she's reading his thoughts, Vira says, "It's not your fault, Rydan. Tymond's been looking for Arden since the day you were thrown in that cell." She takes a shaky breath. "It was bound to happen one way or another."

He breaks his silence. "Be that as it may, we haven't seen your brother in weeks. Shouldn't he be back by now?" He shakes his head. "We came here to tell Arden what we know about her family, and I messed that up. I'm the one who lied to you about searching for her. I'm the one who wasted valuable time. If I had done what I said I was going to do, I could have found her—"

"And in telling her what we know about her brother *and* the Savant murdering her mother," Vira says, her tone matter-of-fact, "she would have fled to Trendalath anyway to get her revenge." She holds his steady gaze. "Like I said, it was bound to happen. There's nothing you could have done."

"But I can now."

"It would be a death sentence, Rydan." She lets out an exasperated sigh. "*Arden* in Trendalath, *you* in

Trendalath. You'd be giving the king exactly what he wants—signed, sealed, and delivered on a silver platter."

The words cut through him like glass. While she certainly has a point, he does too. "Someone has to help her."

"It doesn't have to be you."

His eyes flick to the knife in her hand. "But it should be. I was her partner—"

Vira plunges the blade directly into the cutting board. "She *left* you during that assignment, without the proof you needed, without thinking about anyone but herself. Or have you forgotten? You went into that mission as partners and walked away divided."

Rydan jumps to his feet. He leans over the counter so that his gaze is level with Vira's. "She came back to save me. To save *us*." His jaw clenches tighter with each word. "Without her, we wouldn't be standing here right now."

Vira steadies her hand on the hilt of the knife, her eyes locked on his. Rydan doesn't retreat in the slightest. She pulls the blade from the slab of wood and continues cutting the apple. "Then go to Trendalath," she says, each slice like a jab to his heart. "Because as much as I want to, I know I won't be able to stop you."

CERYLIA JARETH

"HE HASN'T SHOWN his face in days." Cerylia presses her palms into the stone opening of her chamber window, shivering as a cool breeze dances across her neck. "I almost find it amusing how I release him just so he can lock himself in another room," she mutters to herself, but loud enough for Delwynn to hear. When her advisor doesn't respond, she whips around to face him. "Well?"

His voice is pained. "Bear in mind, he *did* just lose his estranged mother, Your Greatness. And at the hands of someone he thought he could trust."

This had certainly come as a shock. When Cerylia had received the news, she'd hardly believed it herself. But, sure enough, Opal had taken her back in time and they'd watched, as bystanders, as Arden's attempt to heal Aldreda had gone terribly, terribly wrong. Cerylia couldn't say she was *upset* that the Queen of Trendalath was dead—rather, the opposite. She'd just hoped it would have been at her own two hands.

With the thought turning in her head, her attention settles back on Delwynn. "Even more reason to surround yourself with—"

"With support?" Delwynn shakes his head, but doesn't say anything further. He doesn't have to.

Cerylia stiffens at the implication—that she's somehow been unsupportive of Braxton. Not only has she welcomed him into her queendom, full well *knowing* his family's history, she's also given him the benefit of the doubt, up until recently—an error on her part that she freely admits to. "If he'd just show his face, I'd have the opportunity to apologize. His stubbornness is proving to be just as infuriating as his father's. Perhaps I should have kept him in there a little while longer." It's meant as a joke, but Delwynn doesn't take it that way.

"As I've said before, I'd advise against that."

She gives him a pointed glare. "I had to do what I thought was right. For the safety of Sardoria. The evidence—"

"There is no evidence," he interrupts. "There's no evidence of Braxton betraying you, or conspiring against you with Cyrus, or with King Tymond." He lifts his shoulders, standing a little taller. "With everything that's happened"—he lowers his voice to a whisper—"with Dane, with the Mallum, with Arden. It's understandable that you'd have your doubts. But assumptions are the devil's work. You know that better than anyone."

As much as she doesn't want to hear it, he's right. As of late, with almost every problem she's encountered, the first logical conclusion that's entered her head has been the *only* conclusion. She'd assumed that Arden's capture and the Mallum's attack had something to do with Braxton because of his family—he has Tymond blood running through his veins, after all. *But* she'd been wrong about Dane's murderer. It hadn't been Darius, but his *wife*. One truth seems to withstand the tests of time: nothing is ever as it appears to be.

The bell tower chimes, signaling the setting sun. She turns her gaze back to the window. "Please escort the Caldari to the dining hall."

"I don't think—"

Cerylia sighs. "I've had my fair share of disagreements for today, Delwynn. Please do as I've requested."

Delwynn opens his mouth as if he's about to say something, then thinks better of it. He bows his head before ducking out the door. Cerylia knows exactly what

18

he'd been about to say—that, more likely than not, she'll be dining alone tonight. And that it'll probably be that way for many nights to come.

BRAXTON HORNSBY

A SOFT RAP on the door wakes Braxton from a longer-than-intended nap. He throws his legs over the uncomfortable chair he'd fallen asleep in, working out a painfully withstanding crick in his neck. The knocking ceases, then starts up again. He stumbles over himself as he makes his way to the door, cursing the unknown visitor, but in his half-sleep daze, answers it without a second thought.

Delwynn's mouth crinkles into a smile. "I didn't think you'd answer."

Braxton stifles a yawn, rubbing the sleep from his eyes. "Did Cerylia send you? Again?"

His smile fades. "She's requested the presence of all Caldari in the dining hall."

Suddenly fully awake, Braxton scoffs, "I suppose it's the perfect opportunity to lock *everyone* up."

Delwynn doesn't respond, but the look on his face is a mixture of indifference and pure exhaustion. "On the contrary, Queen Jareth wishes to apologize and start anew. Mind you, I've only mentioned this every day during my visits for the past three weeks." He raises a brow. "Unfortunately, I've only had the honor of speaking to your door." He knocks on the wood for emphasis. "If you'd opened it, you probably would have known by now."

Braxton taps his fingers against the doorframe. "I'm not hungry. Send the queen my regards."

Before Delwynn can even attempt to persuade him, he shuts the door and turns the lock securely in place. He can hear the old man blubbering about disrespecting elders as he bangs on the door in protest, but he manages to tune it out. If Cerylia wants to speak with him so badly, she can come up here herself.

Not only had she sent Delwynn to release him from the dungeons, she hadn't even attempted to approach him to make things right in the weeks that followed. What she'd done had been unjust and unfair, but it seems her pride had won out.

Reminds him a lot of his mother.

News of her passing had rippled through Aeridon faster than a bolt of lightning. Even though he hasn't seen her in ten years, it'd struck a chord with him. He'd always had a soft spot for his mother, even though she could be worse than Darius at times. Came with the territory. But his mother had been caring, and she'd loved him deeply, wanting only the best for him as any mother would. When Darius had announced that illusié would be banished from the kingdom, she'd supported him—but Braxton could tell she'd sensed the shift in their relationship as mother and son. It was almost as if she'd *known* of her only son's abilities—what he's been capable of all this time.

It hadn't dawned on him until recently that in almost all of his earliest memories, someone had been in the shadows, watching him. He'd felt this presence when he'd deviated a rock that had been thrown at him by a distant cousin. When a handmaiden had gone to scold him with a dishtowel and ended up swatting herself. When his father had lost his temper and thrown a full goblet of wine aimed straight for his head, only to wake up with a nasty bump just above his left temple with no clue as to how it'd happened . . .

Aldreda had known. And she'd prepared him as best she could. He'd only fled because she'd planted the seed at a very young age, telling him stories of the Lands of Aeridon, highlighting the very regions he'd considered fleeing to when he was ten. Bedtime stories had quickly transformed into an overview of each of the regions: Eroesa was barren, Chialka was charming, Lonia was breathtaking, Athia was safe.

Safe had sounded pretty good to a ten-year-old.

She'd known, and she'd done her best to protect him. But now, that unspoken bond between them—between mother and son—could never be rekindled. Whether he wanted it to be or not doesn't matter. Her fate had been sealed, thanks to the one person he'd trusted from the moment they'd met.

Arden.

When Opal had told them—all of them . . .

A flash of fury races across his chest. Whether she'd been captured or not was beside the point. Arden had known his mother had reached out to him. After all this time, he'd been about to get some answers. She'd *known* something—something important—and now he'd never know what that was.

An urge to read her note again courses through him. He goes to his armoire, shuffling through multiple piles of boots until finally locating the right one. Sweeping a small knife from one of the open drawers, he carefully slips the blade where sole meets leather. It creaks open as the two separate to reveal a flattened piece of parchment. With a heavy heart, he unfolds it and begins to read:

JADED SPRING

My dear son,

The time has come to return to Trendalath. There is much to be said for the past, and even more to be gained for the future. I hope you both can forgive me one day.

Your *loving mother*,

Aldreda

He rereads it once, twice—as many times as his eyes can stand—but it's just as cryptic as the first time he'd read it. *I hope you both can forgive me one day.*

Both . . . as in himself and his father? Or someone else? What had she done that needs forgiving?

He stares at the letter until his eyes begin to water. A tear escapes, followed by another, and another. They hit the parchment, swirling with the ink over his mother's signature to make a giant black splotch. Cursing himself for ruining the one piece of his mother he has left, he gently carries the parchment to an empty drawer and places it inside. He leaves it cracked just enough so that the letter can dry.

Perhaps fresh eyes and a new day will help make some sense of the letter. More likely than not, though, whatever she'd been so desperate to reveal had died along with her.

ARDEN ELIRI

AS I FOLLOW closely behind Haskell, I'm starting to wonder where he's taking me. The echo of dried up leaves and twigs crunching beneath our feet is the only sound for miles. We've been walking for at least an hour, deeper and deeper into the forest, without a semblance of a break. I can tell Juniper is growing restless, as am I, but just as I'm about to ask where we're headed, he stops.

Panting, I peer around him to discover what I believe is an entrance—but not to a cave. Built into the black and gray rock is a camouflaged structure. If I weren't standing directly in front of it, I never would have known it existed.

Haskell moves closer before pressing his ear against it. I want to ask him where we are, what's going on, what this place even *is*—but his grave demeanor demands silence. I press my mouth shut to keep from disrupting whatever it is he's doing.

After a few moments have passed, he takes a step back, then knocks his shoulder into the door—one, two, three times. I shudder at the sound of flesh hitting stone, but on his final attempt, the door finally budges. "Watch your step," he says as he disappears into the enclosure.

It takes a moment for my eyes to adjust to the darkness. I can't help but jump when Haskell shuts the door behind me. Dim lighting, although barely bright enough to see, comes into view, and the pitch black that had originally surrounded me begins to fade.

"Follow me."

I watch as Haskell descends an enormous set of stairs, his shoulders and head bobbing with each step. Not wanting to get left behind, I reach for Juniper and swipe her from the ground before carefully touching the toe of my boot on the first step. Even though I can hardly see it, it seems solid enough, so I take the step, using my other senses to journey down to the next landing.

When I finally make it to the bottom, Haskell is waiting for me with a bright flickering torch. "I really should have left these at the top," he mutters, more to himself than to me. "Here, hold this so I can find the rest."

I set Juniper down before taking the torch, making sure not to stray too far from him as he lights each of the wall sconces. Each one illuminates another section of this massive temple we seem to be in. The walls, which are made of smooth brown stone, stretch as high as the sky, and I'm almost certain if I were to yell, a never-ending echo would follow. A whole slew of creatures could be living in the vastness above me and I'd never know it.

Stretching from the bottom of the staircase to the far-reaching corners are uneven columns made of white marble. They immediately remind me of the castle in Sardoria. I'm momentarily distracted by Juniper rubbing against my legs, but when I look down at my feet, I find that I'm standing in the middle of a massive circular indentation in the stone. The lines drawn within it extend outward every which way, but from my vantage point, they seem to be divided into four major quadrants. It bears a striking resemblance to something I've seen before, but I can't quite put my finger on what.

"What is this place?" I ask as I turn in another circle, taking it all in.

"Your *real* birthday present." This makes me laugh, but when he turns to face me, I realize he's dead serious. "I needed a place to keep my research."

I raise a brow. "Research? On what?"

"Our family."

My heart rises in my chest. I watch as he brings a torch to one of the marble columns, then another, then another. Only when I mimic his movements do I realize that there are dozens of metal emblems secured onto each one. He's taken care to only light specific ones, which each emit a different color—purple, green, orange, red. My concentration is broken as he yanks my arm and brings me back to the middle of the circle.

"What are we . . . ?"

My voice trails off as awe sets in. The stones on the outer side of the marble columns begin to rattle and shake, shifting left and right, up and down, until the top of another structure is revealed. It glides through the opening in the ground, rising until it's towering over us.

Haskell releases my arm, motioning for me to stay back. He checks the sturdiness of the structure before angling his head. "Follow me."

I do as he says, making sure Juniper stays close, but seeing as she's on my heels, I don't have much to be concerned about. Instead of descending, like we had when we'd first entered the enclosure, we're now climbing dozens of stairs. I gaze upward at the spiral staircase and how it seems to go on and on. Part of me wishes we had access to the walkways I'd discovered in Orihia.

When we finally reach the top, I'm winded and my legs ache. Haskell also seems to have a hard time catching his breath, which makes me feel a bit better. Before the dots floating in and out of my vision have a chance to become permanent, I pull my canteen from my belt and guzzle half of the container. Instantly, I feel better. As I go to wipe my mouth with the back of my hand, my eyes are drawn to the expansive room in front of me. It appears to be a library of sorts.

I bite down on the inside of my cheek to maintain my composure, but on the inside, I feel like a giddy child. If I thought the library in Orihia was incredible, this library is . . . *miraculous*. Bookshelves, from floor to ceiling, wind around the entire room. There are cabinets with glass doors containing trinkets, artifacts, and other specimens that I can't wait to get my hands on. A multitude of wooden desks with ancient carvings donning the legs hold maps, globes, and rolls of parchment.

But what catches my eye, even from across the room, is a hanging frame. I walk over to it. Pulling both my watch and the folded up photograph from my back pocket, I hold the latter up to compare the two images. Sure enough, they're exactly the same.

A photo of the King's Savant.

The sensation of warm breath on my neck has me whirling around. I immediately take a defensive stance, only to find Haskell jumping backward with his hands in the air, palms facing me. His eyes flick to the frame on the wall, to the photo in my hand, then to me.

"Our father," we both say simultaneously.

I straighten my knees to bring myself to a normal standing position as Haskell lowers his hands.

"Did you know him?" I whisper.

He gives a solemn shake of his head.

"Was this place . . . ?"

"His?" Haskell lifts his gaze skyward before scanning the room. Slowly, he returns his attention to me. "I have reason to believe so."

My breath hitches. With so many questions swarming my mind, I can't seem to formulate a coherent response.

"About a year ago, I found this place—or I suppose you could say I was guided here. At first, I'd been afraid to enter. I could hardly see anything, even in broad daylight. Every day since, I've come back to it." He strokes his beard, deep in thought. "At one point, I'd even convinced myself that it was a death trap. When I finally worked up enough nerve to venture inside, I nearly tumbled down the hundreds of steps. With just a torch and a blade, I started to discover that it wasn't just a bottomless pit."

"How did you know to light the columns? That they'd reveal"—I gesture to our surroundings—"all of this?"

He shrugs. "I suppose you could say I was *shown.*"

I wait for further clarification on what he means, but suddenly realize I don't need it. I know exactly what he's referring to—because I experienced something similar in the Roviel Woods, when my father had appeared and given me his pocket watch. I angle my head at the frame on the wall. "Were you, by chance, guided here by a glowing orb?"

Dumbstruck, his jaw drops. "Yes." He narrows his eyes. "How did you know that?"

"When I departed Trendalath for a mission, I left this behind." I hand him my pocket watch. "Long story short, before arriving in Sardoria, I had a similar encounter with a glowing orb, except"—I struggle to find the words—"my orb transformed *into* something—two men. They seemed to appear out of nowhere." I scan the photograph and point them out so Haskell can see. My voice lowers to a whisper. "Did you see our father, too?"

He continues to stare at the framed photograph for some time. I remain silent until his eyes shift to mine, emerald meeting emerald. He drops the pocket watch back into my hand. "No. Just the orb."

His curt tone is enough to indicate that I've struck a nerve. "I'm sorry. It wasn't my intention to—"

He squeezes the bridge of his nose, then sighs. "It's fine. I'm not mad at you, Arden. I'm just confused, that's all."

That would make two of us. "Do you think he's alive?"

Haskell merely shrugs. "Your guess is as good as mine." His answer is disheartening, but not at all surprising.

"Haskell, he obviously wanted you to know about this place, whatever it is." I walk toward the center of the room, peeking down the endless aisles of shelves as I go. My thumb steadily traces the engraving on the watch. "What exactly *is* all of this?"

"I think it's a collection of"—he pauses, as if unsure how to describe it—"things our father may have found important. There's not much family history—nothing I've uncovered anyway. As you can see, there's a lot to go through."

"How far have you gotten?"

"Not very." He swipes his hand along one of the shelves, then presents the heavy layer of dust covering his hand for emphasis. "Honestly, I've been pretty close to giving up. I've pored over what feels like hundreds and hundreds of texts, but haven't learned anything of value." His jaw clicks to the side. "Or maybe it's all of value and I just don't know what I should be looking for." He falls into a nearby chair. "Wanna have a go at it?"

As soon as he asks the question, I understand how he feels. The thought of looking through all of these books is daunting, to say the least. But I'm convinced the glowing orb isn't a coincidence. Our father has been trying to communicate with us—to tell us something— albeit I don't know what.

I'm determined to find out.

DARIUS TYMOND

RAIN POURS FROM the sky. The deafening sound is a welcome reprieve from the usual chatter of the Trendalath merchants and townspeople. The clouds above are so dense that, to the naked eye, they've formed a singular gray silhouette. A bolt of lightning illuminates the dreary canvas, and thunder roars soon after. From the confines of his window, Darius can see the dirt roads flooding, transforming into gushing streams. They carry dismantled carts, soaked linens, and baskets of wares down, down, down, until they finally dump over into the Great Ocean.

And so, it's an ideal day to venture into the depths of the castle, although he's not particularly fond of whom he'll have to face. The man who impregnated his late wife. The man who continues to betray him over and over again. The man he cannot kill because he's destined to serve a higher purpose.

Clive Ridley.

Darius pushes himself away from the window and begins his descent to the dungeons. He gives a hasty hello to the guards on each floor, which is more than he usually does in a given month. A swell of anger surges through him as he passes Gladys's old chambers. At least her face is one he won't have to see.

As if to add insult to injury, he'd assigned Gladys's execution on the very same day he'd set Aldreda's body adrift on the Great Ocean. Although she'd pledged her loyalty to the Tymonds, Gladys had always preferred Aldreda over him. Seeing as he and the late queen had been in conflict for most of his reign, it came as no surprise that Gladys would eventually betray him and side with his late wife. Unfortunately for her, whatever veil of protection Gladys had hoped for had never existed in the first place.

As satisfying as her execution had been, Darius had hoped she'd show some remorse for the actions leading up to that moment. But she'd been so stoic, so unwavering in her conviction, that she'd maintained eye contact with him until the very moment the blade had severed her head. Even more unnerving had been the level of indifference in her expression. No guilt. No shame. No fear.

Just a woman facing her fate.

He releases the thought as he reaches the door to the dungeons. Even from the outside, he can feel the dank, musty air seeping through the cracks of the door. He grabs hold of a torch from a nearby wall sconce before twisting the appropriate key into the lock, using his shoulder to push through the weighty entrance. A phantom draft sweeps across the back of his neck—impossible, given that there are no windows and little airflow in the dungeons. He shakes off the uneasy feeling, drops the key back into his pocket, and continues onward.

The smell is even worse than he remembers. Hands of all different sizes reach for him through the metal bars, some begging for his forgiveness, others cursing his name. The majority partake in the latter, which fuels him even more. He holds the torch high, looking each one of them in the eye as he passes by the cells. Young, old, weak, strong, illusié or non—it doesn't matter. This is *his* kingdom to rule as he sees fit. Any level of misconduct is punishable, as long as he deems it so.

Finally, he arrives at the end of the long hallway. Clive's cell is just steps away. As quietly as he can manage, he secures the flickering torch in the nearest wall sconce. Locking up illusié, especially one with Clive's level of abilities, isn't simple by any means. Most of the time, the guards end up severely injured or dead, which is why his Savant had taken the reins. But the Savant locking up one of their own? Not exactly something he'd been inclined to ask.

Darius remains on the edge of the cell, intentionally not revealing himself. After news of Clive's indiscretion with Aldreda, his Savant had obeyed his directive to bound, gag, and blindfold him. Removing his ability to see, speak, or move was the only way Darius knew how to suppress his casting capabilities. He's about to find out just how effective that had been.

With his back against the wall, Darius cautiously peers around the edge of the cell. At first glance, it's so dark that all he sees is a vast sea of black. He keeps his eyes trained on the center of the cell, waiting for them to focus. Although barely discernible, a figure comes into view. He appears to be sitting at the very back of the cell, but Darius can't tell if he's awake or asleep, bound or free.

"My old friend."

His voice is distinct, not muffled in the slightest—which means he's no longer gagged. Out of habit, Darius traces the shape of the stone in his ring, remembering the power he holds in his very hands. It instantly makes him feel at ease.

No longer hindered by his own hesitation, he brings himself in front of the cell door. Hazel eyes meet his own. He follows Clive's gaze as it falls down his arm, to his hand. "Don't worry," he says, the contempt in his voice clear as day. "I'm not foolish enough to try anything." His mouth presses into a firm line. "I know what you're capable of."

This is not at all what Darius had expected. The man in front of him *should* have been in a frenzied rage after everything that had transpired. He'd lost his love. He'd lost his unborn child. And he'd lost them both at Darius's hands. Clive should be writhing with fury and vengeance, cursing Darius's name and weaving the most horrific illusions his twisted mind could conjure.

Who was this pathetic, defeated shell of a man?

"Time and time again, you continue to betray me." A ghost of a smile touches the king's lips. "Aldreda is dead. Perhaps now, you'll finally understand how it feels. What the two of you did"—his voice catches in his throat—"I want to hear you say it. Tell me she's dead."

Clive just hangs his head.

"Look at me," Darius hisses. "And say it out loud."

He keeps his eyes on the ground.

"Say it!" Darius shouts, his voice echoing.

With tear-stained cheeks, Clive lifts his head. His lower lip quivers as he whispers, "Aldreda is dead."

Broken. Fragile. If only she could see him now.

Darius flings his robes to his sides, leaving Clive's view as he retrieves the torch. As he walks toward the exit, he yells loud enough for everyone to hear. "After all this time, you're well on your way to getting what you deserve. But believe me when I say that the worst is yet to come."

RYDAN HELSTROM

TO PROVE TO Vira that he wasn't leaving, Rydan hadn't left the house in days. He'd hoped that this truce would remove the tension between them, but it'd only grown worse. That is, until today.

Today is the first day Vira seems even remotely cheerful. He's in the middle of reading a fictitious tale based in the Crostan Islands when suddenly, she swings around the corner, her golden plaited hair catching in the light. Dangling from her arm is an ornate woven basket, and, almost immediately, Rydan senses what she has in mind.

"I need to go into town to pick up a few things." Her eyes twinkle like stars in a cobalt sky. "Care to join?"

Rydan knows she's just extended an olive branch. He also knows he'd be stupid not to take it. "Sounds great," he says, closing the book and setting it on the table.

"What were you reading?"

The question comes as he follows her out the door. It's obvious she's making polite conversation to try and smooth things over, which is fine by him. They've had enough confrontation as of late. "Just a tale about the Crostan Islands. Nothing special."

At this, her shoulders tense. "The Crostan Islands?"

Rydan can feel the discomfort mounting yet again. "Yeah. It's pretty interesting, actually. It's a tale of deceit between two sisters and their partners, except they come to find out that their partner is the same person. Betrayal leads to slaughter which leads to vengeance. Pretty dark stuff."

She seems to ease up a little, but her voice remains rigid. "Sounds delightful." He doesn't realize how far they've walked until she turns around to face him. "We're here." Indeed, they've arrived in the bustling streets of Lonia. She sticks her hand out, palm facing upward. "Do you happen to have any extra riyals?"

A shadow flickers in her eyes, and it's then he realizes that this is a power play. Vira's felt out of control ever since Xerin delivered the news about Arden being held captive in Trendalath—ever since Rydan suddenly switched gears. He'd gone from lying about searching for Arden to wanting to risk everything to ensure her safety. It's no wonder Vira feels jerked around. He had, too, when he'd discovered that Arden had ultimately left him for dead.

He digs around in his pocket, presenting more than a few amber-colored coins. With a blank expression, he drops them into her open palm, watching as her fingers close securely around them. She gives a quick nod of appreciation before wandering off into the crowd, her braids bouncing with each step.

He loses track of her as quickly as his thoughts run away from him. He shoulders his way through the horde of people, scanning the sea of bronzed faces for her delicate porcelain one. Finally, he locates her at a familiar merchant stand—a fruit cart.

At first glance, he's instantly taken back to his first trip to the Isle of Lonia . . . with Arden. Vira's standing in front of a hooded figure and when it raises its head, even from a distance, he swears violet eyes search his own. He blinks and the mage is gone. The merchant standing in front of Vira is no more than a middle-aged man with a potbelly and a crooked grin. He approaches with caution as she waves him over.

Rydan realizes that there is no hood.

The man's eyes are a deep brown, not violet.

Vira doesn't seem to notice his blatant concern. Her

conversation goes on with the merchant as she picks through the assorted fruits, adding a few to her basket, then putting some back and repeating the entire process.

Rydan doesn't take his eyes off of the man.

"Four more riyals?"

He doesn't even realize she's speaking to him until her hand appears at eye level. "What?"

"You didn't give me enough." She shakes the basket for emphasis. "I need four more riyals."

She's intentionally trying to test his patience, which would normally have him up in arms, but he can't seem to snap himself out of his past-present daze. He checks his front pockets, then the back, before producing the exact amount she's asked for.

"Thank you," she says with an exasperated sigh, dropping the coins onto a ledge atop the merchant's cart. He nods in appreciation before sliding the riyals into his hand and out of sight.

The rest of the day is an endless cycle of Vira rushing to the next merchant and asking for more riyals, not hesitating to spend every last one. Wash, rinse, repeat. Rydan's so caught up in his own head that he mindlessly follows her around, obeying her every command without a single objection. There's only one scenario playing in his head.

Arden suffering in Trendalath.

When they finally return to their dwelling, the sun has set. Rydan shuts the door behind him, noticing that they've returned home with more baskets than they'd left with.

"I'll get dinner started," she says as she unpacks them.

"I'll go wash up," Rydan says with a forced smile before turning a corner and heading into the nearest bedroom. Quietly, he secures the door behind him, then rakes a hand through his salty, windswept hair. He hardly notices the burning sensation on his forehead and nose after spending an entire afternoon in the blazing sun. He can hear soft whistling from the kitchen as Vira begins to prepare their next meal.

Correction: *her* next meal.

His eye catches the strap of a knapsack poking out from underneath the bed. He pulls the bag out and rifles through it until he finds what he didn't even know he was searching for.

His black Cruex uniform.

He glances back over his shoulder at the closed door, his grip tightening on the fabric. He runs his finger over the stitching of the familiar symbol. The place that had been his home for almost a century.

Yes, Arden had left him behind during the Soames mission, but she'd come back for him. She'd risked everything to break him out of Trendalath. Most importantly, she'd accepted him—as Cruex, and again as illusié—when he'd refused to do so himself. To stay here, at a time like this, would be unforgiveable. *The sin of all sins.* And, thanks to Tymond, he already has enough of those under his belt.

Vira's voice echoes from down the hall. He stuffs the Cruex uniform back into the knapsack before shoving it under the bed. He rises and goes to the door, hesitating to open it. He knows what it'll mean if he walks through that door.

Is he really willing to risk losing her for good?

CERYLIA JARETH

CERYLIA SITS AT an empty table for what must be the fifth night in a row. She finishes her meal, then refills her goblet with the last of the verdot. She'll have to send for more in the morning if she's to get through the foreseeable future. If it weren't for the howling wind outside, she'd swear she was stuck in one of Opal's inversions. At this point, she wouldn't mind being *anywhere* else—anywhere but here.

She guzzles the verdot as if it's water, almost knocking over the bottle as she pushes her chair from the table. The lack of social interaction has her drinking more than usual—it helps her to cope with the fact that, as gracious as she'd been to let the Caldari in, they'd only ever intended to leave. Seems that had been their end game from the start—she'd been a pawn, nothing more.

Her aggravation rising, she pushes the doors to the White Room open, full well ignoring the bustling servants as they rush past her to clear the table of its unused dishes. What a waste.

She snakes her way around the castle with no clear direction—that is, until she winds up walking down a corridor she'd learned to avoid many, many years ago. Even in her semi-inebriated state, she realizes the door to Arden's old room is just around the corner. And around the corner from that is another room—one she hasn't dared venture into for over a decade. Even so, she's carried the key with her all this time, never letting it out of her sight.

It would seem the verdot has given her an ounce or two of courage because in mere minutes, she's approached the door and inserted the key into the lock without a second thought. A gentle nudge and the door creaks open. Carefully, she sticks one foot inside, followed by the other, until her entire body is engulfed in darkness. She leaves the door cracked before slinking to the center of the room. An armoire with glass doors stares her in the face. Two different sized robes—one larger, one smaller—hang limply inside.

Their Trendalath robes.

On the shelf above are two jewel-encrusted crowns.

Sadness overcomes her as she kneels, placing both hands on the glass. She presses her forehead against the cool surface, allowing tears to fall for the first time in months. Her husband hadn't deserved this fate. She hadn't either. She'd envisioned such a different life for them, for Aeridon. Trendalath had been *their* home, *their* kingdom.

As she rises, she doesn't wipe her tear-stained cheeks. Her breath catches in her throat at the sight of her own two hands pulling on the doors of the armoire. Suddenly, the Sardorian robes are splayed out on the floor, the circlet next to them tilted on its side. The silver and navy robes of Trendalath—*their* Trendalath—are now flung around her shoulders, the crown somehow both heavy and weightless on her head.

She closes the glass doors, catching her reflection in the moonlight. Her eyes are wet, her lips are stained crimson, and her hair is a tangled mess in the crown. She tears her gaze from the pathetic woman reflected in the glass and moves to the open window.

As beams of moonlight shine down on her, she can't help but feel his presence—in the last crisp air before spring, in the steady breeze whirring through the trees, in the glinting stars overhead. He'd promised to always stay with her, until the end of their reign. Until the end of time itself. And with those words, she'd felt her heart split in two. Because even then, she'd known the truth—that, with him, no length of time would have been long enough.

BRAXTON HORNSBY

THE KNOCKS ON his door have been relentless and, already, Braxton's lost track of the days. He's been holed up in his chambers for lords know how long, only allowing servants inside to drop off his meals. He'd even gone so far as to arrange a distinct knock for the servants, so as to not accidentally answer the door and have to face Cerylia or the other Caldari. No one had yet caught on to his arrangement with the servants. The last person he'd spoken to had been Delwynn—a conversation he'd tried to erase from his memory.

Every time a knock sounds, he's had to restrain his curiosity from getting the better of him. Might it be Opal?

Cerylia? Felix? Estelle?

Arden?

Surely if Arden had returned, one of the servants would have notified him—but then again, for Arden's safety, perhaps they'd been directed to keep the news to themselves.

One thing's for certain. If he doesn't get out of this room, and soon, he'll surely go mad.

His next move is completely up to him, and yet, indecision plagues him. All of the options he's come up with are less than favorable. His least favorite among them? Making amends with Cerylia.

After the way she's treated him, without even a fragment of respect . . . His blood boils at the thought. He *could* flee Sardoria, an option that's certainly more favorable in his eyes. But where would he go? He could return to Athia and try to start over—but would the Caldari ever truly let him be?

He retrieves his mother's letter from the drawer of the armoire, reviewing the flowing script for what feels like the thousandth time. Recently, another option *had* presented itself, albeit unexpectedly—one he'd quickly dismissed and never deigned to think of again. And yet, here it is, reappearing. Calling to him.

It's downright risky and could result in the end of life as he knows it, but he *could* choose to return to Trendalath. To find the answers he seeks—about his mother, the ring, the Mallum, the loss of his abilities. *But*, in order to do so, he'd have to face his father. Rebuild a relationship that had hardly existed in the first place. Solidify his father's trust in him. And then exploit it, just as his father had done to countless others.

The edges of the parchment crinkle in his grip as his father's face floats across his mind. It wouldn't be sustainable. Darius would see right through it. The master of deceit would know immediately what his estranged son was up to. But even with all the odds stacked against him, it seems like his best shot—which is really saying something . . .

His thoughts scatter at the sound of rattling at the window. He folds the parchment into a small square and slips it into a book atop the dining table. He hurries toward the window to find a falcon with beady red eyes pecking incessantly at the glass. He hadn't even noticed the impending storm. He forces the window open, and a blustery wind sweeps the bird inside.

Braxton heaves a jagged breath as the window clicks into place, then turns away as a yellow glow illuminates the room. "Think you could give a little warning next time?"

His jab is ignored as a familiar voice asks, "Do you happen to have an extra pair of trousers?"

Braxton goes to his dresser and retrieves his last pair from the drawer. With his back still turned, he tosses them blindly toward what he thinks is the window.

52

"Appreciate it. You can turn around now."

Braxton does just that to find a shirtless Xerin standing before him. "Next time," he says as he retreats to the armoire, "ask for both trousers *and* a shirt." He tosses one over, which Xerin hastily pulls over his head.

"What are you doing here?"

"I—I heard what happened in Trendalath. With Queen Tymond and . . . "

"Arden," Braxton finishes for him.

Xerin bows his head.

"I wasn't expecting company and, to be frank, I'm not really up for it." He angles his head toward the door, then the window. "Must be nice to have two points of exit. I can't even seem to find one."

"I'll be brief."

The way he says it indicates that he knows something Braxton *wants* to know. He feigns disinterest as he sits in an armchair. "Let's hear it then."

"Your mother was laid to sea." A shadow flickers across Xerin's eyes. "Did you know this?"

"No. How do you?" Braxton counters.

Xerin extends his arms, making a soaring motion. "I was flying over Trendalath, over the Great Ocean, when I saw a canoe filled with lilacs floating by its lonesome."

Braxton feels a lump form in his throat. Lilacs had been his mother's favorite flower. Although he'd only been a child, he distinctly remembers the lengths she'd gone to attain them in the colder seasons. Vases adorned with the purple flowers had covered almost every surface of the kingdom—a welcome, colorful respite during those gray winter months.

"Where is she now? My mother?"

"I'm afraid she's drifted northwest . . . "

Braxton's heart sinks. "To Drakken Isle?"

"Yes, but in a cavern, just off the coast."

For the first time in weeks, Braxton feels a flicker of hope. Perhaps *this* option will do.

ARDEN ELIRI

I'VE SPENT THE past few days perusing the items in our father's alleged . . . well, I don't know what to call it. Hideaway? Sanctuary? Library? My persistence in wanting to come here every day had finally forced Haskell to take the initiative to show me how to enter and exit the enclosure on my own. As much as I've enjoyed spending time with my brother, it feels nice to be here without supervision.

Alone.

The legs of the chair screech as I push it back from the bolted desk. Across from me, one of my most prized possessions wobbles, nearly falling off the edge, but I grab it just in time. I turn the wooden carving over in my hands, trying to keep my thoughts from wandering to Felix, but it's no use. They go there anyway.

Lords do I miss him.

News travels fast in Aeridon. By now, I'm sure he's heard about Queen Tymond. About *me*. About what I've done. *What he must think of me now.* A shiver snakes its way down my spine.

Before my thoughts can spiral any further, I reach down and open my knapsack, dropping the ship inside. Needing to distract myself, I shut the book in front of me, rise to my feet, then throw it on top of a nearby stack. Piled nearly eight books high, I slide it towards me, then return to the aisle where I'd originally retrieved them.

It's not surprising that being here, surrounded by all of my father's things, makes me feel even more connected to him in ways I can't really explain. Every time I open a book or study a map or spin one of the globes, I can *feel* his presence. After so many years of not knowing what had happened to my family, I'd come to believe that they were dead—and yet, my brother is alive.

I get the sense that my father might be, too.

The archives I've reviewed point to an infinite number of possibilities, but I can't seem to find a connection—if there even is one—to my father nor our family. I'm so desperate for guidance that I find myself daydreaming about that glowing orb coming to visit me again, as unsettling as it was. Now that I have some reassurance that it *is* indeed my father, I feel differently about it. Why hasn't he tried to make contact again?

I return to the desk with another stack of books and drop them onto the table. I fall into the chair and lean back before closing my eyes. My thoughts are neither here nor there, and it dawns on me that I don't know how much time has passed since I last left Haskell in Lirath Cave. Time is a foreign concept when you're surrounded by stone walls with no windows.

With a sigh, I press my shoulders into the chair and arch my back, digging around in my pockets for my watch. My fingers wrap around the chain as I lift it to eye level. I click it open to find that it's a few hours past sundown—much later than I'd thought. I'm a little surprised Haskell hasn't come to check on me, but he's probably enjoying the non-company, relishing the alone time—just like I am. I flip the watch open and closed a few times, my eyes flitting from the engraved metal to the looming stack of books before me. If I go through them tonight, I'm almost certain I won't give them the attention they deserve.

I lift my gaze, my eyes unintentionally landing on the wall with the framed photograph. Although it's at a distance, I know exactly which person I've inadvertently chosen to focus on. I think back to my encounter with my father in the Roviel Woods. His words echo in my mind. *It's good to see that you're doing well. Casters are some of the most dangerous illusié. You'd do best to remember that.* After tossing his pocket watch over, he'd said, *Let this token serve as a reminder.*

Casters.

I look down at the watch, then back up at the photograph. As much as I don't want to, I force myself to recall Tymond's words in the Daegrum Chambers. Bile rises in my throat at the memory of shockwaves coursing through my body. The sheer pain and immense fire I'd felt blazing through my veins. The seemingly endless explosion of sparks that had careened across my vision. The inability to form thoughts, words, or feelings. Somehow being both inside and outside of my body and mind simultaneously. My throat burns. What had he called him—that member of his Savant?

I rack my brain, playing with different words until one feels right. *Conjurer.* He'd *conjured* the elements—a bolt of lightning to be exact. In uttering a single word, he'd directed it straight at his target—*me*—until I'd almost lost consciousness.

And then there'd been the man in the maroon mask. Somehow, his ability had been worse than the Conjurer's. My blood goes cold as I envision Elias and his helpless expression—and me, a predator, approaching him with a longsword. Any semblance of my thoughts, my actions, my *intentions*, had been gone. Those whispers, of someone else pushing at my mind with such intensity . . . forcing them away had been near impossible. I'd been so close to killing Elias, even though I'd already spared his life in the Thering Forest. I'd felt controlled. Cursed, in a way.

Curser.

The man in the maroon mask had invaded my mind. He'd taken hold of the very threads that make me who I am, weaving them in such a way to ultimately play out whatever scenario he so desired. And I'd been able to do absolutely nothing about it. To me, *that* had been worse than the Conjurer. Hell, I'd take being fried to my core any day over losing control of my mind.

Conjurer. Curser. My father had clearly said to keep an eye out for Casters—but the only other incident that springs to mind is . . .

I whip my head toward the frame, focusing on another familiar face. I rise from the chair, recalling each unique feature with every step I take. The wiry copper hair. The bright hazel eyes. My breath catches in my throat as I shuffle backward. It's the same man that had appeared next to my father after the orb had disappeared. And again in the Thering Forest, when Estelle had brought me to the injured fawn.

The illusion this man had wrapped around me had been horrifying. I'd been in an enclosed space, unable to breathe, suffocating. I'd pounded my fists on the walls, opening my mouth to scream only to find that no sound would come out. There had been no cracks, no fissures—

no light or air of any kind could have possibly gotten through.

And yet, *something* had found its way inside.

I'd been enveloped in blackness, not just spatially, but also from within. It'd trickled across every surface, seeped into my every pore, entwined itself with every sensation, every memory, every underlying thought. I'd twisted and jerked from its relentless grasp, trying to salvage anything that was left, but it had prevailed. Forced to merge with this unforgiving entity of darkness, I had become everything and nothing all at once.

An obscure rebirth into an unparalleled form.

There's no doubt in my mind that what I'd experienced that day in the forest had been the deviant work of a Caster.

I pull myself away from the frame, eyeing a roll of parchment on a nearby surface. I unfurl and flatten it, using some of the heavier books to secure the edges. With a freshly inked quill, I begin to record my findings. Seeing as the recollections are at the forefront of my mind, the words flow from my fingertips with ease. When I've finished, I realize it's not much, but it *is*, to some degree, inside knowledge into the King's Savant and their abilities—well, *three* of their abilities.

As I reread what I've just written, a startling realization dawns on me. If Casters create illusions, then that day in the woods . . . had my father actually been there? Or had it merely been an illusion, a trick of the mind? Even more concerning, how had he known something so personal about me—like who my father is?

With these questions roiling in my mind, I impatiently wait for the ink to dry before tightly rolling up the parchment. I secure it with twine and stuff it into the waistband of my trousers. With everything in me, I'm hoping that Haskell's still awake.

Something tells me he'll want to see this.

DARIUS TYMOND

DARIUS WAITS BY the side of the castle, scowling at the empty dirt path before him. He adjusts his oversized hood, tightening it to hide his face from any lurking townspeople. "Where is he?" he mutters to himself. The darkening sky above indicates it's well past their agreed upon meeting time, and he's quickly losing patience.

The sound of hooves in the distance does little to calm his nerves until he eyes Cyrus atop a black steed, a carriage rolling behind him. Darius rushes forward as he approaches, wanting to get out of sight as soon as humanly possible. What a difference being outside the castle is—he can *feel* the filth and grime as if he's just bathed in it.

"You're late."

Cyrus opens his mouth, surely in an attempt to apologize for his tardiness, but Darius raises his hand to stop him. "To Volkharn." He pulls the carriage door shut and hits the top twice with his amethyst ring, anxious to get moving. The horse neighs as they take off down the long and winding road.

Dusk is fully upon them as they arrive at the base of the Volkharn peaks. Just west of the Vaekith Mountains, Volkharn doesn't stretch as tall or as wide, but it's large enough to house something very sacred to Darius—something only he and a select few know about.

The door to the carriage swings open. Darius delicately places both feet on the ground. He turns to Cyrus and, without a moment's hesitation, says, "You are to wait here until I return."

Cyrus bows his head in submission before retrieving a wooden staff, the top curving into a clear glass sphere. "If I remember correctly, you'll be needing this."

Darius takes it from him. The moment it touches his hands, the sphere glows a pale green. "This very spot." He points to where Cyrus is standing. "Do not move until I return."

"Yes, Your Majesty."

With nothing but the sphere lighting his way, Darius begins the skyward hike into Volkharn.

RYDAN HELSTROM

BEFORE DAWN BREAKS, Rydan's up and moving around Lonia. He roams the streets until he's off the beaten path, in search of a secluded spot—but no matter where he goes in this damn town, people always seem to be nearby.

After dinner with Vira the other night, he'd returned to his room to finish packing his knapsack. He'd been seconds away from leaving when, without warning, sparks had shot from his fingers. While he'd been able to put out the small, unexpected fire, it was in that moment that he'd realized something. If he left now, he'd be sending himself on a suicide mission.

He isn't ready . . .

To face Tymond. To face the Cruex. To face the King's Savant.

As much as it pains him to admit, his illusié abilities as an Ignitor give him a certain . . . edge. He doesn't know what horrors he'll have to face once he's arrived in Trendalath, but having the ability to instantaneously create fire—and knowing *how* to control it—could very well be the deciding factor in a life or death situation. And so, he needs to practice.

Hence the search for a secluded area.

Upon reaching a familiar crossing—a giant oak tree—he chooses to go left instead of right. The day prior, he'd gone right, and had been led to another small town. Sure, there had been less people around, but it hadn't been secluded enough, and he certainly doesn't need anyone asking questions.

As he treks further into the woods, a shoreline comes into view. The coast gleams in the rising sun as pale pinks and yellows are cast upon it. Rydan surveys his surroundings, hardly believing his luck. There isn't a soul on the beach. No fishermen on the rocks. No ships in the distance. It's as if he's struck gold. Not only can he practice his igniting abilities in peace—there's also an endless source of water mere steps away, in case something goes awry.

Standing where dirt meets sand, he removes one of

his shoes, then the other. His shirt follows. He places them at the edge of the woods, within view. The soft grains cushion the short journey as they slide between his toes. He can't remember the last time he stepped foot on a beach—or got into the water, for that matter.

He strips off the rest of his clothes before running in, diving headfirst into the water. The salt stings his eyes and, even though the water is still slightly chilled from the winter months, he finds that he's enjoying himself more than he has in weeks. When he comes up for air, he can't help but whoop loudly, relieved that his mind is clear and free of Trendalath—of anything, for that matter. He floats on his back for some time, observing a colony of ring-billed gulls as they fly overhead.

Rydan dips underneath the surface a few more times, only getting out once the sun has reached its full ascent. Vigorously, he shakes his head to free the salt particles from his hair. He wipes the remaining water droplets from his arms and legs before pulling his trousers back on. In his Cruex days, he would have considered *relaxing* to be a waste of time—but now . . . now he views it as absolutely essential.

He laughs to himself as he plops down on the beach and digs his feet into the sand. It immediately sticks to the tops and undersides of his feet, but he pays it no attention. His focus is currently on his hands. He turns them over so that his palms are facing up, studying the many lines that lead to his fingertips. They look so ordinary and yet they hold so much power.

How is that possible?

It's then the childhood memories come crashing in like the waves before him. He's always assumed that his mother and father had been non-illusié. If they had been "like him", surely they would have fought back. Surely they would have used their abilities . . .

He squeezes his eyes shut, forcing the tears back. A low groan stirs inside him, begging to be released—but he clenches his jaw to silence the pain. His eyes shoot open, glassy and exposed.

Slowly, he brings himself to his feet. His focus steady on the crashing waves before him, he brings his palms together, simultaneously pushing his parents' lifeless faces from his mind. His eyes travel to the tips of his fingers.

Even if I had known, I couldn't have saved them.

Emotions well up inside of him—rage, guilt, vengeance—but his fingers remain still. Unmoving.

The sparks refuse to come.

CERYLIA JARETH

I T ' S   A   F O G G Y   day in Sardoria, or perhaps it's just in her mind. Unable to sleep the night prior, Cerylia had awoken earlier than usual, before the dawn. Her nightly routine of pouring multiple glasses of verdot has not only left her wine cellar empty—it's also left her with a persistent headache that won't seem to go away no matter how many different herb concoctions she forces down.

With a hooded cloak and her riding boots, she approaches the stables. Perhaps a bit of exercise will ease the lingering pain. Normally, she'd have Delwynn prep her favorite horse, Briar, but when she arrives at the stall, she discovers that it's empty. Alarmed, she runs out into the open field, looking in every direction to see if Briar had somehow run off. She glances over her shoulder once more, taking note that the gate is closed—which means someone must have taken him out. It seems unlikely, given the hour, but the thought of taking one of the other horses isn't the least bit desirable. Not to mention, she's curious to know who's taken her horse without her permission. She spots a nearby barrel of hay and sits, quietly waiting for Briar and the perpetrator to return.

As dawn breaks, Cerylia's nearly dozed off again, but the sound of pounding hooves jolts her back to consciousness. She rises from the haystack and goes to the end of the stable. From a distance, she can see her beautiful bay horse come into view. Its chestnut coat catches the light of the rising sun as its obsidian mane rustles in the breeze.

Cerylia smiles as the majestic creature trots closer, but that smile quickly fades. Atop the horse is a familiar figure in a jade cloak, pools of silver hair spilling out from underneath the hood. She's immediately reminded of the first time she'd met Opal—when she'd arrived in Sardoria claiming to be a member of the Caldari and Cerylia had almost turned her away . . . before she'd known the girl was an Inverter.

Ever so slowly, an idea begins to form.

Opal gently pulls on the reins to bring Briar to a halt. She gives him a loving pat, then pivots her right foot out of the stirrup before bringing her leg over the back of the horse, dismounting with ease.

"Early morning ride?"

Opal doesn't meet the queen's eyes as she strokes her fingers through Briar's mane. "Forgive me, Your Greatness. I didn't think you'd fancy a ride at this hour, let alone be awake." She gathers the reins and extends them to Cerylia. "I'm headed back inside."

The queen ignores the gesture. "He rides well, doesn't he?"

Opal glances at the castle before finally making eye contact. "Indeed. He's a lovely creature." She brings her gaze back to Briar. "I've ridden some of the other horses, but none of them seem to listen the way he does."

"It appears we have similar observations," Cerylia says as she reaches into a nearby pail to produce some hay. Briar's ears twitch as she extends her hand. He lowers his head to take the hay from her palm. "I've always favored him. Dane and I used to squabble over who would get to take him out in the mornings." An overwhelming sadness burrows in her chest. "I'd usually let him win. It was his horse anyway."

Opal remains silent. She walks over to where Cerylia is standing, then takes the queen's palm in her left hand. With her right, she digs into her pocket and pulls out two sugar cubes. "He seems to like these." A small smile tugs at her lips as she places the cubes in the queen's hands.

Cerylia closes her fingers around them.

Silence ensues.

"I suppose I should get going. I promised Felix I'd help him with something—"

"How is he doing?" Cerylia interrupts. She bites the inside of her cheek, hoping not to sound too desperate. Not only does she have no idea what's going on with the Caldari under her own roof—she also fears that she's lost their respect, and that any sort of alliance they'd once had no longer exists.

"After Arden left without a trace? Not well, I'm afraid."

"Can you see her in your inversions?"

Opal shakes her head. "No."

"So we haven't any idea where she is?"

"I wish we did." She turns to leave.

"And what about you?" Cerylia asks, not wanting the conversation to end. "How are *you* doing, Opal?"

When she turns back around, there's nothing but concern etched in her expression. "I'm fine, Your Greatness. I'm doing just fine."

Cerylia opens her mouth to respond, but Opal turns again before she can get the words out. She watches in vain as the girl retreats to the castle, to the place that had once been the Caldaris' safe haven. As of late, it doesn't feel like anything of the sort.

.

BRAXTON HORNSBY

BRAXTON CAN FEEL the intensity of Xerin's gaze as if it were searing a hole in the back of his head.

"Almost ready?"

Braxton turns to face him. "Just about." He tosses the final few items in his knapsack before throwing it over his shoulder. "I thought you would have shaped by now."

Xerin regards him with curious eyes. "Into what, exactly?"

"Well, seeing as we're going to Drakken Isle, I figured you'd shape into a dragon and . . . " His voice trails off as Xerin clicks his tongue against the roof of his mouth.

"Shaping into a dragon and flying over Trendalath wouldn't be wise. Not now, what with the king looking for us"—he pauses, looking him up and down—"*all* of us."

"What would you suggest then?"

"Riding horseback, of course." He pulls a map from his back pocket and splays it across the table. "We'll ride together through the Roviel Woods, to the edge of the Vaekith Mountains. We'll pass through Volkharn and once we get to the shore, I'll shape into a dragon and take you to Drakken Isle." He stops, seeming to consider the validity of his own plan. "The mountains should provide enough coverage."

Braxton follows his finger as he traces the path once more. "Think it's discreet enough?"

He nods. "Should be. It'll take us a few days though."

"We best get moving then," Braxton says, heading for the door.

"Have you told anyone that you're planning to leave?"

His hand falters on the door handle. Feeling foolish, he turns around to face Xerin. "The window?"

"Unless you want Cerylia, Delwynn, and the rest of the Caldari on your ass," he retorts, "yes, the window is probably your best bet." Xerin answers his next question before he can get the words out. "Don't worry, you won't plummet to your death." He goes to the armoire and pulls out a long knotted rope with a detachable harness that Braxton hadn't even realized was there.

"How—?"

Xerin puts his hand up as if to silence him, then starts assembling the harness onto the rope. "Do you remember when I brought you here to speak with Cerylia about providing a safe haven for the Caldari?"

At the mention of it, Braxton can't help but flash back to the first time he'd met the queen—alone. Xerin had taken him here, told him what to do, and then had vanished into the bushes . . . or so he'd thought. "You broke into the castle *before* she agreed to house us?"

A shadow flickers across Xerin's blood-red eyes. "I wanted to make sure we were well-equipped with an escape route, in case we ever needed one."

"How did you know what rooms we'd be staying in?"

"I didn't." He clasps the final buckle and throws the contraption over to Braxton.

"Are you saying there's a harness hidden in *every* single room of this castle?"

A ghost of a smile touches Xerin's lips. "Just about."

Braxton shakes his head as he locks the door and secures the rope around the leg of his dresser. He pulls it taut, knowing that it won't go anywhere with that monstrosity holding it down. He eases into the harness before throwing the rope out the window. "See you down there."

A buttery glow fills the room as Xerin shapes into his tried-and-true form—the falcon. Braxton ducks as he soars right past his head and out into the darkening night sky. He braces himself against the window, holding the rope for support. His heart almost stops when he assesses the distance from where he's crouched.

It's a long way down.

The falcon glides by the window, its wings almost swiping his cheek. "Okay, okay," he says, cautiously lowering himself over the ledge. With his feet pressed firmly against the stone and his hands wrapped tightly around the rope, Braxton begins his descent.

ARDEN ELIRI

"IT'S TOO DANGEROUS."

My gaze meets Haskell's. I look down at the piece of parchment, the one where I've written out my knowledge of the Savant and their abilities. "Please, will you just hear me out? This is *something*, but I know it's not enough. We need to learn about the other Savant members if we ever stand the chance of—"

"Of what?" he interrupts, his tone callous. "Of overthrowing Trendalath? Of killing Tymond?" He throws his hands in the air. "Are you even listening to yourself? You and I alone can't defeat him. And perhaps you're forgetting that you *are* the most wanted illusié in Aeridon right now."

I narrow my eyes at him. "You didn't let me finish." He doesn't realize that I'm basing what I want to share next solely on his current reaction—and it's not looking good. Perhaps now isn't the best time to point out that it all *may* have been an illusion . . . but that theory only applies to my situation. It doesn't explain whether the orb that led him to our father's hideaway was real or not. I decide to keep it to myself.

"Arden," he says with an exasperated sigh, "the only reason I was able to find you was because Xerin told me where you were. I almost didn't believe it—that you were actually *alive*. All this time, I'd thought I was the only Eliri left. You have no idea what that news meant to me. I didn't risk everything just to go and risk everything all over again."

I see his point, but I'm not budging. "I know you risked everything in going to Trendalath, in rescuing me from Tymond . . . from death. I am so grateful for that." I pause, knowing my next words won't be received well. "But if we aren't going to get the answers we need to defeat him, it will all be for naught. And Trendalath—hell, even *Aeridon*—will remain exactly as it is."

Haskell knocks his fist on the table, sending a few quills flying off the sides. He squeezes the bridge of his nose, then takes a long, steady breath. "Do you know what happened to our mother?"

The question comes as a shock. I open my mouth to respond, but the words elude me.

"The King's Savant murdered her."

His icy gaze chills me to my core. "How?"

"There are multiple theories, none of which have been verified. Not surprising," he scoffs, his disdain for Tymond more evident than I've ever seen before. "But what I *can* tell you is that she didn't deserve it."

"Do you remember her?"

His voice cracks. "Only slightly."

"I need to show you something." I go to my knapsack and gingerly remove the folded photo I'd stolen from Braxton's childhood room. I walk to him, slowly, and wait for his eyes to meet mine before handing it over.

At first, his expression remains blank, but it quickly turns to disbelief. "Where did you get this?"

I ignore his question. "That's you, isn't it?" I ask, pointing to the young boy in the photo. "And that's our mother."

His stunned silence is the only answer I need.

Clutching the photo in one hand, he reaches behind him with the other, searching for something to sit on. I guide him toward a bench, sitting next to him as he processes the information.

"Where did you get this?" he asks again.

"Trendalath castle. From"—I stop myself, not knowing if Haskell knows who Braxton is—"the prince's room." I point to the picture of the other young boy in the photo. The one with white-blonde hair.

He flips the photo over. "Your birth date."

I nod, not knowing what to say next. We're both at a loss for words, and rightly so.

After a stretched silence, I whisper, "Does this mean—?"

"—that we share blood with the Tymonds?" The photograph drops from his hands, fluttering to the ground. "Hard to say."

A lump forms in my throat. "What do we do?"

But I already know how he'll answer. For the first time since I've met him, Haskell doesn't know *what* to do.

And neither do I.

DARIUS TYMOND

THE TREK INTO Volkharn takes every bit of two hours to complete, but it's time well spent. Panting, Darius arrives at the gates, hardly stopping to catch his breath. He holds his ring in front of the enormous metal structure, smiling as the glow from the amethyst unlocks the entrance. The gates swing open to let him pass.

As he ventures further into the mountains, it grows darker and darker, the green light from his staff doing little to light the way. The sound of rushing water greets him, and he knows he's getting close. He steps onto the floating stones below him, going the distance until he crosses over to the other side. His gaze settles on a wall covered in vines. He reaches out in front of him with both hands, fingers spread wide, searching as they brush against leaves and sprigs, stems and flower petals. Finally, he senses the invisible veil that's separating him from where he wants to be—where he *needs* to be. His ring pulsates the moment it comes into contact, and the veil is lifted.

The reflection of moonlight in the vast body of water illuminates the entire mountain cavern. Varied rock formations scale the sides, and a series of breathtaking waterfalls cascade down the mountain. They flow into multiple streams, dancing along the bank's edge, until finally pouring into the expanse of cerulean before him.

He has arrived.

Breathing in the crisp air, Darius leans his staff against the wall. He removes his robes, gently laying them near the entrance. He locates the sturdiest edge of a triangular shaped stone, testing it with a quick press of his toe, then steps onto it. With his feet firmly in place and his arms extended outward, he slowly floats to the center of the water. The waterfalls cease and everything around him stills.

The formation halts, securing itself into place below the water. Darius joins his hands, interlacing his fingers, as he stares intently into the vast space, the energy in his ring humming violently against his skin. He closes his eyes and waits. Although he can't see it, he senses the shift.

His eyelids flutter open just as a familiar black mist begins to take shape above the water. It grows larger and denser, to the point where it blocks his entire view of the cavern. His gaze unrelenting, he waits patiently until the tip of a red cloak emerges. It breaks through the mist, floating toward him with tremendous speed. As discreetly as he can manage, he braces himself, waiting until it gets just close enough.

Three.

Two.

One.

At just an arm's length away, he stoops down, his reflection clear as day, and thrusts his hand into the water. The amethyst ring glows from beneath the surface, and it only takes moments for the red cloak to halt in its tracks and dissipate entirely.

A radiant black orb takes its place.

His heart swells as it glides toward him, leaving red wisps in its wake. He reaches for it, but it doesn't come closer. "It is done."

A faint glimmer is the only response.

"It is only a matter of time until we meet again." His voice catches. "You have my word."

Without warning, the orb begins to retreat.

Panic rises in his chest. "Stay," Darius commands as he reaches out. "Please."

He feels a flicker of hope as it lingers in the air, but it's instantly extinguished as the orb crashes into the water, disappearing from view.

"No!" Darius cries, plunging his hand back into the water over and over again. "Please!" But no matter how rapid his movements, no matter how desperate his pleas, the orb does not return.

He remains on his knees, clutching the edge of the stone until the water stills once more. Slowly, he lifts his head, his eyes meeting his own tormented reflection.

His jaded spring.

RYDAN HELSTROM

ANOTHER EARLY MORNING.

Rydan slinks around the corner of the house, cringing as the door to Vira's room creaks. He waits a moment before poking his head inside, relieved to see that Vira's body is still rising and falling rhythmically beneath the sheets. Still sound asleep.

Gently, he closes the door behind him. Determined not to make a sound, he tiptoes to the kitchen, swiping a ripe red apple from the basket on the countertop, then heads out for the day. The sun is rising faster as spring draws nearer, and today is already much brighter than the few days prior. He picks up the pace as he hikes toward the hidden cove he's visited every morning for the past week—but when he arrives, he's dismayed to find that someone seems to have discovered *his* private beach.

Staying hidden in the dense thicket, Rydan steps around fallen branches and clusters of pebbles until he reaches the edge of the forest. With a sturdy oak tree as his only cover, he slowly peers around it, trying to make sense of the commotion going on near the water's edge.

A dozen or so people are huddled together in a semi-circle, talking quietly amongst themselves. Rydan scans their faces—the ones in his line of sight, anyway—to see if he recognizes any of them. No recollection, but then . . .

His eyes widen as his gaze lifts to the beached ship on the shore. He couldn't forget the name of it even if he tried. *The Corsair.*

Avery Bancroft's ship.

As if on cue, an auburn head pops up from the middle of the circle. Rydan can't hear exactly what he's saying, but he appears to be giving directions. *Who are these people? And why are they on the edge of the island instead of at the main dock?*

He watches intently as, one by one, the group dwindles. Rydan considers following them to see where they're headed—that is, until it becomes clear they've intentionally broken off into different directions. Defeated, he slumps down against the tree. He racks his brain, replaying the conversations between Avery and Vira, hoping that something of interest will stick out, but he comes up short. All he remembers is Avery saying he comes to Lonia often, but he'd never mentioned carrying stowaways. Then again, why would he?

When Rydan turns back around to check out the beach, Avery is nowhere in sight. He scans the length of the shore, his eyes landing on *The Corsair*.

Does he dare?

Rydan takes off in a sprint, jumping over rocks and bushes as he approaches the vessel. He makes it to the other side—the one he couldn't see from his original vantage point—and heads toward the back. He stops in his tracks when he realizes there's no rope or ladder thrown over the side. A breeze rustles in the leaves above him. He watches as one breaks free and drifts down the stern.

Looks like I'm climbing a tree.

Any hope for his plan falters as he runs his hand along the smooth white bark. *Of course* it would be a birch tree—one that's nearly impossible to climb without some sort of assistance . . .

He assesses the distance between the tree and the exterior of the ship. Fortunately, it's close enough. Whether this is a good idea or not, it's the only one he has. He grabs the bottom of his shirt, then rips it over his head and wraps it around the base of the tree, just above shoulder height. With his back pressed against the metal frame of the ship, he bends his arms inward so that the shirt grows taut. Steadying himself, he puts one boot on the tree, the other just below it. With almost all of his weight behind him, he begins to walk his feet, one at a time, up the trunk. Each time he's almost parallel with the ground, he leans forward and methodically wiggles his looped shirt further up the tree and, like an inchworm, continues the climb.

When he's finally level with the railing of the ship, he bends his knees even more and quarter-turns his chest. He pushes off the tree, releases the shirt, and extends his arms, spinning in the air until his fingers meet the cold metal, legs dangling beneath him. He glances over his shoulder as the shirt flutters to the sand. The immense effort of scaling the tree already has his arms shaking, and he's convinced they're just seconds away from giving out entirely. With a final grunt, he pulls himself over the railing, flopping onto the deck like a fish out of water.

Panting, he rolls over onto his back and closes his eyes. Salty air fills his lungs as he takes a deep inhale, followed by another, and another. Once his breathing returns to normal, he smiles, almost laughing aloud at his foolish, yet effective plan. But the moment he pulls himself upright, his smile fades.

Arms crossed, Avery stands before him. His mouth twitches into a smirk. "Didn't fancy seeing you here."

CERYLIA JARETH

IT'S BEEN ABOUT a week since Cerylia's short interaction with Opal, but every morning since, she's woken up early and gone to the stables, hoping to find Briar out of his stall. It's strange, feeling disappointed seeing him there, waiting for her—but she'd hoped to continue her conversation with Opal, to open up the line of communication again and rebuild her trust. Whether that's even remotely a possibility at this point remains unclear.

Briar greets her with a warm neigh, nuzzling against her hand as she pets the side of his face. "Good morning to you, too." She opens the stall and guides him to the edge of one of the many trails that leads into the forest. A sigh escapes her. Another morning ride alone.

She secures the saddle before mounting the horse, then situates herself and grabs hold of the reins. Yellows and oranges light up the sky and, just below the horizon, the mountains are cast in a mesmerizing glow of indigo and violet. With the tops of the trees blooming green, the sight before her could easily be mistaken for a grand illusion—she, of all people, would know. Not even the most skilled illusié could conjure up something so beautiful.

With a slight tug on the reins and a light squeeze of her knees, Briar takes off along the dirt trail. Like her cloak, his mane billows in the crisp air, and if it weren't already wrapped around her, she's certain it'd fly away. One by one, she ducks underneath the low hanging branches, keeping her eyes focused on what awaits at the other end.

The trees begin to grow taller and, along with them, the branches. Delicate flowers of various colors bloom all around her, signaling she's getting close. With a giant leap, Briar's hooves leave the forest behind before landing in a grassy meadow. It's both strange and comforting being able to see for miles and miles, with only a faint shadow of the Vaekith Mountains protruding from the skyline.

Briar slows down as Cerylia pulls on the reins. Once he comes to a complete stop, she dismounts, then feeds him a few sugar cubes and strokes his mane. She pulls the hood of her cloak over her head and slowly turns to face the endless expansion of tall grass and rolling hills. Reins in hand, she and Briar trudge through the meadow with no aim and no purpose other than to walk . . . and to think.

About halfway into their third or fourth circle around, she stumbles upon some lovely blue and purple wildflowers. She plucks a few from the ground, admiring their simplicity and beauty, but just as she's placing them in her pocket, she hears the pounding of hooves in the near distance. Briar seems to sense the incoming intrusion as well because his ears twitch and he kicks against the ground, breaking up the dirt underneath.

"Shhh," Cerylia soothes. She pats his nose, then the side of his face, but neither do much to comfort him. Seeing as they're on the outskirts of the meadow, near the edge of the forest, she decides to secure the reins around a nearby tree. The sound of hooves grows louder, then stops altogether. With caution, she steps in front of Briar so that half of her body is in the woods, the other half visible to whoever's out there. For some reason, she feels a slight urge to shout and reveal herself—but something tells her to keep quiet.

Relief washes over her as a familiar jade cloak rides in on Penny, her warm-natured and docile Percheron.

Opal clearly spots her from a distance but, strangely enough, doesn't trot over to her. Instead, she remains completely still in the middle of the field.

With slight hesitation, Cerylia swallows her pride and loosens the reins from around the tree. She mounts Briar and they cautiously approach Opal and Penny. Briar stops just past Penny's head so that she and the queen have no other choice than to look each other directly in the eye.

Opal speaks first. "When I saw Briar missing from the stables, I figured you'd taken him."

An odd thing to say, seeing as Briar is *her* horse, but Cerylia ignores the girl's condescending tone. "Yes, it's a lovely morning for a ride. I was surprised to find that you hadn't taken him out already." She almost adds that she knows Opal hasn't ridden Briar since they'd last spoken, but thinks better of it. "How's Penny?"

Opal gives the queen a wry smile. "I think you know the answer to that. Like I mentioned last time, I'm partial to Briar."

Cerylia narrows her eyes. "Did you come here for a reason, Opal?"

"Yes." Her expression darkens. "I need to speak with you."

"About?"

For the first time in a long time, Opal seems uncharacteristically uncomfortable. "The last time we spoke, I—well, I believe I know what it is you wanted to ask me . . . what you were thinking."

Surely she hadn't been *that* transparent. The idea had only formed in her mind just moments before their last conversation. She hadn't hinted at or mentioned inverting back to that day—at least she *thought* she hadn't. "Care to divulge?"

Opal's grip tightens. "I know you want me to take you back to the day of Aldreda's death. I know you want the opportunity to kill her before Arden can—to get vengeance for Dane, for what she did all those years ago." She takes a deep breath but doesn't say anything further.

"Wouldn't you?" Cerylia feels her own grip go rigid, her shoulders tensing. "It isn't just about Dane."

Opal tilts her head, curious. "What else is it about, then?"

Her question is met with a deafening silence. The queen averts her gaze, looking to the sky to keep her rage from surfacing.

Opal doesn't ask a second time. "I cannot invert and take you back, Your Greatness. I cannot allow you to redo what has already been done." She shakes her head. "We'd be risking too much."

Cerylia shoots her an icy glare. "In what way exactly? *How* would we be risking too much?"

"The Mallum," Opal whispers. "For starters, I'd lose my abilities and . . . "

"And what?"

With a knowing look, she says the one thing Cerylia never expected to hear. "And you'd lose *yours*, Your Greatness."

BRAXTON HORNSBY

BY THE TIME they reach the stables on Sardoria grounds, only one horse remains. Braxton follows Xerin inside, watching in amusement as he throws his hands in the air. "There were at least three when I last checked!"

Braxton gives him a slap on the shoulder, then walks over to the only full stall. He reads the text aloud on the iron nameplate. "While I hop on ol' Whitley here, looks like you'll be shaping into a horse after all."

Xerin mutters something indiscernible before opening the empty stall next to Whitley. "We'd better make this fast. I'm guessing Cerylia's out riding now. She likes to go in the mornings." Braxton's about to ask him how he knows this, but Xerin seems to read his mind. "I've flown over a lot of places and I've seen a lot of things. Trust me when I say that the queen likes to take her horses out before dawn, and she usually goes northeast to a nearby meadow."

"Is that the route we were going to take?"

Xerin nods. "Instead, we'll take a slight detour, head south. Once we're a little ways into the Roviel Woods, well past the meadows, we'll head north again before turning east."

When he doesn't say anything else, Braxton gives him an affirming nod, even though he's not familiar with the area—or their travel plans, for that matter.

Xerin places his hand on the horse's side. "For lords' sakes, turn around, would ya?"

"Oh, right," Braxton says as he averts his gaze. The inside of the stable flashes yellow, and when he looks back, there are two horses instead of one. "Perhaps you should have left your stall open," he says with a laugh, but when Xerin gives him a harsh nudge on the shoulder that nearly knocks him off his feet, Braxton's no longer smiling. "It was only a joke. Take it easy," he says, swinging the gate to Xerin's stall open.

Xerin sways his mane and trots out, hardly giving Braxton a chance to mount his horse and follow. Fortunately, Whitley is a calm, even-tempered creature, and he finds himself following Xerin's hoof-prints in no time.

~§ ~§ ~§

About an hour into the journey, Braxton's already wishing he'd taken the time to have a proper meal—and that he'd worn a heavier coat. The spring leaves on the trees have already created a thicker canopy than usual for this time of year, blocking out most of the sun's warmth. Fragments of sunlight shine through the leaves but don't quite make it down to the forest floor. That, coupled with the crisp gusts of wind, makes for a less-than-ideal journey. Xerin, of course, wouldn't notice this because, well, he's a *horse*.

When they finally reach a crossing at a stream, Braxton yells out a warning to Xerin, then brings Whitley to a stop. He jumps off, searching for berry bushes and fruit trees—hoping that *something* might be ripe given the early season—but no such luck. He swipes his canteen from his knapsack and goes to the stream to fill it. Keeping his focus on the container, he shouts over the rushing water, "I may need you to turn into a bear or a wolf or something and catch us some food. I can get a fire started . . ."

But when he turns to look over his shoulder, Xerin is nowhere to be seen.

ARDEN ELIRI

THINGS BETWEEN HASKELL and I have been . . . awkward, to say the least. Even though we're in this together—what with finding out we *may* share a bloodline with the Tymonds—things have been tenser than ever. If he's feeling anything like I am, then he's probably convinced himself that he's completely alone in this and that it's something he'll have to deal with on his own. A solitary endeavor.

It's not a good place to be, believe me.

Today is a rare day because we happen to be in the woods. *Together.* Every time Haskell transports to get supplies, he's asked me to come along, mostly in case something goes wrong. It's not the most honorable of intentions—transporting to different regions to steal food, clothing, and weapons—but as refugees hiding out in Lirath Cave, we don't have much of a choice. I do give him credit, though, because seeing as spring is upon us, his first attempt is always to catch his own game to cook for our meals. It's only when he doesn't succeed that he prepares to transport.

Today is one of those days.

"You'll only take what you need?" Even though I'm staring at the back of his head, I can sense his eyes rolling. "Haskell, did you hear me?"

He briefly glances over his shoulder. "Yes, only what *we* need."

I stop in my tracks as Juniper skips ahead of me. "I wish you wouldn't say it like that—like I'm completely useless or something."

"You know that's not how I meant it." He continues walking. "You have to remember, I've been doing this for a long time. I just need you to trust me."

"Maybe one of these days you'll actually take me with you because you *want* to, instead of seeing me as just back-up," I mutter under my breath.

Clearly having heard me, he turns around. He slowly crosses his arms, as if to emphasize how immature my behavior is. "Your job is to wait here until I get back. I'm sure there will be plenty for both of us to carry. Can you do that for me?"

I shrug before reluctantly nodding my head.

"Where to this time?" I ask, hoping he doesn't say Trendalath. I'm getting tired of the stale bread, mealy fruit, and day-old fish. I could really go for some ripe mangoes and apples, and fresh fish that actually *tastes* like fish. "What about the Isle of Lonia?"

He shakes his head. "No can do. I'm afraid Lonia is off limits."

I roll my eyes. "Is Lonia also *too dangerous*?"

"If you really must know, I would love to go to Lonia, but I've never been. And if I've never been, I'm unable to transport there."

It all makes sense now. "So that's why all the food tastes the same—because it *is* the same." I sigh. During my time with the Cruex, I'd gotten to know the neighboring towns of Trendalath pretty well—Declorath, Chialka, Miraenia—and I'd also learned that each one heavily depends on the kingdom to provide food. Aldreda had made it her mission to ensure that the kingdom's leftovers were rationed on a weekly basis between the three towns—although after the feud with Miraenia, perhaps they were only rationing between two. But, with Aldreda now gone, I'm guessing any goodwill has been removed entirely.

"Could you at least try Miraenia?" I plead. "We'll have a better chance of scoring fresh game and ripe fruit."

He raises a brow. "It's usually harder to come by, but I'll do my best." He keeps his distance from me, readying himself for the journey ahead. "Please. Do us both a favor and stay put."

I heave a loud sigh as he disappears from view.

෯   ෯   ෯

I must have dozed off because when I wake, it's nearly sundown. I'm immediately shaken from my hazy state when I realize that Haskell still isn't back—at least, I don't think he is.

He can't be. He would have seen me. I listened to him and stayed here, just like he asked.

A tremor of panic rises in my chest, even more so when I realize that Juniper isn't anywhere near me. My senses heighten as I begin to search the woods.

"Juniper!" I call out. "Haskell!"

Each step brings with it a new level of unease.

I rush back to Lirath Cave, hoping with every fiber of my being that my brother will be there cooking dinner, with Juniper curled up in her usual spot underneath the bench by the fire. But when I arrive, the cave is completely dark. No flickering torches. No ash floating in the air. No campfire smell.

Fear surges through me.

I race back through the trees, returning to the spot where I'd last seen Haskell. I heave a jagged breath as I frantically search the area. I look for footprints, both human and animal, but come up short. I extend my search deeper into the forest, cursing the descending sun for setting so quickly.

And then . . . twilight falls around me.

I've been here before.

I know this feeling.

I brace myself for what's next, but it doesn't come. Confused, I spin in a circle, yelling out Haskell's name, only to be greeted by silence. I sink to my knees and smash my hands against the ground. An array of broken twigs, leaves, and wilted flower petals stick to my sweaty palms. I try to get a grip on myself, but it's all just too much. My family—my *real* family—is gone.

DARIUS TYMOND

AS HE'D INSTRUCTED, Cyrus is waiting for him at the bottom of the Volkharn cliff. He jumps to attention at the sight of the king, hurrying over to retrieve his staff and usher him into the carriage. Darius subtly expresses his gratitude before leaning back into the velvet-cushioned interior, gazing out the window as Cyrus readies the horse to head back to Trendalath.

Between twilight and the dim lighting in the carriage, Darius ought to have fallen asleep, but his mind is reeling. He goes back and forth the entire ride, not realizing they've arrived at the gates until the horses come to a sudden halt.

Keeping his irritation at bay, Darius composes himself before sticking his head out of the carriage. What should have been a dull, quiet evening has been replaced with absolute chaos. His stationed guards are not in their usual positions, and, furthermore, the drawbridge is lowered with no one keeping watch. He bites down on the inside of his cheek, nearly drawing blood. He exits the carriage, motioning for Cyrus to follow him.

"What in lords' name is going on?" Cyrus shouts as he rushes toward the entrance, just steps behind Darius.

"Do you think I'd be running if I knew?" he shouts back. He rushes up the stone steps, nearly colliding headfirst with Hugh Darby.

"Your Majesty," he says, eyes wide, "please forgive my lack of attention. There's an emergency. There's an intruder in the castle."

"Where are the rest of the Cruex?" Darius snaps.

"They're upstairs, on the third floor . . . near the forbidden wing."

Darius's breath hitches. "In what room?"

Hugh shifts uncomfortably between his feet. "In—er, well," he stammers.

Darius grabs him by the shoulders. "You are wasting my time. Spit it out."

"In the prince's childhood room," he says quickly. "They're doing their best to apprehend the intruder." He glances over his shoulder, then lowers his voice to a whisper. "It isn't proving to be easy. He's one of *them,* Your Majesty. A *Caldari.*"

Darius shoves the babbling Cruex member out of the way before darting up the steps, climbing two at a time. He rushes down each corridor, only slowing down to catch a quick breath before taking off again. The hallway grows darker and darker until he reaches the one place in the castle that he hasn't visited in over ten years.

Braxton's old room.

The door is wide open, and there are sounds of a scuffle inside. He can hear his Cruex members grunting with every missed swing of their weapons. *And they call themselves assassins.*

Without delay, he marches to the entrance, twisting his amethyst ring so that it's flush against his palm. Between the darkness in the room and the Cruex clad in black, it's nearly impossible to see. "Show yourself!" he commands. At the sound of his voice, the Cruex lower their weapons. "I said show yourself!"

The heavy breathing stops.

Darius takes a cautious step forward into the room.

No one moves.

He can't see, but he can sense something approaching from the side. He turns his head, a twisted grin creeping across his face. With the Mallum at his fingertips, he is the furthest thing from afraid. "Show yourself," he whispers.

A gruff voice says, "Coward."

Darius blindly lunges, but the intruder is too quick. An enraging flash of green follows.

ARDEN ELIRI

JUST AS THE tears are about to come streaming down my face, I hear a yip a short distance away. *Juniper.* I jump to my feet and turn toward the sound. A blinding flash of jade follows.

My senses heightened, I race toward the fading green light, my legs moving faster than they ever have before. When I arrive on the scene, my chest tightens. Lying on the ground is my brother.

Covered in blood.

"Oh my lords, oh my lords," I say, dropping to my knees. Juniper yips again, and I can see her, shaking and hiding behind a tree. "It's okay, Juni," I say unevenly, even though I don't believe my own words. "Everything is going to be okay."

I look down at the red heap before me. Gently, I grab my brother's shoulders and shake them. "Haskell, can you hear me?"

He doesn't stir.

I try again. "Haskell?"

His eyes remain closed. His chest doesn't move. I notice there's a drop of crimson trickling from his mouth.

Dead. Dead. Dead.

I try to quiet the debilitating whispers swarming my mind. Even in my panicked state, I remember my abilities. "I can fix this," I say aloud, hoping that the words will affirm my actions. "I can heal you."

As I set my hands over his chest, I take a deep inhale. On the exhale, I close my eyes. I begin to search for my light, just like I had with Aldreda, begging for it to come forth, to reveal itself. For what feels like an eternity, I remain still, peeking out of my left eye every now and again, hoping to see that glowing light.

It doesn't come.

I try again, but notice I feel . . . empty.

Devoid of everything.

Despair washes over me. I retract my hands, bringing them back to my sides, my eyes trailing over Haskell's eerily still body.

Why can I no longer heal?

"No," I say aloud. "This is not how this ends." I did not reunite with my brother only to have him taken from me . . . again. I push back a wave of tears. "I can still fix this."

I look down at my useless hands before noticing something strewn off to the side of the forest. Even through the glassiness of my eyes, I can see that it's a bag full of supplies.

The one he'd left with.

I don't hesitate to rush over to it. "Come on," I say, digging through the contents. "There has to be something in here." Something clinks at the very bottom. I pull out a vial of golden liquid, recognizing it immediately. I remove the cork from the top and take a whiff, my eyes watering at the putrid smell—and yet, I feel a flicker of hope. It's the same liquid Harrod Oakes had administered after the unwelcome infliction I'd experienced in the Daegrum Chambers. *A brew to heal severe injuries caused by illusié.* It isn't lost on me that finding the vial in his bag means that Haskell had gone to Trendalath—and that someone had tried to kill him.

I bring the vial to my brother's mouth, parting his lips just enough to ensure the liquid doesn't trickle out. The empty vial drops from my hand and rolls onto the ground next to me as I wait.

And wait. And wait.

He doesn't move.

I press my hands to my forehead, covering my eyes, feeling the tears once again as they threaten to fall. I squeeze them shut as a whimper escapes me.

Please come back. Please.

While I can't be certain exactly how much time passes, it feels excruciatingly long. Just when I think all hope is lost . . . his chest rises.

RYDAN HELSTROM

RYDAN GAZES UP at Avery with what is surely a fool's expression. Slowly, he pushes himself to his feet.

"Lose your shirt along the way?"

"Had to get up here somehow."

"You're trespassing."

Rydan angles his head. "So are you."

Avery throws his head back in amusement. "And in what way am *I* trespassing? Might I remind you, you're on *my* ship."

"Merchant ships are supposed to dock at the harbor. Does this look like a harbor to you?" He gives a sarcastic sweep of his hand.

"Not that it's any of your business, but I can do as I damn well please." He rolls his eyes before angling his head toward the beach. "Now get off my ship."

"I saw you the other day."

Avery's face falls.

"Who were they?"

The once confident man before him fades. "I don't know who you're talking about."

"The dozen or so people you brought here on this very ship," Rydan clarifies, his tone razor sharp. "I saw you from the woods. You huddled everyone together and then had them break off, one by one."

Avery just looks at him, stunned.

"Who were they?" Rydan repeats.

He fumbles for words. "They're, well—they're just some people who needed a ride to Lonia."

Not good enough. "Where'd they come from?"

Avery presses his mouth into a firm line, his eyes narrowing. "Why are you so interested in people you've never even met? Shouldn't you be focused on your own relationships?" He moves his head from left to right, scanning the area. "Speaking of, where's Vira?"

"You're avoiding my question." His voice doesn't waver. "Who were they and where did they come from?"

Avery takes a few steps forward, stopping just inches from Rydan's face. "That's none of your concern."

Rydan's voice comes out as a whisper, speaking the one truth neither of them can ignore. "They're illusié, aren't they?"

Avery's eyes go frank and cold.

Rydan already knows the answer to his next question, but he asks it anyway. "You are too, aren't you?"

Avery shifts uncomfortably between his feet.

"You know, this would go a whole lot faster—and be a lot less painful—if you'd just open up and talk to me." A sharp pain shoots through his chest as he recalls that he used to say the exact same thing to Arden after their Cruex training sessions. It'd usually worked and she'd spilled whatever was on her mind.

Hopefully it'll work on Avery, too.

Avery steps back, studying him for a moment before saying, "I'm only telling you this because of my trust in Vira. If she's chosen to spend time with you"—he looks Rydan up and down—"then I have to assume it's for good reason."

Rydan ignores the less-than-subtle jab and waits for him to continue.

"Yes, I am illusié, and so are the people I brought here." He lifts his arms and shrugs. "Is that what you hoped to hear?"

Rydan shifts his gaze from Avery's face so that he's looking just past his shoulder, out at the vast ocean. The color of the sky and the water match almost perfectly,

114

essentially eliminating any distinction between the two along the horizon. He prolongs the pause, choosing his next words carefully. "The way you brought them here— out of sight, away from the public—it suggests that they're fugitives of some sort. That they're not supposed to be here."

Avery shakes his head. "On the contrary, they *are* supposed to be here. This is their home."

"Then why the secrecy?"

He sighs. "Because there's a good chance I'm going to have to take them back."

"Back where?" Rydan presses, feeling his frustration rise with every cryptic answer.

Avery looks skyward as a dark cloud rolls overhead, then observes the shore and the forest with furrowed brows. The sudden shift in his demeanor is more than noticeable. "Come on, let's talk about this inside."

Rydan follows him along the edge of the deck, plodding down the stairs that lead to the galley. Avery pulls a nearby crate out from underneath a cabinet, gesturing for Rydan to do the same. "So?"

"We'll talk about the people I brought here in a moment, but first I need to know . . . what's your ability?"

The question hits Rydan right between the eyes. "I'm sorry?"

"Your illusié ability. What is it?"

"Oh." He lifts up his hands so that his palms are facing him. "I'm an Ignitor."

Avery sits back on his crate, amused.

"What about you?"

Avery mimics the motion of Rydan's hands with one glaringly obvious difference—the flames dancing at his fingertips. "Looks to me like we're cut from the same cloth."

CERYLIA JARETH

"HOW COULD SHE possibly have found out?" Cerylia paces back and forth across the White Room. "I've been so careful. I can't even remember the last time I—" She stops in her tracks, her gaze resting on Delwynn's perplexed face. She knows she's been rambling on for hours about this, refusing to leave the room like a stubborn child would, but logic defies this situation.

"Your Greatness, Opal's abilities have only gotten stronger since she's arrived. She's sharp, clever, and adaptable. Frankly, I don't know how she *didn't* find out sooner."

His response does little to placate her. In fact, it does just the opposite. "Please fetch me some tea."

"I can have one of the serv—"

She shoots him a pointed glare before he can finish his sentence. Without another word, he bows and exits the room. She waits until the doors click into place to indicate that she is truly and utterly *alone*. Her throne calls to her, but she can't sit at a time like this.

And so she paces.

Back and forth.

Back and forth.

The tea arrives too soon.

Delwynn wheels the cart over to the window, only to push it back the way he came as the queen changes direction. "Your Greatness, if you'd take a seat, I can serve you properly."

Cerylia halts, then turns on her heel. She knows he's just doing his job—doing *exactly* what she's asked of him—but in her current state, she'd like nothing more than to flip the cart over and bring the dishes and flatware crashing to the ground. As titillating as that would be, it would also be wildly inappropriate; and so she subdues the thought and retreats to her throne.

Sensing her growing irritation, Delwynn works quickly to prepare the tea. The cup and saucer shake in his hands, the scalding liquid nearly sloshing over the sides as he climbs the steps to serve her.

She eases into her seat the moment the brew hits her lips. It soothes her from the inside, her nerves calming, tone softening. "Thank you."

Delwynn bows his head before walking back down the steps. He waits for her to finish before saying, "Perhaps it'd be wise to just speak with Opal, tell her what she already knows. You confided in her once before and it brought you the truth about Dane . . . " His voice tapers off at her deepening frown. "She is a loyal ally, Your Greatness. I wouldn't take that lightly, nor would I take it for granted."

Before she can formulate a response, the doors to the White Room burst open. Startled, Cerylia jumps from her seat as Delwynn stumbles backward, nearly tripping over the tea cart. She regains her composure, setting her steely gaze on the guard before her. "What is the meaning of this interruption?"

"Follow me," is all the guard says before rushing out of the room. Flummoxed, Cerylia gathers the bottom of her robes, trailing the guard all the way out of the castle and down the hill to the stables. He gestures to a bare stall. "Whitley is missing, Your Greatness."

Cerylia rushes inside to see for herself, grabbing hold of the metal bars. Sure enough, the horse is gone. "When did you first take notice?"

"Not but ten minutes ago. I came to you as soon as I realized it."

"Any sign of anyone leaving the castle?"

He shakes his head.

One glance at the ground reveals a pair of footprints leading away from the stables. "Then how do you explain this?"

The guard merely shrugs.

A pit forms in her stomach. Without saying another word, she pushes past the guard and hurries back to the castle. She climbs the many steps to Braxton's room, only to find that it's locked. She calls for Delwynn, full well knowing that he can't hear her, but stops as she sees another guard rushing toward her.

"Open this door immediately!"

"Your Greatness, I don't have a key."

"What good is your armor if you can't bust down a door?"

He seems to consider this, then bashes into the door—one, two, *three* times—but it doesn't budge.

"Again," she orders.

He switches sides, aiming for the weakest part of the door with his left shoulder. *Four, five, six.* She's about to kick the damn thing down herself when it finally flies open to reveal exactly what she'd feared.

Yet another Caldari has fled Sardoria.

BRAXTON HORNSBY

DUSK IS UPON him and there's still no sign of
Xerin. Where he's gone, Braxton hasn't even the slightest
inkling, but he's made sure to scour every inch of the
perimeter. Much to his dismay, he's alone—besides the
company of Whitley.

The horse neighs upon his return. Braxton gives her
a soothing pat on the side of her face, then grabs the
reins and secures them to a low-hanging branch.
Realizing that he'll probably have to settle in for the night,
he begins to scout the area for some shelter. He's
nowhere near the mountain range, so caverns aren't even
a remote possibility. There are a few streams and small

burrows dotted along the bank, but the likelihood of finding a hollowed out cavity to sleep in is dismal. He gazes upward at the many trees surrounding him. In this part of the woods, the branches are thick enough to hold him—but he'll have to rig together some sort of hammock if he hopes to get any sleep.

The sun continues its descent at an increasing speed, and Braxton works quickly to see what supplies he'd been smart enough to throw into his knapsack. He pulls out the harness he'd been able to detach during his escape from Sardoria, but not the lengthy rope that had aided him in landing safely on the ground. His hand sweeps over a wrinkled linen, and fortunately, some knotted rope. It's not as much as he'd hoped, but if his time in Athia had taught him anything, it's that he can do a lot with very little. He pulls the linen from his bag, sizing up the length. It's narrow, but a little over his height.

The chirping of crickets signals the impending nightfall. He doesn't have much time. On a whim, he chooses a set of trees with the thickest branches. They look sturdy enough to hold him, and they're close enough in proximity to set up his makeshift bed for the evening. He stuffs the items back in his bag and approaches the tree that looks the easiest to scale. With an underhand grip on one of the branches, he braces his left foot against the bark, then his right. With his other hand, he grabs the branch diagonal to him and repeats until he's shimmying his way up the tree.

He's panting and sore by the time he reaches the halfway point, having used muscles that an average innkeeper would *never* use. He peers below to ensure that Whitley's still there. Even from this distance, it appears she's fallen asleep standing up.

For the first time in my life, I envy a horse.

Refocusing, Braxton wiggles his knapsack off and retrieves the necessary items. He works quickly to knot the ends of the linen to make a small loop on either side, then expertly weaves the rope through the openings. He pulls the ends of the linen taut, but the only way to test its sturdiness is to attach it to the tree and apply weight.

Meaning he has to lay on it.

He narrows his eyes, squinting in the fading daylight, as he secures the rope around two trees opposite one other. Fortunately, there's a thick branch right beneath him to catch his fall—if it comes to that. He places his hand in the middle of the linen and presses down, but, as assumed, it doesn't give much indication as to how much weight it can hold.

With a grunt, he keeps one hand on the branch he's currently sitting on, then scoots his body until he's completely engulfed in the fabric. His heart nearly stops as he feels the linen sink lower and lower, but eventually, it reaches a stopping point. He loosens his grip on the branch, squeezing his eyes shut as he allows the hammock to absorb the full weight of his body. He tries to still the persistent images of plummeting to his death in the middle of the night to no avail. When he opens his eyes again, twilight has fallen all around him. His gaze travels to the sky. From up here, the thickness of the canopy isn't nearly as full, making the stars and constellations shine ten times brighter than if he were on the ground. The sight nearly takes his breath away, and it immediately reminds him of when he used to live in Athia—when he'd sneak away from the inn and go fishing late at night at Lake Ipcea.

He'd loved going there for the silence, the oneness he'd felt with nature. He'd sit there for hours, sometimes delaying his fishing because he hadn't wanted to disrupt the stillness of the water—a perfect reflection of the night sky with its glowing moon and flickering stars. It'd always been a pleasant experience, going to Lake Ipcea.

Except for that last visit.

When he'd met Xerin.

The memory flashes across his mind—of the young boy with crimson eyes who'd greeted him that night. A shiver works its way down his spine.

Where had Xerin gone tonight? Why hadn't he said anything? Why hadn't he returned? And how was he able to disappear so quickly, so *quietly*, without so much as a trace?

He braves another look over the side of the linen in

hopes of seeing another horse, or better yet, another human—but there's only Whitley. With a sigh, he carefully rolls back onto his shoulders, then folds his hands and places them underneath his head.

Xerin is not tonight's problem—sleep is.

He inches down until his left foot makes contact with the tree, then pushes off with it. The hammock begins to sway, rocking steadily, left to right, right to left, until his eyes finally close, engulfing him in a sea of black.

ARDEN ELIRI

AT A TIME such as this, how I *wish* I had a way to utilize Haskell's abilities. I've frantically been running back and forth from the cave to where Haskell lay, bringing all the supplies my arms can carry. I dump the most recent haul onto the ground next to my brother. I kneel to check his pulse. His heart's still beating, and he's still breathing, but he remains unconscious.

After he'd taken his first breath, I noticed he hadn't opened his eyes. Hadn't said a word. I'd tried to speak with him, to lift his head and get him to make some other voluntary movement, but he'd been still as a board. I'd known then that I was in trouble—with his burly frame, there was no way in hell I'd be able to get him back to the cave. So I'd brought the cave to him—or tried to, anyway.

Juniper sits patiently near the top of Haskell's head, watching me as I organize the items currently littering the forest floor. The still-lit lantern flickers in the night, but even so, I'm having trouble seeing what I'm doing. I know I need to make shelter, so I unfold four or so linens and gather some rope. I eye the trees around us, devising in my head how to use what minimal supplies I have to make a fort.

Suddenly, I feel inadequate, wishing for everyone else's abilities—Estelle's cloaking to hide us from any potential threats; Rydan's igniting to start a fire to keep us warm; Haskell's transporting so that I wouldn't have to do any of this in the first place . . . and my own abilities that, for some reason, have decided not to make an appearance when I need them most.

Frustrated, I throw the linens to the ground and kick them with my boot—which only makes things worse. They wrap themselves around my ankle as if they have a mind of their own. I yelp as I trip and fall backward onto the ground, kicking my feet in the air to free myself from the tangled trap.

When I finally stop flailing, my arms and legs are splayed out in a starfish position. I heave a loud sigh as I gaze up at the night sky. A waning crescent moon is the only thing illuminating the black abyss—not a star in sight.

I angle my head toward Haskell and the array of items sitting next to him. I push myself onto my elbows. "You're an ex-Cruex and a Caldari," I mutter to myself. "You can make a damn fort."

I roll over onto my stomach and spring to my feet. The crumpled linens and knotted rope are in my hands before I know it. Working meticulously, I knot the ropes together to make two separate lines, then secure each end around four different trees. I cross them over one another to form an *X* above Haskell's body. I then shake out the linens and begin to place them methodically over the ropes. It takes a few adjustments, but eventually the top is completely covered and the sides are enclosed.

I duck down and crawl underneath. None of the linens seem to be sagging and, even though it's a little off center (and clearly made by an amateur), it does the job. I lay on my stomach and finish organizing the various items I'd brought from the cave—books, spare clothes, parchment, wax, canteens, and two loaves of bread. Realizing my hands are shaking from lack of sustenance, I grab one of the loaves of bread and bite into it. Even though it's on the verge of being stale, I devour most of it anyway. Juniper rubs up against my arm, so I break her off a small piece. "Sorry Juni. No berries tonight."

❧   ❧   ❧

I wake to a sliver of sunlight peeking through a gap in the linens. I blink, feeling disoriented, and it takes me a minute to remember where I am and why I'm here. I turn my head to the left to see Haskell still lying there—still unconscious. The rising and falling of his chest is more noticeable—surely a good sign—but his eyes remain closed. I sit upright and stretch my arms overhead before crawling to the edge of the fort. I poke my head outside.

No sign of anyone.

I'd slept with my boots on as a precaution, in case an unexpected visitor had decided to show in the middle of the night. I can feel my hair matted against my forehead and the back of my neck, my shirt sticking to my skin. The thick linens overhead really restrict the airflow. "Keep an eye on him," I say to Juniper as I grab a spare shirt and trousers. I'm about to head out to bathe in a nearby spring when I eye the canteens. I take three empty ones with me.

It's not a far walk, maybe about ten minutes or so, but it feels so much longer. Needless to say, I hadn't slept well, so when I finally reach the spring, tucked way back in the trees, I feel as though I've been walking for hours. I pull my boots off and throw them to the side before dipping my toe in. *The perfect temperature.* I smile, pleased that at least one thing's going right, then strip down and wade into the water.

JADED SPRING

The cool rush over my shoulders is enough to make me shudder with delight. I swim to the center of the spring, to the deepest part, then shake my hair loose. I tilt my head back so that it's completely immersed, all the way up to my forehead. Slowly, I lift my right leg up, then my left, so that I'm floating on my back. Water pools onto my stomach, just above my belly button, before spilling over the sides and back into the spring. Eventually, I'm so still, my breathing so shallow, that everything around me becomes still too, as if I've become one with the spring.

With my ears bobbing at the surface, I gently close my eyes, listening to the ethereal sounds both above and below. The swishing of minnows darting to and fro. The soothing sway of bulrushes and cattails. The low hum of toads and the chirping of crickets. The subtle droplets of rain as they hit the water.

When I open my eyes, I'm surprised to see that a dark cloud has rolled overhead. I sigh, knowing I should probably get back to Haskell. Somewhat reluctantly, I swim to the edge of the spring. I pat myself dry with a linen before fastening my damp hair into a side-braid. I pull on a fresh shirt and pair of trousers, followed by my boots. Grabbing the canteens, I walk back over to the spring, kneeling to fill the first one. As soon as my hand touches the water, I stop. The hair on the back of my neck rises and a chill works its way down my spine.

It's here.

Slowly, I lift my gaze. A familiar cloak hovers over the motionless water, its red reflection scattering throughout the spring like a viral disease. The canteen drops to my side as I rise. I stand in place, waiting for it to move toward me, but it remains where it is.

Watching.

Waiting.

My words find me. "I can't give you what you want if you don't tell me what it is."

Except for the rustling of its sleeves in the breeze, it doesn't move.

I try again. "You ask me to join you and I—I've been tempted." I choose my next words carefully. "But I need to know what you are, why you're here, and why you've chosen me."

Without warning, it begins to slink toward me, like a serpent after a small mouse. My mind screams at me to take a step backward, to run—but I stand my ground. It stops just inches from my face.

Close your eyes.

The words aren't spoken, yet I can hear them all the same. I do as it says.

Now open.

I'm met with darkness. I stick my hands out in front of me, trying to force my eyes to adjust, but it's useless. I can't see *anything.* I reach for the creature, but my hands only grasp the air. Just as I'm about to speak, a reel of various images appears before me. I scan each one as they draw closer, finding a small recognition in every frame.

This one.

Suddenly, as if I'm somehow being pulled in all directions, vivid colors zoom at my face, swirling around me until I'm moving so fast, they all become a blur of beige and white. My insides scream as if they're being ripped apart, my head throbbing from the intensity, until I finally manage to squeeze my eyes shut.

I land in the middle of a field with a thud, the sun above me blindingly white. As I sit up, I'm almost certain I'm about to vomit, but the bile doesn't make it past my chest. I peek over the long strands of grass. It's then I realize . . . I've been here before. From a distance, I can see a small child—a young boy—running around with a toy, just like last time. Something catches his attention, and he darts off.

The boy vanishes from my sight as he enters a small cottage. Recalling my steps from before, I spot an open window on the side and, as discreetly as I can, run over to it. I rise just high enough to see over the ledge, and spot the young boy sitting on the floor, moving his dragon figurine along a handwoven rug. I hadn't known who he was before, but this time, the recognition is immediate.

The russet hair.

The striking emerald eyes.

It's my brother . . . *as a child.*

Which would mean that the woman to his left, with her back facing me . . . is his mother. *My* mother

Our mother.

My assumption is further confirmed as she turns to the side, her plump belly bulging. A lump forms in my throat as I realize who she's carrying. *Me.*

"Go wash up," she instructs Haskell.

Without any reservation, he does what she says.

I scan the small cottage, looking for any sign of our father, but it doesn't seem to exist. No large boots by the door. No overcoat. No photographs or portraits. Nothing.

I get a sinking feeling as I prepare to be whisked back to the present, but the memory keeps playing out. Haskell returns with a smile on his face as our mother prepares a bowl of rice, lamb, and a bread roll for dinner. Just as they're about to start eating, a knock sounds at the door.

I can sense a shift in the room almost immediately.

"Hide," she tells Haskell. "Now."

As he drops his wooden utensils onto the table and rushes into another room, she's swiftly removing his bowl and toys from sight. I strain my neck as she makes for the door, wondering who it is.

But I don't make it that far.

Within seconds, I'm pulled away from the image, in another blur of beige and white, and plopped back into reality. Where my mother and the door should have been,

I find myself staring at the spring—no cloak hovering above it. But in its place is something *much* more disturbing: dozens of putrid, rotting fish, their yellow underbellies floating at the surface. The stench is so overwhelming that I frantically snatch the drenched linen beside me and the half-full canteen from the ground. I try not to gag as I dump the water out, then race back toward the fort.

Fear grips me so tightly that I can't even begin to process what I've just seen. Part of me hopes that Haskell is awake, but a larger part hopes he's still in his unconscious state. I just need a little more time to think about this—to figure it all out—but when I arrive back at camp, it's apparent that time is not on my side.

RYDAN HELSTROM

AVERY HAD GIVEN his word that he'd stay a couple more days in Lonia. Rydan hadn't been able to tell if his reasoning had been for the many people he'd dropped off earlier that week, or for something else; but learning that Avery was also an Ignitor had given him a sense of hope. If they spent enough time together, perhaps he'd be willing to teach Rydan a thing or two about his newfound ability.

Sneaking out of the house every morning has only gotten easier—that is, until today, when he runs straight into Vira in the kitchen. She turns to face him, intrigue lining her eyes. "You're up early."

"I just woke up not too long ago. How did you sleep?"

She looks him up and down. "You're already dressed. Going somewhere?"

"I was going to go into town." He hesitates, hoping she won't see through his lie. "We were running low on"— he scans the countertop—"apples. And bread."

She stifles a yawn, then finishes drying a bowl and turns to place it in an overhead cupboard. "While you're out, do you mind grabbing some more tea?"

He'd been so focused on the inevitable interrogation his lie would bring about that he almost blows his façade entirely. "Tea. Sure. What kind?"

"Lemongrass and mint, please."

He makes a mental note. "Will do. I'll be back soon."

She glances back and gives him a lazy smile.

With a small wave goodbye, he's out the door. As he's about to turn off to head to the private beach, he thinks better of it and decides to do as he's promised and go into town first. He digs in his pockets for some riyals, pulling out three, hoping that it'll be enough to get Vira's tea.

Not surprisingly, the town is bustling with activity. He scans the crowd of people, being jostled and bumped every which way, before locating an herbs and spices stand. As he approaches, he senses that someone is watching him. He stops in the middle of the crowd, looking left and right, hoping that his erratic behavior won't be noticed, but everyone seems to be going about their business. There's nothing out of the ordinary, so he advances toward the merchant's cart with a charming smile plastered on his face.

After some slick negotiating, he exchanges the riyals—the exact amount he has on him—for one small jar of lemongrass and mint tea, tucks it into his knapsack, and carries onward. Even through the forest trees, the rays of sunshine beat down on him so that by the time he reaches the beach, all he wants to do is run directly into the ocean. But first, as he always does, he checks the perimeter to ensure that no one is around.

The moment his feet hit the sand, he flings his knapsack off, fumbling to remove his boots. His trousers and shirt follow soon after, leaving him in nothing more than his undergarments. Without a second thought, he darts into the ocean, diving underneath the crashing waves. He swims out a little ways, the crisp water a respite from his burning skin.

Only when he looks at the ship does he notice Avery at the stern motioning him inward—and just as he was starting to enjoy himself. Rydan sighs before ducking under again, then takes his time swimming back to shore.

"I was starting to think you weren't coming," Avery says as he throws a rope ladder over the side of the ship.

Rydan rakes a hand through his tangled hair. "Had to stop into town first." He gathers his clothes and tosses them up to Avery, then swings his knapsack over his shoulder and begins to climb. This time, he doesn't tumble onto the deck, but gracefully throws his legs over the side and lands on his feet.

"Still no Vira?"

Avery had asked about her every day since they'd started meeting regularly. As much as Rydan wants to include her, he also wants to learn more about their shared Ignitor abilities, as well as what Avery's gotten himself into with the dozen illusié he'd brought here on this very ship. "Not today, I'm afraid. I was actually hoping we could talk more about illusié."

Avery takes a seat. "Did you have something specific in mind?"

Rydan leans up against the railing, considering which topic he should bring up first—igniting or the other illusié. He goes with the former. "I was hoping I could learn more about igniting. It comes so easily to you."

"It doesn't for you?"

Rydan shakes his head. "To be honest, I was sort of a prick when I first found out I was illusié. I didn't want much to do with it. Nothing at all, actually."

Avery shoots him a sidelong glance. "You have no idea how to use your abilities, do you?"

Rydan laughs. "Think you can you teach me?"

Avery studies him for a moment. "Well, I'm not much of a teacher, but I *can* show you. You know what they say, experience is the best teacher. Perhaps you'll pick up on something."

Rydan extends his hand in gratitude. "Thanks."

Avery meets his grip. "No problem. Anything in particular you want to know?"

"Well, I haven't exactly been able to wield my abilities, like *at all*. I noticed before that if I felt angry or upset, they'd appear almost instantly."

"You discovered you were illusié on accident, didn't you?"

Rydan gives a sheepish nod.

"The key to handling our particular ability is to focus on the point of contact." He raises his hands in the air. "The fire is produced from our fingertips, correct?"

Rydan nods, mimicking Avery's movement.

"Imagine being able to ignite with just your mind."

Rydan lifts his gaze. "Is that possible?"

"I've seen it firsthand." His face falls. "I'm not quite there yet, though."

"I'm sure it takes practice," Rydan says as he focuses on his own two hands. "I should probably master the basics first."

"That would be wise."

"So, I focus on the point of contact—then what?'

Avery snaps out of his daze. "Right. You'll want to find something that will raise your body temperature. I've found it to be the easiest way when you're first starting out."

Rydan gives him a blank stare. "I'm not quite sure I understand."

"You just said that, in the beginning, you could only wield your abilities when you felt angry or upset."

"Right . . . "

Avery rises from the crate. "What happens to your body temperature when you get angry or upset?"

"I tend to get flushed, warm—" Rydan stops himself as the pieces come together. "You're saying I have to recall unpleasant memories in order to use my abilities?"

Avery shrugs, his mouth pulling to the side in a childish smirk. "Or hope that you're somehow always near a fire or that the sun's out." He gestures to the entrance of the galley. "In Lonia, the latter isn't really a problem, but up north," he shakes his head, "hate to break it to you, but you'll be fully dependent on those memories."

"Sadly, I have enough unpleasant memories to last a lifetime." Rydan doesn't realize he's said it out loud until he catches the grim expression on Avery's face. "So," he says, quickly changing the subject, "should we head back up to the deck so I can give it a shot?"

"I'm surprised you're letting me off that easy."

Rydan has no idea what he's referring to until he catches a glimpse of a crumpled up blanket at the far end of the galley. *The other illusié.* "Now that you mention it, I have to ask." He motions for Avery to sit again. "What can you tell me about the others you brought here?"

"Right," he says. "Where to start? Well, they used to be illusié until they were attacked by," he lowers his voice to a whisper, "the Mallum. Legend has it that when illusié is used in defense of or to attack the Mallum, it absorbs those abilities."

Oddly enough, this angers Rydan. And here he'd thought he'd be happy to know there actually *was* a way to rid him of his abilities—but that was *before* realizing what a selfish fool he'd been, and that the only way to help Arden might be the very thing he despises about himself.

"When I took your friend"—he pauses, recalling the name—"Opal, back here, we had an encounter with the Mallum." He winces, as if the memory causes him physical pain. "I dodged the attack, hid out here, in the galley. Your friend wasn't so lucky."

Rydan's throat goes dry as he realizes that Avery is talking about *Arden*, not Opal.

"It's strange, really. It seemed to be fixated on her—like it was dead-set on getting something from her."

Rydan knows he should ask for specifics, but the processing of all this information keeps him from doing so.

Avery doesn't seem to notice his deep state of contemplation. "It's rumored that there *is* a way to get those lost illusié abilities back, although no one's been able to prove it, dare I say even *attempt* it," he continues.

"There are two freshwater springs, one in Volkharn and one in the Crostan Islands. With the proper provisions, one can immerse themselves in the spring and restore their abilities."

Rydan leans forward, resting his elbows on his knees. He studies Avery's face carefully. "What sort of provisions?"

"That's just it. Some say you need a mixture of different herbs, others claim elemental magick should be used, and others have interpreted the restoration to involve draconic magic."

Rydan raises a brow. "Draconic?"

"Working with dragons."

"So basically, it's a free-for-all?"

Avery shrugs. "Seems to be. A sure way to tell if your illusié abilities have returned is to go to Orihia."

"Dare I ask what Orihia is?"

Avery lets out a long sigh. "I didn't realize this was illusié orientation."

Rydan feels a faint warmth bloom in his neck. "I'd be remiss if I didn't tell you that when I found out about my abilities, I panicked. I ran away from the very people that could have taught me and helped me." He bites the inside of his cheek, hoping he hasn't revealed too much. "I really appreciate the information, Avery."

A small smile tugs at his lips. "Well then, to answer your question, Orihia is home to all illusié—and *only* illusié can access it."

"And it's here? In Lonia?"

"Just east of the Thering Forest." He angles his head, strands of auburn sticking to his temple. "You've never been, have you?"

"Afraid not. This is the first I've ever heard of it."

"Well, how about we change that?" He hops forward on one foot and grabs Rydan by the arm, yanking him from his seat, before darting up the steps. Rydan hardly has a chance to process what's happening when he suddenly bumps into the back of Avery's head. He clutches the railing to keep from falling backward. He has no idea what's caused Avery to stop so suddenly—until a familiar voice floats down to him.

"Well, this is an unlikely pairing if I've ever seen one." Vira stands at the top of the deck with her arms crossed. "Why didn't you tell me you were meeting with Avery?" She looks between the two of them. "I thought you hated each other."

Rydan slinks out from behind Avery's shadow and climbs the last few steps. "You heard everything, didn't you?"

She nods reluctantly, as if he's just taken some sense of vindication from her.

"Well, we were just about to head to Orihia. Have you ever been?"

Vira casts her gaze toward the ground. "I've always wanted to. Never had the chance."

Rydan climbs the last step until he's directly in front of her. He lifts her chin with his index finger, her cerulean eyes poring into his—searching. He smiles. "Looks like you showed up at just the right time." He turns toward Avery. "Ready?"

"Ready as I'll ever be," he says, breezing past them. "I'll meet you on the shore."

As Avery disappears over the edge of the ship, Rydan retrieves his knapsack, then walks back over to Vira.

Her voice is strained. "I take it you never made it to the market?"

He grabs her hand, then slides something into her palm. She raises a brow before looking down to find exactly what she'd asked for.

"On the contrary," Rydan says with a smile, "I aim to please."

DARIUS TYMOND

AFTER THE INCIDENT in Braxton's old room, Darius calls a meeting not only with his Cruex, but also with his Savant. The men file into the Great Room, one by one, hurriedly taking their positions as Darius observes from his throne. The guards slam the double doors shut, indicating that everyone has arrived.

Slowly, Darius rises. The stillness in the room only grows, the silence deafening. He glances downward at the steps, but doesn't take them. Instead, his gaze moves across the room as he scans each one of their faces. Timid, no—but he *does* sense a slight unease.

"I don't feel it's necessary to discuss at full length what occurred in the far eastern corridor the other night." Two of the Cruex shuffle uncomfortably between their feet, momentarily drawing his attention away. "Those who need to know already do. What's done is done—but I'd like to emphasize, once again, that the entry of unpermitted individuals into Trendalath Kingdom is unacceptable." One of the Cruex steps forward, but the king ignores him. "Any trespassers must be brought to the Daegrum Chambers immediately upon capture—"

"Your Majesty." The voice comes from the Cruex who'd stepped forward, apparently still standing his ground, although Darius's ignoring him had been quite obvious.

"Do not interrupt me, Sir Garrick."

Percival bows his head in apology. "Forgive me, but there seems to be a larger force at work here—one that we"—he gestures to the rest of the Cruex—"are ill-equipped to handle." His voice is strained as he adds, "Perhaps in the future, any misconduct pertaining to illusié should be handled by the Savant."

Although the statement angers him, Percival does have a point. Up until now, he's sent his Cruex on countless missions across the lands of Aeridon—missions specifically targeted at illusié. While the majority of the missions have been successful, there's always been an underlying risk—of magick being more powerful than even the most skilled assassin.

Darius swallows his pride. "You make a fair point, Sir Garrick." An arrogant smile flashes across the Cruex's face as he steps back into line. "*But*, given the current state of things, I need the support of everyone in this room—illusié or otherwise."

The members of the Cruex give the Savant a sidelong glance, but they're so focused on Darius, they hardly seem to notice.

"From this moment forward, you will behave as equals. You will be given similar tasks and you will work *together* to capture the members of the Caldari." He narrows his eyes. "Every last one of them."

CERYLIA JARETH

DELWYNN COMES RUSHING into the White Room followed by none other than Felix, Estelle . . . and Opal. She almost expects to see Braxton trailing behind them—until she remembers he's fled the grounds.

"I assume you've heard the news?" Her tone matches exactly how she feels. Hopeless.

Opal shoots her fellow Caldari a sidelong glance before looking at the queen. She drops her gaze immediately under Cerylia's icy stare.

"I demand to know the last interaction each of you had with him." She fixes her attention on Felix first.

"It's been at least"—he pauses, eyes rolling skyward as he counts in his head—"a week or so since I've spoken with Braxton."

"Same here," Estelle chimes in.

The queen's gaze travels to Opal.

"It's been longer than that for me," Opal says. "Two weeks, maybe more."

Which leaves Delwynn.

He looks at Cerylia with a pained expression. "You're already aware of my last encounter with him."

"Did you intentionally exclude any details?" She raises a brow. "Did he give any sort of indication of fleeing?"

"If he had, I would have told you." He takes a step forward, angling his head at her. "You believe that, don't you?"

"Quite frankly, I'm not sure what to believe anymore." She leans back into her throne, shoulders slumped. "Between Rydan and Elvira fleeing, then Arden, and now Braxton"—she notices a glimpse of sadness in Felix's eyes at the mention of Arden's name—"I'd just hoped another conversation like this one wouldn't be necessary."

From the sudden shift in Estelle's stance and the fiery look in her eyes, it seems she wants to speak—and say something that's been on her mind for a while. "How can we trust you?" Felix nudges her in the side, but she continues. "After the way you treated Braxton? Locking him up on a mere assumption? And he's *royalty*, for lords' sake!" She gestures to Felix and Opal. "We're just Caldari. Based on what we've seen, this 'safe haven' doesn't feel so safe anymore."

Normally, a statement like this would have Cerylia reeling—but Estelle is right. She *had* mistreated Braxton. She'd panicked and acted out of fear, the one thing she'd sworn to Dane she'd never do. If he could see her now, he'd be ashamed—completely and utterly ashamed.

"I don't condone my behavior." She inhales a shaky breath. "It was irrational and uncalled for, and Braxton certainly didn't deserve any of it. I should have listened to him, should have taken him at his word." She nods at Estelle in solidarity. "I hope that you can forgive me and that you will continue to stay and train here—"

"And what exactly are we training for?"

Cerylia's gaze shifts to Opal. Her arms are crossed, feet shoulder width apart, jaw clenched. The hood of her jade cloak frames her face, matching the color of her narrowed eyes. The expression she wears is fierce.

Unrelenting.

Ruthless.

"You, of all people, should know the answer to that."

The queen's response doesn't seem to rattle her. "Are we training to fight Tymond and his Savant?" She takes a step forward. "Or does this go deeper than that?"

Slowly, Cerylia straightens. She removes her hands

from her lap and places each arm beside her, fingers gripping the edges of the throne until her knuckles turn white. "What are you insinuating?"

Opal doesn't hesitate in the slightest. "I think you know more about the Mallum than you've let on. And if you want us to stay"—she looks from side to side at her friends—"you'd better start talking."

BRAXTON HORNSBY

VOICES CARRYING THROUGH the woods jolt him awake. Braxton starts to sit upright, momentarily forgetting he's swinging tens of feet above the ground in nothing more than a linen and some rope.

"Damn it," he mutters before holding his breath and sticking his foot out to steady it against the tree. The hammock ceases its swaying. He listens carefully as the voices draw closer, hoping that, perhaps, he'll recognize one of them. But, knowing Xerin, he's probably traveling alone.

Meaning that *others* are approaching.

He strains his ears, trying to place the voices.

Possibly Felix. Could the other voice belong to Rydan? He'd hardly spent any time with him in Sardoria, so it's hard to tell.

"Well, look what we have here," one of the voices says from right underneath him. "What a beautiful horse."

If he weren't trying to move, Braxton would slap himself on the forehead. He'd completely forgotten about Whitley. *It's only a matter of time before they start looking around . . . and up.*

"Someone left you here all by yourself," one of the strangers coos. "Shame, really. We'll bring you back with us."

A wave of sheer panic washes over him. Not only is he miles and miles from civilization, he hasn't even the slightest inkling as to where the next town is. No direction whatsoever. Without that horse—or Xerin, for that matter—he may as well just call it quits now.

Perhaps these men would cut him a break.

"I reckon King Tymond has never seen a horse this magnificent. Must be from up north."

Braxton's blood runs cold. Nope, revealing himself is certainly not in his best interest. These men, whoever they are, would definitely *not* cut him a break.

Feeling more on edge than before, Braxton looses the breath he's been holding in, but in doing so, his foot slips down the tree. Contact with the bark is lost, and the hammock begins to sway back and forth from the sudden movement. He winces as he brings his foot down, back inside the confines of the linen, hoping and praying that the men won't look up and see him.

Wishful thinking.

As if intentionally trying to work against him, the rope begins to creak, even as the swaying slows. The chatter below him stops. Braxton can sense them looking skyward, up through the many branches, until their gaze lands on the underside of the concaving linen.

"Who's up there?"

Shit.

"Reveal yourself!"

Shit. Shit. Shit.

"If you don't willingly come down from there, we'll have to force you," one of the men says. "And trust me, you wouldn't want that. Very painful for you."

"Quite painful," the other voice echoes.

Seeing no other choice, Braxton musters up the courage to poke his head over the edge. Although it's hard to see exact details, he can tell the men aren't armed.

They're not Trendalath guards.

They're not members of the Cruex.

Which means they're part of the King's Savant.

Braxton curses the Mallum under his breath for taking his deviating abilities. *With* them, he might have actually stood a chance against these two. Without them, he's at a total loss. "Don't attack," he shouts as he leans over the other side to grab hold of the tree branch. "I surrender."

He gazes up at the sky, fervently praying that a dragon with ruby-colored eyes will swoop down and take him away. But the sky is empty, save for a few swallows.

He curses Xerin, too.

Not bothering to take down the hammock, he throws on his knapsack before descending the tree. When he reaches the last branch, he pushes off the trunk and hops down, his gaze landing on two ornate colored masks.

The taller one takes a calculated step forward. "Well I'll be damned, do my eyes deceive me?" He pauses before scanning Braxton's white-blonde hair and light blue eyes. "You're not who we're looking for."

The other man steps in line with his cohort. "You're even better."

ARDEN ELIRI

THE SOUNDS COMING from inside the fort are unlike anything I've ever heard before. I'm completely out of breath by the time I reach it, cringing at each dreadful groan. I swing one of the flaps open and crawl inside to find Haskell, pallid and shaking.

"Shhh, it's me. It's Arden." My attempt at soothing him is futile.

He continues to writhe in pain. I have no idea how long he's been like this, how long he's been awake.

I wasn't here for any of it.

Guilt consumes me as I look for something to help him. I check the vial to see if any tincture remains, but it's bone dry. I grab his forearm and squeeze it, but he doesn't look at me. His pupils dilate and roll out of sight before coming back again.

He doesn't even realize I'm here.

"Haskell," I say once again, trying to soothe him. "It's me, Arden. Your sister. You had a healing potion with you when you transported back here." The seizing slows momentarily. I take full advantage, hoping that he can actually hear what I'm saying. "I administered it as soon as I found you. For a minute, I thought I'd . . . " My voice catches in my throat. "I just need you to be okay."

By the time I finish speaking, he still isn't looking at me, but something tells me he's registered what I've said. His eyes flutter as a bit of drool trickles from the corner of his mouth, then they close. Feeling panicked all over again, I check his pulse. His heartbeat is steadier than it was before—a good sign.

I sit back on my heels, the vial rolling from my fingertips. I look at Juniper, the dismal expression on her face matching my own. All there is to do is sit and wait.

❦   ❦   ❦

Five hours have passed, and while my stomach is rumbling, I refuse to leave Haskell. He still hasn't awoken since his last episode, and all I can do is think about my most recent encounter with the cloaked figure. I know I should eat something, but the thought of food is both unsettling and unappetizing. The only thing I can manage to get down is water—and I'm running out of that, too.

For what feels like the hundredth time, I replay in my mind what had happened earlier this morning. Without a shadow of a doubt, I'm certain that the boy in the memory was Haskell and that the woman was my mother—and that *I* was the bulge in her womb. Where had my father been? Who'd been at the door? How did the cloaked figure have access to these memories— memories I don't even have because I hadn't been born yet?

Those three questions have plagued my mind for the past few hours and all I want to do is tell Haskell. To ask him if he recalls the memory. If he can tell me who was at the door. Given his current state, I know I'll have to be patient—not exactly my strongest quality.

A deep inhale grabs my attention. I catch the end of Haskell's chest rising before it falls again. I go to him and place my hands over the afflicted area. I've attempted, at least a dozen times today, to bring forth my healing abilities—but each time, I'm met with a void.

When no white light appears, I retract my hands and close my fists at my sides. I squeeze them until my knuckles turn white, then loose a frustrated grunt. Just as I'm turning away, I hear something.

"Arden."

It's little more than a croak, but it's him.

He's conscious.

And he knows I'm here.

I hover over him so that he doesn't have to angle his head. His eyes travel—not to the ceiling, not to the back of his head—but to my own. A small smile tugs at his lips, but disappears as soon as he coughs.

"Can you help me sit up?"

My eyes grow wide as I assess his current state. "I'm not sure that's such a good—" I'm only halfway through my sentence when he begins to push himself upright, whether I'm going to help him or not.

"Careful," I say, gently lifting his shoulders. Another strained groan escapes him, but he continues until he's all the way up. I hand over the one full canteen I'd saved specifically for him—the one *not* filled from the highly questionable spring. He gives a slight nod of his head before drinking its entire contents.

"I tried to get more . . . " I'm silenced by the shaking of his head. I watch and wait until he's ready to speak.

"I'm just happy that you're here. And that you're safe." The inhale that follows is shaky at best. "I was worried they'd somehow transported back with me, catching you off guard and"—he eyes my chakrams—"well, at least not defenseless."

It's so nice to hear his voice again, to see him awake, that I hardly remember to respond. "Who? Who did you think came back with you?"

"I thought they were guards, but they weren't wearing armor. They were clad completely in black—"

I don't hear the rest of the sentence because I know exactly to whom he's referring. *The Cruex.* "Can you describe them, what they looked like?"

He wrinkles his forehead, deep in thought. "Two males. One was tall and lanky, the other short and stocky. The latter gave me this." He lifts his shirt to reveal a jagged gash along his ribcage. If it weren't for the healing potion, I'm certain it'd be festering and becoming even more infected. I recognize the wound immediately, having gotten one many years ago during my first Cruex training session—from a serrated scimitar.

Ezra Denholm's weapon of choice.

"I know who gave you that." I swallow. "And the tall one? Do you remember what he looked like, what weapon he had?"

"Blonde hair. He had a lance with a long pointed end. Poor sap couldn't get near me fast enough to use it though."

"It was a glaive." Percival Garrick's weapon. My hands curl into fists at my sides. So Ezra and Percival had tried to kill my brother. *How fitting.*

"After seeing that photo and knowing you'd gotten it from Trendalath, from the prince's room . . . I had to see for myself. See if there was anything else in there that might point to our history with the Tymonds." We both shudder as he says it. "I shouldn't have gone alone. For that, I apologize."

"At least you had the sense to grab a healing potion."

His brows furrow. "What do you mean?"

"The healing potion—you had one on you when you returned. That's how you survived."

"I didn't grab a healing potion. I didn't even know such a thing existed until now."

A chill lodges in my chest.

"You didn't use your healing abilities?"

I try to process my thoughts, but my mind is whirling. "I tried, but it didn't work."

Haskell runs a hand down his face. "Oh, Arden."

I meet his timid gaze. It's an unsettling sight.

"That day, in the Trendalath healing ward with Aldreda . . . how much do you remember?"

"Honestly, it's all starting to blend together, but," I bite my lower lip, "I know for a fact that I'd started to heal her. She'd taken a breath. Her chest had risen. I could *feel* her coming back to life—"

"But then it went away. Or it felt like it did."

I regard him with increasing curiosity. "How do you know that?"

"There are others who have encountered what you faced that day. The Mallum."

My mind goes blank.

"You don't know about the Mallum?"

I shake my head.

"The Mallum is rumored to be one of the greatest forces of evil in Aeridon. It exploits illusié by drawing them in and absorbing their abilities, but only if said illusié uses those powers in defense of or in attack on the Mallum itself."

I suck in a sharp breath. *The cloaked figure.* "It was there, when I was healing Aldreda. It absorbed the healing." I look down at my hands, turning them over. "Does this mean I'm no longer illusié?"

"Afraid so."

His words cut through me like glass. "But you were also there. You saved me by transporting. And yet, you still have your abilities?"

"I know." He shakes his head. "As a Healer, my guess is that your abilities provided a shield of sorts. So while the Mallum was absorbing your abilities, I had the opportunity to appear, undetected, and transport you away from it. Apparently, I wasn't fast enough."

My shoulders slump.

"But there are others, like you." He coughs, his chest heaving with the sound. "And there's also a way to get them back."

My heart picks up pace. I can see he's fading fast, but I have to know if I've heard him correctly. "Are you saying that I can become a Healer again? How?"

He coughs again, motioning for me to help him lay back down. "I need to rest," he says, each word a strain on his throat. "But yes, there is a way to get your abilities back."

That single sentence is all it takes for newfound hope to surge through me. *Finally.*

RYDAN HELSTROM

"YOU TWO ALMOST ready?" Avery's voice echoes down the hall.

"Just a few more minutes!" Vira calls from one room over.

Rydan discreetly pulls his full knapsack out from under the bed. He's attempted to delay as much as possible—pretending to gather items that have already been packed—before finally heading into Vira's room. He leans against the doorframe. "I'm ready whenever you are."

She's kneeling next to her dresser, rummaging through one of the drawers, when she stops and turns to look over her shoulder. "That was quick."

"I'm a guy." He shrugs. "I don't need much. Plus, I don't imagine we'll be staying there for too long."

"A-ha!" She pops up after finding whatever she'd been looking for, then throws it into her bag. "You may be right about that, but you never know. Best to be prepared."

He waits patiently for her to finish packing and, when she approaches with her arm extended, he gladly links his with hers. "Avery seems anxious to get moving."

The living room is vacant, but the front door is wide open. Avery's messing with something on the front porch, muttering under his breath, hardly even noticing their presence. Only when they're a few steps away does he look up. "There you are. Got everything you need?"

"Think so," Vira replies, "although I'm not really sure what to bring to a place like Orihia."

Avery seems to notice Rydan eyeing the wooden trellis that wraps around the porch. "I fixed it for you." He knocks on the wood. "It was uneven. Drove me nuts when we first got here."

Rydan breezes past him, patting him on the shoulder. "Thanks. You didn't have to do that."

"The pleasure was all mine," Avery says as he follows them down the front steps. "Ready to head out?"

"Lead the way," Vira says with a smile.

❦ ❦ ❦

Two hours into their trip has Rydan wishing Vira had summoned a dragon to take them to Orihia—but when Avery had blatantly pointed out that it would have drawn too much attention, Rydan couldn't argue. He wipes his brow as sweat drips down his temples, wondering if Avery and Vira are struggling as much as he is. "Can we take a quick break?" he calls out from behind them, his voice raspy.

Avery turns around, compass in hand. "Now? But we're almost there."

Rydan ignores his plea to keep going the moment he spots a large shaded area to his right. He slides down the base of the birch tree, then leans forward and wriggles his backpack off. The metal canteen clinks against the other items in his bag. Mouth dry, he unscrews the lid and takes two giant gulps.

Vira motions for Avery to follow as she backtracks to where Rydan is sitting and joins him. Avery refuses and stays exactly where he is, reluctantly leaning against a nearby tree.

"What's his deal?" Rydan says, taking another swig of water.

"I think he's just eager to get there," Vira responds absentmindedly as she searches through her own bag. "You have to remember, he's basically responsible for all those people he brought here. If they head back to the ship and he's not there . . . " She shrugs. "I've known Avery for quite some time. He's not one to go back on his word. If he says he's going to do something, that's that."

Rydan rigs his mouth to the side as he studies Avery from afar. "Good to know."

She laughs before playfully punching him in the shoulder. "Break's over. We should probably get—" She doesn't get to finish her sentence because Avery's suddenly yelling as he dashes into the forest.

"What the hell?" Rydan shouts, springing to his feet.

"Where's he going?" Vira asks.

"Come on," he says as he helps Vira up. "We have to follow him."

They take off down the trail, dodging tree branches and bushes as Rydan does his best to track Avery's movements. They go until the footprints stop, but Vira makes a sharp left and continues running at full speed. Stumbling over his own two feet, Rydan follows a few paces behind her until she suddenly halts in her tracks.

Seconds later, he arrives next to her, eyes widening at the sight before them. Avery falls to his knees and Rydan feels he might do the same. The people he'd brought here on his ship, fellow illusié . . .

They're all dead.

CERYLIA JARETH

HER LAST CONVERSATION with the Caldari certainly hadn't ended the way she'd hoped. After Opal's accusation, she'd gotten up and stormed out of the room. In hindsight, she probably could have handled things a little better. Is it true she knows more than she's let on about the Mallum? Yes. Do the Caldari need to know every last detail? No.

If they want to flee, so be it. She only has half their strength anyway, what with Rydan, Vira, Arden, and now Braxton leaving, so really, what's the point? Is it even worth the hassle anymore?

She's starting to think not.

The gardens are usually so droll this time of year, but given the earlier arrival of the spring season, the grounds are alight with vibrant color. Burgundy poppies and white orchids line the trail she walks along, the contrast between them reflecting her innermost thoughts. There are times when she wishes she could confront the Mallum, but it's an impossible task. At least, without that amethyst ring it is.

She sweeps her robes to the side as she bends down and plucks a few of the poppies from their place. They'll look nice in the White Room—a splash of color to represent spring's awakening.

And new beginnings.

She's arranging the small bouquet to her liking when she suddenly senses someone watching her. With a subtle tilt of her head, her eyes rove the castle grounds, the alcoves, the balconies. Nothing seems out of place— that is, until her gaze lands a few stories up. Albeit brief, she swears she catches a shadow as it disappears behind a wall.

One guess, knife to her throat—it's Opal.

Cerylia has never felt so insecure in her own queendom. Certainly Opal's ability to invert had been of great use to her, but now that it's being used to essentially *spy* on her, to gain *inside knowledge* on her and her past . . . Cerylia can't help but find the ability downright despicable.

She has half the nerve to storm up there right now and demand punishment, to lock her in the dungeons just as she'd done to Braxton. But with the Mallum and most of the Caldari at large, she fears she'll need the girl's abilities sooner rather than later.

Her eyes fall to the bouquet in her hands as it drops lifelessly to the ground. *Fear*—the driving force ever since Dane's death. Fear of invasion. Fear of loss. Fear of nonexistence.

The last one she's already nailed down. She hasn't *truly* existed for years. A mere shell of the woman she used to be—just going through the motions, day in and day out. Doing her best to lead by example when, in her heart, she knows she's the worst example of all.

A roll of thunder booms overhead, sending her gaze skyward. A raindrop hits her cheek, followed by another, and another. Within seconds, the clouds open up, pouring all over her—soaking her hair, her face, her robes. And like she's done every night that week, she weeps along with it.

BRAXTON HORNSBY

HIS HANDS BOUND with rope and tied to the back of Whitley's saddle, Braxton reluctantly trudges behind the two Savant. He knows exactly where they're headed and desperately looks up at the sky for some sign of Xerin.

No falcon soaring in the sea of blue above.

He scans the area to his left, then his right.

No horse hiding in the brush.

He's completely alone.

The skin around his wrists is starting to chafe. He's tempted to ask how much longer they'll be walking in this lords-forsaken forest, but the last time he'd spoken, the men had elbowed him in the back, bringing him to his knees. "No more questions," they'd said in unison. The spot between his shoulder blades is still sore. He's kept his mouth shut since then.

The horse begins to pick up speed and so does Braxton, whether he wants to or not. He can feel the sweat as it beads along his hairline. His mouth is dry and his legs are shaking, but even so, he continues onward.

A bird caws nearby, causing him to search frantically for the source of the noise. Xerin's usual form is a falcon, but it's possible he could have turned into a crow . . .

Isn't it?

He focuses forward again, his eyes following the back and forth movement of Whitley's tail. How ironic to have fled Sardoria with the intention of paying his respects to his mother, only to be captured and brought to face the very man who'd failed in protecting her. He stifles a laugh of pure disbelief, shaking his head instead.

After what feels like hours, they finally reach the edge of the Roviel Woods, Trendalath Kingdom in plain view. Braxton can't help but shudder as he takes it all in. The place he'd been forced to hide who he really was. The place he'd fled because he didn't feel like hiding anymore.

Only to return and have to hide again.

Braxton wishes Whitley would slow down or neigh for water or food or *something*. She's gone the entire trip without making a sound—surely the most self-sufficient animal Braxton's ever seen. His stomach drops the closer they get to the castle.

He can't help but notice that the Savant don't take him through town, but instead along a backroad that stretches along the side of the castle. Much to his surprise, he finds he's quite familiar with this trail. His eyes wander to a small hill that overlooks the ocean, the waves crashing against the jagged rocks—the very spot he'd used to go fishing as a child.

Being here is like being forced to relive his worst nightmare all over again.

The two Savant men arrive at a side door—another undisclosed area of the kingdom Braxton knows all too well. Without knocking, the door swings open and they're ushered inside. The man on the horse hops down, quickly untying the rope that's currently connecting Braxton to Whitley before wrapping it around his own hands instead.

"Come on," he grunts. "King's waitin'."

Braxton wishes more than anything that he still had his deviating abilities. He'd rile the men up to the point where they'd have no choice but to attack him, only to find that they'd be attacking themselves. The thought brings a smile to his lips.

"*Move*," the man repeats, tugging at the rope.

With his head hung lower than low, Braxton follows them up the castle steps to the misery that surely awaits.

DARIUS TYMOND

AS TWO OF his Savant approach the throne, Darius can't help but notice the white-blonde head of hair bobbing up and down behind them. He strains his eyes for a closer look. Surely he's mistaken.

It can't be.

The boy is brought forward, pale blue eyes searching his own. It's like looking into a mirror.

"Where?" His tone is brusque.

"In the southeast quadrant of the Roviel Woods."

Darius angles his head, looking from the Savant to his estranged son. "This is unexpected." He waits for

Braxton to say something in response, but he doesn't—he just glares at the king with those ice-blue eyes.

"Anyone else?"

"Just the kid and a horse." A nameplate clatters at his feet. "Whitley."

Darius recognizes the name. To keep himself from spiraling into a full-fledged rage, he presses his lips together, then firmly grips the sides of his throne. "I should have known you'd flee and make allies with the enemy."

Braxton finally speaks. "Cerylia isn't the enemy."

Darius scoffs as he leans back. "I see you're on a first name basis." He crosses his arms. "I'm surprised she let you anywhere near Sardoria." He notices Braxton's gaze shift to the amethyst ring on his finger. Almost instantly, he brings his arms back to his sides. "Tell me, dear son— is your life everything you'd hoped it'd be?"

Braxton remains expressionless. "Is it true Arden Eliri killed my mother?"

Darius's face falls. *How does he know about Arden?*

Memories of the failed execution day flood his mind. Although Arden hadn't physically been there that day, in the town square, he'd sensed that she'd been the one to free Rydan—to break him out of the dungeons. It seems Braxton had been involved with the Caldari.

Just like Arden.

Braxton repeats his question.

"Yes," Darius says, the lie slipping easily from his tongue. "Arden Eliri killed your mother."

ARDEN ELIRI

HASKELL'S BEEN IN and out of consciousness for what feels like a century, and all I can seem to do is replay the last conversation we had. Recently, he'd woken long enough to be able to walk—or, more accurately, *limp*—back to the cave, but as soon as we'd arrived, he'd collapsed and fallen asleep again. I've been checking on him somewhat regularly to ensure his wounds are healing properly, but it's slow going. Just like everything else around here.

I finish eating the last of my dinner—some trout I'd caught in a nearby river—and place the other filet on a separate plate for Haskell to eat once he wakes. Walking back to the cave had taken a lot out of him, but the few times I've tried to get him to eat, he just waves his hand in the air and says, "Maybe next time." But *next time* hasn't come yet.

I'm starting to worry.

I swing my legs over the bench and walk outside the cave to clear my plate. Even though it's growing dark, birds fly above. I have no doubt they'll pick whatever meat is left from the bones.

I head back inside and set the wooden dish on the table. Juniper raises her head at the sound. "Sorry," I whisper. "Go back to sleep."

As if she understands what I've just said, she lowers her head and burrows back into her tail. The fire next to her crackles. I consider putting it out since I've finished cooking, but she seems to be enjoying the heat. I won't deprive her of this small luxury.

I make my way across the cave to where Haskell is, not surprisingly, still sound asleep. I'd advised him to not wear a shirt—especially since his are dingy and haven't been washed in days—so as to not increase the chance of infection. He hadn't exactly been of sound mind when I'd made the suggestion, but as I gingerly lift the blanket, I'm glad to see he'd listened.

Doing my best not to wake him, I inspect the wound. It's definitely in need of an antibiotic. I sigh, carefully replacing the blanket back over him and trudge to the kitchen area. I scour the cabinets for turmeric, rifling through the different herbs and spices, hoping it's something he'd thought to pick up during one of his transports. I smile as a jar of burnt orange powder, tucked in the very back, catches my eye.

I stand on my tiptoes to grab it, leaning so far forward that I almost fall into the cabinet itself. "Gotcha," I say as my fingers close around it. It isn't labeled, so I pop off the lid and waft its scent. Mild traces of orange and ginger. I dip my little finger in the jar and bring it to my lips. I recoil at the pungent, bitter taste.

Yep. Definitely turmeric.

As I retighten the lid, remnants of an unwelcome memory surface. I roll the bottle back and forth between my hands, trying to ignore it, but it's no use. It wraps itself around me.

Rydan had just finished his sparring session with fellow Cruex member, Ezra Denholm. I'd watched him closely as he'd wielded his weapon—the ripples in his back, the clenched jaw, the determined eyes—each swing of his longsword graceful, like watching a well-rehearsed dance between two perfectly synchronized partners. I'd been so captivated by the fluidity, the *ease* of movement, that I almost hadn't realized I was up next.

"Good luck," he'd whispered as he'd headed for his next round with Percival. He'd walked away without a scratch, and even though his words had filled me up, I wasn't convinced I'd be so lucky—certainly not the best state of mind to be in before walking into a sparring session with one of the most merciless Cruex.

I'd stepped onto the platform, into the rectangular ring we'd be sparring in, chakrams at the ready. King Tymond had stood just across the room, watching, waiting—albeit I hadn't known for what.

My damp uniform clung to my skin, strands of hair stuck to my forehead—though none of it had bothered me. I'd looked Ezra directly in his cobalt eyes, smirking when Cyrus had finally given us the signal to begin.

Ezra hadn't gone easy on me. He'd come at me full force—with a vengeance. Up, down, side to side. I'd successfully blocked every single one of blows, his serrated blade slicing through the air at lightning speed. I could hear his heavy panting and grunting with each defiant swing of his arms. I'd been on the defensive most of the time and knew I needed to take my shot, especially with Tymond watching.

We'd almost come to a stalemate. Cyrus had been on the verge of calling time when I'd found my opportunity. Something had briefly distracted Ezra, causing him to shift his focus from me to something *behind* me. I'd seized that moment for all it was worth, flinging one of my chakrams at his left shoulder. It'd spun through the air, slicing across the top layer of his skin.

Ezra had looked down at the injury, at my weapon clattering to the floor, then up at me with fury like I've never seen before. He still held his scimitar in his good

180

arm, and I should have known in that moment that Ezra Denholm was not one to accept defeat. He'd hurled the blade at me—his cowardly final strike—and it'd soared through the air, slashing the fabric of my uniform across my left tricep.

My hand had flown to my arm as blood gushed from the laceration and, for some reason, I'd turned my head toward the king, expecting him to call foul play—but, with his back already facing me, he'd retreated from his post.

Rydan had rushed over, jumped onto the platform, and shoved Ezra into the wall. "First hit wins," he'd said through clenched teeth as he'd pressed Ezra harder against the stone. "You can't strike back once you've been hit."

Dots had floated into my vision as I'd watched it all unfold: Ezra trying to wriggle free from Rydan's grip; Rydan's aggression rising with each shout; Ezra spitting in Rydan's face . . . Rydan punching him square across the nose.

I'd passed out then.

When I'd regained consciousness, I found myself lying in my bed—in my private quarters—but not alone. Rydan sat next to me with a small wooden bowl, delicately applying an orange powder to the cut on my arm. "He got you pretty good," he'd said.

"Not as good as I got him."

A splitting grin. "Damn right."

With my chin tucked down, I'd rotated my arm. "That stuff smells awful. What is it?"

"Turmeric. A spice for cooking *and* healing."

"How appetizing."

"Try to avoid training for a few days. And make sure to apply this two to three times a day, especially at night before you go to sleep. You should be healed in no time."

"And if I'm not?"

A raised brow. "Then next time, you can spar with me."

"As long as you promise not to go easy on me."

"Challenge accepted."

And that was the day I became friends with Rydan Helstrom.

With the turmeric in hand, I venture back over to Haskell, treading as lightly as I can manage. Still asleep, I kneel beside him before pulling the blanket just past his ribcage. I hold my breath as he stirs, but doesn't wake. I remove the lid from the jar and sprinkle some of it onto the gaping wound. Only when it's thoroughly covered in the orange powder do I stand, not bothering to return the blanket to its original position.

I stay there for a few more minutes, hoping that maybe he'll wake so we can talk—he can tell me all about how to regain my abilities. And I can tell him about the strange encounter I'd had with the Mallum.

Without so much as a warning, the other Caldari

impede my thoughts—specifically Felix. I wonder if he's known about the Mallum all this time.

If he's faced it before.

If he's faced it recently.

If he's in the same predicament I'm in.

Surely he would have told me, a quiet voice nags. *The Caldari share everything.*

But Felix had seen it from the very beginning—the growing darkness in me. The inevitable force I've been able to hide from everyone but him.

Perhaps he *hadn't* told me—and for good reason.

Exhausted, I stifle a yawn before falling into a nearby chair. I don't want to think about this anymore—or ever, really. Fortunately I don't have to, because the moment I lean my head back and close my eyes, my thoughts cease altogether.

RYDAN HELSTROM

"WHAT IN LORDS' name happened here?" Rydan hardly recognizes the voice as his own as the question leaves his lips. Vira comes up beside him, gingerly taking her hand in his. The warmth provides temporary solace as their fingers interlock—his rough and callused, hers petite and dainty. Avery remains on the ground, hands covering his mouth.

Reluctantly, Rydan breaks his grip from Vira, stepping past Avery to examine the scene further. The bodies don't appear to be injured or wounded in any way—no open cuts, no bruises, no bleeding. It's a strange sight—almost as if they'd all mistakenly dropped dead somehow—but something tells him this wasn't an accident. *This was intentional.*

Avery finally speaks after an extended silence. "The Mallum." He pushes himself up from the ground and slowly walks over to one of the fallen. Rydan and Vira follow.

The girl's golden hair is splayed out across the dirt, having already collected broken twigs, wilted leaves, and withering flower petals. Her eyes are wide open, as is her mouth—an indefinite stare into the eternal sky. A single tear sits at the corner of her eye, fully formed and ready to slide down her cheek. It hadn't even had the chance.

Rydan watches as Avery bends down and brushes the tear away with the back of his hand. Then, with his index and middle fingers, he gently sweeps across her eyelids so that they close. Her lips are barely parted, as if she'd just taken her last breath.

Rydan and Vira follow Avery in complete silence as he performs the same ritual on each of the fallen illusié. Rydan's convinced that it'll get easier as they move through them, but the opposite is true. He squeezes Vira's hand as she chokes down a sob, feeling as though, at any minute, he might do the same.

When Avery closes the eyes of the last illusié, he rises, turning to look at the two of them. He bows his head, his voice faint. "Welcome to Orihia." Rydan's not sure what it is he's referring to until he looks past his small frame and into the deep unknown. "The Mallum attacked them just outside of their home. Of *our* home." He takes a shaky breath. "I'm the one who brought them here, who gave them hope. And now look at them." He whirls around in an angry circle. "Dead. Dead. Dead—"

Vira grabs hold of his shoulders. "This is *not* your fault, Avery. Surely you must know that." Her attempt to console him is utterly useless as he continues to mutter incomprehensibly under his breath. Even so, she tries again. "If they had been able to see Orihia, they should have made it inside, before the Mallum could attack. It can't go in there, remember?"

"The jaded spring. It . . . it didn't work."

Vira shakes her head sadly. "They were no longer illusié, Avery . . . and so the Mallum took them for itself."

Rydan watches their interaction, hearing the words but not understanding them. They may as well be speaking a different language.

"We have to burn the bodies." Avery's tone is flat, decided. "We have to respect what we've lost here."

"Of course." Vira gives his shoulder a light squeeze. "It's a good thing we have just the person for the job." She shoots Rydan a sidelong glance.

"*People*," he corrects.

At this, Avery looks up.

"You're an Ignitor, too?" Vira says incredulously.

He gives her a slight nod of his head.

"It's settled then," Rydan says with a forced smile, extending his hand to Avery. "So, how about that lesson?"

CERYLIA JARETH

"IF YOU DON'T say *something*, they're all going to leave."

Her advisor's words slice through her like glass. "I know."

Delwynn marches over to her with purpose, a determined look in his eyes. Even though it's old news, it's still strange to see him fully upright and walking without a limp. *Suppose he has Arden to thank for that.*

"If you know, then why haven't you done something about it? Why are you prolonging it even further?"

From the bell tower, she keeps her gaze on the vast mountain range. The peaks are still covered in a thick layer of snow, but specks of green protrude through the canvas of white. Winter is dying. Spring is reborn.

Surely a metaphor for her life.

"What I *do* know about the Mallum is very limited. It won't change anything. It won't help them nor hurt them."

Delwynn stares at her in bewilderment. "Then tell *me*, Your Greatness. Confide in *me* and I will help you decide whether it's worth sharing."

She gives him a small smile, well aware of what he's trying to do—what he's *been* doing ever since she first appointed him as her advisor. She won't fall for it again.

Not under these circumstances.

"Perhaps another time, Delwynn."

She turns to leave, but not before his sturdy grip meets her wrist.

"You *will* lose them. For good." Desperation lines his voice. "After everything you've worked for, don't let this be it. Don't give up now."

"I must say, I'm rather disappointed." She gently tugs her wrist from his grip, then turns away from him. "It's always been about the timing, Delwynn. By now, I thought you would have known that."

DARIUS TYMOND

HE'D HAD EVERY intention of locking Braxton up with the rest of them in the dungeons, but with Clive there, lurking, waiting . . . he hadn't wanted to risk it—especially since he still hasn't decided exactly what he wants to do with his estranged son.

Not yet anyway.

As much as he despises Braxton for leaving all those years ago, he's still his *son*. The only heir to the throne. Perhaps he could find a way to confront him—to rebuild the father-son relationship they'd never had the chance to cultivate. Seeing as he's already lied straight to his face about Aldreda's death, he's off to a *great* start.

No, he hadn't locked him in the dungeons. Instead, he'd done the only other thing he could think of: locked him in his childhood room. Hardly cruel and unusual punishment. It could have been so much worse. The dungeons are most certainly not for the faint of heart—and neither are the Daegrum Chambers.

Darius stands just outside the door to Braxton's room. He raises his hand to knock, then thinks better of it, given the late hour. Instead, he presses his ear to the door, wondering if he's asleep. The padded footsteps pacing back and forth across the room answer his question.

Apparently not.

Darius heaves a sigh before stepping away from the door. If he were to knock and Braxton were to answer . . . what then? What would they talk about? If his son's demeanor during their last conversation is any indication, Darius would be the only one talking. But he has so many questions.

How well does Braxton know Arden? When did they meet? Did he flee to Sardoria originally? Is this a ploy executed by none other than Queen Jareth?

The uncertainty is enough to make his head spin. He isn't prepared for this—and he has a feeling that Braxton isn't either.

Perhaps tomorrow will be a better day.

And if not, perhaps the day after that.

It's not like he's going anywhere.

BRAXTON HORNSBY

BRAXTON STOPS PACING the moment he senses someone's presence. Slowly, he turns to face the door. Shadows dance back and forth from underneath as if caught in an eternal draft. Even as he holds his breath, they don't falter. They continue to sway rhythmically.

It has to be his father.

He wonders why Darius is here. If he's alone or surrounded by guards. What he's thinking. What he wants to say to his only son after banishing him from his own home.

He wonders if the coward will ever knock.

Braxton stares at the door handle. It doesn't move.

As a prisoner, he should be readying himself to fight whatever's on the other side of that door—to bolt, to flee—but that isn't what he's thinking at all. Instead, something unfamiliar roils inside him.

An urge to *belong.*

He'd trusted Cerylia and she'd locked him up.

He'd trusted Arden and she'd killed his mother.

What if I have it all wrong?

Even if he had half the nerve to fling the door open, it wouldn't matter, seeing as it's locked from the outside.

Whether this interaction happens or not is completely up to Darius—like everything else.

Does he even want his father here? And if that door *does* open, would they sit in strained silence? Or would Darius share information that could be useful to him?

He quiets his mind. *Come on, you coward.*

As if to spite him, the shadows stop. They sweep past the door one last time before the sound of footsteps carry down the hall. Not surprising in the least.

Braxton turns away from the door and resumes pacing. The dance continues.

ARDEN ELIRI

I'M HALF ASLEEP when a loud groan shakes me awake. My eyes flutter open. I grit my teeth as I shift from my diagonal position in the chair—not the most comfortable way to fall asleep.

"Arden."

It's faint, barely a whisper, but it has me stumbling over myself to get to Haskell's side. "I'm here."

He shoves the blanket down, offering me a quick look at the wound—which appears to be healing nicely—but my attention is drawn elsewhere when he croaks for water. I scramble around the room, frantically looking for the canteens, but they're all empty.

"Hang on!" I yell over my shoulder as I rush to the kitchen area. I scan every surface, cabinets included, before my eyes land on a bottle sitting upright next to Juniper. My feet can't move fast enough. I swipe it from the ground and head back toward Haskell.

He's found a way to sit upright and is wincing when I re-enter the room. I rush over to him, unscrewing the cap, and tilt the bottle to his mouth. He takes a few large gulps before raising his hand to take it from me. I take a step back and study him—his expression, his breathing, the strength of his stare. From the outside, he appears to be healed, but I have no idea what's going on in that head of his.

I silently curse myself for losing my healing abilities.

He angles his head, eyes meeting mine, as if he's heard my every thought. "I'm feeling much better." He glances down at the fading orange powder sticking to his glistening skin.

"Turmeric," I say. "Something I learned in my Cruex days."

"Thank the lords for that." He wipes his dripping forehead with the back of his hand. "It's hardly spring and look at me, already sweating profusely."

"You're just sweating out the toxins." I recall what Harrod had told me. "Whether you like it or not, the healing potion causes you to release any and all toxins from your system—from prior incidents as well as recent ones."

He grunts. "Wild guess . . . with illusié altercations?"

I nod.

"That explains a lot." He leans his head back against the wall. "Probably best to get it over with now rather than later on down the road."

I study him quietly for a few moments. He seems coherent enough so I ask, "Do you remember what we talked about last? What you said?"

He furrows his brows, deep in thought. "You may have to jog my memory."

"About the healing potion . . . you said you'd never heard of it, that you hadn't grabbed one when you transported back to Trendalath."

He stills for a moment, then nods.

"So where did it come from?" I press.

"I wish I knew the answer to that, Arden."

I try not to show the disappointment on my face. I know he's not lying to me, so I move on to the next question. "Okay, well you also mentioned that there was a way for me to get my abilities back. Do you remember saying that?"

He nods again.

"Can you tell me how?" My hand slips into the pocket of my trousers. I squeeze my pocket watch, the metal cool against my hands. I can't help but think about how much time I've wasted, sitting here, when I could have been working toward regaining my abilities.

"Yes, but only if you promise me one thing."

"What's that?"

"If I tell you, you have to take me with you." A crooked smile spans the entire length of his face. "No exceptions."

He says it as though we have to *go somewhere.* Rightly so, I hesitate before saying, "I can't promise that until you tell me what it's going to take."

"Arden," he cautions, "I need your word."

I sit back and cross my arms. He's not budging. As much as I don't want to, I know I have to. "Fine."

"*Fine* . . . what?"

I roll my eyes. "I promise I'll take you with me."

"Good." Haskell sits up even straighter. "I assume you've heard of Volkharn and the Crostan Islands?"

I think back to my days in the Cruex. We'd never been assigned to missions in either location. The Crostan Islands had always been a bit of a mystery to me—hardly any of the texts I'd studied even remotely covered the area or its history. Volkharn, while less of a mystery, had never been of interest to me. At the base of the Vaekith Mountains, it was dreary and dismal with little to no activity—essentially an assassin's worst nightmare.

"Heard of them, yes," I respond, "but I'd be lying if I said I knew anything about them."

"I figured that'd be the case." He rakes a hand through his greasy hair. "It's rumored that Volkharn and the Crostan Islands are home to two springs."

I can't help but shudder at the word, and it immediately reminds me of my most recent encounter with what I now know to be the Mallum. It also reminds me of the fact that I haven't told Haskell what I've seen— but that's a story for another time. I've been waiting for what feels like ages to finally get this information from him so I wait, patiently, for him to continue.

"It is said that any illusié who has been attacked by the Mallum—and subsequently had their abilities absorbed—can immerse themselves in the spring and restore those lost abilities."

"Lost?" I scoff. "More like stolen."

He waves a flippant hand in the air. "However you look at it doesn't matter. The solution remains the same."

"Okay, well that leaves just one question, then," I say, starting to pace back and forth. "Which location is closest?"

A shadow falls over his face. "Volkharn."

"Once you're healed, we can go." I know as soon as the words leave my mouth that it won't be that easy. Given the look on his face, it's clear that there's more I don't know—*much* more.

RYDAN HELSTROM

RYDAN HAS NEVER seen a place so beautiful. Breathtaking. Awe-inspiring. There are no words to describe the beauty of Orihia—and yet, for some reason, it's desolate. Not a soul in sight. Well, except for him, Vira, and Avery—and the cart of the deceased he's currently lugging behind him. When Avery had mentioned burning the dead, Rydan figured he'd meant doing it *outside* of Orihia, where they'd been slain. Apparently, Avery had meant something entirely different.

"Over here," he says, walking down a pebble-lined path. Rydan is just steps behind Vira, who is closely following Avery.

The path transitions from smooth dirt to a rocky one. The rickety cart sways violently behind him as the wheels meet the new, less welcoming walkway, but Rydan hardly notices because flying above his head are fluorescent-colored butterflies. Swirls of indigo and magenta dodge in and out of his view. The sound of the cart must have startled them, causing a flurry of excitement.

He's so busy looking at everything around him—the hundreds of giant trees, the multiple levels of dwellings tucked into each branch line, the oversized glowing mushrooms surrounding the perimeter, the star-dotted night sky overhead—that he nearly trips over his own two feet. It crosses his mind to ask Avery and Vira to stop for just a few moments to afford him the chance to take it all in.

"Just up there," Avery calls from behind his shoulder. "Not too much farther."

Instantly, there's a shift in his surroundings. The vast expanse of nature that was once before him dwindles to walls of sprawling vines and ivy—even the ground is covered in them. The poor wooden cart seems to have even more trouble adjusting to this new road, or lack thereof.

Rydan adjusts his grip on the cart's handles, making sure to stay close to Vira. It's almost as if they've entered a maze—he can't see anything to his left or his right or ahead, just skyward. If it weren't for the stars above, they'd be engulfed in complete darkness, impossible to navigate. They wind through the maze, some of the turns wider, some narrower, until they finally reach what appears to be their destination. The maze spits them out at the foot of a long stone staircase that leads to a round platform. From his vantage point, he can see four sizeable columns with floating spheres lining the perimeter and, at the far end of the dais, the largest tree he's ever laid eyes on. Its branches and its many leaves tower over the platform, completely blocking out the view of the night sky.

As Avery begins to climb the steps, Rydan realizes that the cart can't exactly go with them. "Should I just leave this here or . . . ?"

Avery doesn't respond. When he reaches the top of the platform, he removes one of the floating spheres and carries it back down the stairs. He secures it underneath the cart, and Rydan watches in awe as it rises from the vine-ridden ground. He releases the handles as the cart begins its ascent—perfectly balanced on the floating sphere until it reaches the top.

Vira extends her hand. Stunned into silence, Rydan takes it and climbs alongside her, stride for stride. At the top, Avery stands next to the cart, which is no longer floating, but instead sitting on its wheels on yet another raised platform. The floating sphere has been returned to its column.

"Take the end opposite me."

Rydan doesn't question him as he moves a few paces behind the cart. There's a deep indentation in the stone that runs from the center of the platform to where he now stands.

Vira takes a step back so that she's parallel with one of the columns.

"I need you to start thinking of something that makes you angry or embarrassed," Avery instructs, his gaze steady on Rydan.

Rydan glances at his hands before raising them. "You mean right now?"

"You said you wanted a lesson." Avery's mouth tilts in a faint smile. "Here it is."

Rydan shakes his head. "I know I asked for this, but this isn't right. You want to give me a lesson during an illusié ritual for the deceased?" At Avery's bemused expression, he quickly adds, "Or whatever this happens to be?"

"They're already dead." Blunt, honest words. "You don't have to impress anyone here."

"Okay, fine. You've made your unnecessarily morbid point." He notices Avery's expression turn serious as he seems to gather his own thoughts and emotions. Rydan joins the tips of his fingers together, then presses his mouth into a firm line, arms extending outward.

Knowing that *he's* the one they're waiting on, Rydan goes back to the one situation that angers him the most.

Waking up with a giant knot on his head in the middle of the Soames's house after Arden had fled from their mission. The back of his neck burns at the memory, and that warmth climbs past his chin all the way to his cheeks until he feels as though his eyes are on fire.

Without blinking, arms still extended, he brings his palms so that they're facing one another and splays his fingers. He can feel it—*the igniting*—coursing through his veins, pumping through his heart, pulsating in the very essence of his soul. He keeps his focus on that memory, on the abandonment he'd felt. His eyes draw to his fingertips as sparks ignite.

"Now!" Avery shouts.

Fire shoots from his fingertips into the indentation, traveling along the stone at a rapid speed until it reaches the raised platform. The cart bursts into a fury of orange and red flames. Rydan takes a step back, shielding his eyes as it grows brighter and brighter.

Vira runs over to him and takes his hand again. He wants to look at her, but he's so mesmerized by what he's just created—or rather, *co-created* with Avery. It's absolutely magnificent. His jaw drops as the orange and red blaze transitions into a deep purple, rising higher and higher, until the flames vanish entirely. Thousands of tiny multi-colored ashes appear in its wake, but they don't float to the ground. Rydan takes a step closer. The ashes appear to be frozen in time.

From the other side of the dais, Avery holds up a hand, cautioning him to remain still. Rydar stops moving, his eyes fixed on the sight before him. In the blink of an eye, the ashes fall to the ground before shooting skyward into the massive tree. He cranes his neck, hardly believing what he's seeing. Within seconds, tiny, but fully bloomed orange, red, and purple flowers adorn the branches. The simple beauty of it brings a smile to his face, and when he looks to his left, he's pleased to see that Vira is smiling, too.

She grips his hand tighter.

Avery tilts his head toward the stairs, but doesn't say a word. There's no need to.

What they've just shared says it all.

BRAXTON HORNSBY

TONIGHT MARKS THE fifth consecutive night that Darius has shown up outside his door without knocking—and every time, Braxton's been tempted to break down the door just to see the look on his face, but he's resisted. Tonight is no different.

As the shadows begin their routine of swaying, to then retreating, from underneath his door, he hears something out of the ordinary. He rushes over to the door, and presses his ear against the wood—but the voices are muffled.

Frustrated, Braxton crouches, then lays flat on his stomach. At first, he tries to see what's going on with just one eye, but the effort is futile. He places his hands underneath his chin and presses his left ear against the bottom sliver in the door.

The voices are faint, but he's able to make out some of what they're saying.

"You must go talk to him, Darius. This has gone on long enough."

A male's voice—or a very, *very* deep voice of a woman. The former is more likely.

"I don't have anything to discuss with him."

The response is hushed, but Braxton catches the end of it. " . . . a means to an end."

"As long as you keep it in your possession . . ."

The rest of the conversation is inaudible. Braxton knocks his forehead against the floor, then pushes himself to his feet. With the bits and pieces he's just heard, there isn't much to be gleaned. Some fragments may contribute to the whole, but not when half of them are missing. It also doesn't help that he has absolutely no idea who'd been on the other side of the conversation.

His eyes scan the room. He hates it in here. He would have much rather been locked up in the dungeons than in his childhood room. Okay, perhaps that's a slight exaggeration. There is *one* good memory—of his mother reading him stories before bed—stories he'd never cared for. But, nonetheless, they'd done their job in putting him to sleep.

He meanders over to the bookshelf, taking a quick inventory of the different texts. He pulls out a familiar book with a navy spine and blows the dust from the cover. A sad smile pulls at his face. This one had been his mother's favorite—about dragons and kingdoms, kings and queens. As a child, she'd read it to him almost every night before bed, to the point where he could practically recite it word for word.

He's on his way to take the book over to the bed to settle in for the night when something catches his eye. Dried blood on the far corner of the bookshelf. He draws closer, alarmed to see that there's more than just a drop of blood—there's a whole *spray* of it. He inspects the area around the shelf, but there's no sign of blood on the floor or on the walls. The glossy reddish-brown color indicates that whatever happened here . . . was recent.

Braxton runs his hand along each of the shelves with a sense of urgency, observing each item carefully. Nothing appears to be out of place—but then again, how could he possibly know that? He hasn't been in this room for over ten years. There is, however, something that does seem a little out of place. A gold figurine of a dragon.

How odd.

He'd refused to take anything with him when he'd fled, not just because he'd wanted to forget everything that reminded him of this place, but also because he couldn't risk being caught, especially after creating a new alias for himself—Braxton Hornsby. It'd sounded like the perfect name for an innkeeper's apprentice . . . and it had been.

As he examines the figurine further, he notices what looks like . . . more dried blood. He scratches at the fleck and it comes off in particulates, further confirming his suspicions. A stark realization washes over him. Someone had broken into this room—recently—and, whether intentional or by accident, they'd left this behind.

He scours the bookshelves even further, going so far as to open up the many different texts and flip through the pages. He checks some small containers and wooden wares, turning them upside down and shaking them. He even goes to the dresser and rifles through the drawers, but nothing unusual pops out at him.

With a defeated sigh, he retreats to the bed. He sets the dragon toy on his nightstand before pulling the blanket over his legs. He sets the thick navy book on his lap, absentmindedly thumbing through the pages. Try as he might to focus on the text, he's too distracted by the gold glinting in his periphery. He reaches over and swipes the figurine from the wooden table, turning it over in his hands. "Where did you come from?" he mutters, noticing how strangely familiar it feels. It's not long before another distraction surfaces.

A knock at the door.

DARIUS TYMOND

DARIUS STANDS JUST outside Braxton's door, wondering whether or not his son had heard him knock. In most circumstances, he usually announces his presence—but in this particular situation, he has a feeling that subtlety is more likely to work in his favor.

He takes a step back, looking underneath the door for any sign of light or movement, but it's completely still. He resumes his position, raising his hand to knock, yet again, when a voice sounds from the other side.

"Who is it?"

Darius hesitates, momentarily considering not answering, but then the door would never open. Although if he tells his son it's him, he may not open it either. Lose, lose. "It's your father."

He can almost *feel* the cringe on the other side of the door.

A prolonged silence follows.

"I'm coming in."

Knowing the door won't open on its own, Darius retrieves the key from an inner pocket of his robes and unlocks it. He opens it slowly, deliberately. The hinges creak. Braxton's disheveled head appears. He's sitting on the bed, not even bothering to get up and greet him. "You finally knocked."

Darius stands in the doorway, one foot in, one foot out, flummoxed. It would appear that Braxton's noticed his nightly journeys down the corridor. "I wanted to give you some time to process everything."

It's partly the truth.

Braxton turns and shuffles something underneath the sheets, then rises from the bed. Darius can't help but feel slightly taken aback because Braxton is so much taller than he remembers. He hadn't paid much attention when the guards had brought him in—the fact that he'd been kneeling hadn't helped either—but looking at him now, in wrinkled trousers that appear to have been worn for days, hair unkempt, eyes tired but determined . . .

He realizes that this is not the foolish boy who'd fled Trendalath ten years ago. This is a man—a man who's seen and experienced more than Darius could possibly fathom.

"Why are you here, King Tymond?"

The formality is a dagger to the heart. A fleeting urge to imprison his son surfaces, but, like dust, it vanishes the moment Darius recalls his recent conversation in the hall. As uncomfortable as it is, he decides to assume the role of father instead of king. "Seeing you here, like this . . . you're no longer a child." He runs a hand over his mouth, stopping at his chin. "You've grown more than I ever could have imagined."

Braxton remains silent, but his eyes soften.

"When you unexpectedly showed up in the town square that day," Darius carries on, "I was shocked, yes, but I was something else, too." He smirks. "I hate to admit it, but I was actually *glad* to see you. For a decade, I didn't know if you were even alive."

"Is that why you sent your Savant?"

"My Savant do—"

"—whatever you order them to do," Braxton finishes.

Darius crosses his arms. *He's not going to make this easy.*

"You sent your Savant to kill your only son."

Darius wags a finger in the air. "Not kill. No, if I'd wanted you dead, it would already be done."

"Like with Arden?"

He can feel his face pale at the remark.

"Answer me."

"Arden Eliri killed your mother." The lie rots on his tongue. "Of course I want her dead."

The words seem to snag on something in Braxton's mind because his expression grows lighter.

Although unspoken, Darius catches onto his son's train of thought. *He wasn't aware that Arden is still alive.*

"Well, are you going to come in or are you going to just linger in the doorway?"

Darius glances at his feet, just now realizing that he hasn't fully entered the room. He pulls on the front of his robes and clears his throat before shutting the door behind him.

Braxton gestures to a nearby chair, then takes the one opposite him. He studies his father with curious eyes. His gaze eventually settles on the ring.

Darius shifts in his seat, purposely bringing his hands beneath his robes. He casts his eyes to the floor. "I know why you left all those years ago." His voice is passive—almost forgiving. "When you emerged in the town square and showcased your abilities . . ." His voice trails off as he looks at Braxton, who seems to be wincing, as if waiting for some sort of punishment. "Well, to be frank, I thought it was just magnificent."

Braxton sits back, eyes wide. "Not what I expected to hear—and from you, of all people," he responds, his shoulders dropping in relief. "You've always hated illusié."

Darius lets out a small laugh. "There's a difference when you're *royal* illusié.

Braxton considers this. After a few moments, he leans forward, propping his elbows on his knees. "That shouldn't matter. I'm not surprised, though, that you hold something so insignificant in such high regard."

"One day you'll understand," Darius says coolly. And then, to add insult to injury, "I certainly wouldn't expect that day to be today."

Braxton doesn't seem fazed. "Well, *father,* I suppose you've gotten what you've always wanted." He sighs. "A non-magickal heir to the throne."

Darius is about to tell him that he's wrong when a guard suddenly bursts through the door. "Your Majesty, please forgive the interruption. You are needed in the dungeons immediately."

"Can't it wait?" Darius huffs, not taking his eyes off of his son.

"No, Your Majesty."

Darius waits until Braxton shifts his gaze back to him. "To be resumed at a later time?"

A flash of disdain darts across his son's eyes. "We'll see."

And just like that, their entire conversation—all that they'd started to rebuild—disappears without a trace.

CERYLIA JARETH

N O   M A T T E R   H O W   hard she's tried, Cerylia hasn't been able to shake Delwynn's warning from her mind. *You will lose them for good. After everything you've worked for, don't let this be the end. Don't give up now.*

She pulls a bottle of verdot from the freshly stocked cabinet in the dining hall. It'd taken weeks for the shipment to arrive. In the meantime, she'd substituted tea for wine, but it'd hardly done the trick—although the mornings *have* been more enjoyable. No fogginess. No nausea.

Seeing as it's nearly dusk, she uncorks the wine and is about to pour herself a glass when a shadow darts across her vision. Eyes fixed on the spot, she tilts the bottle upward and sets it down. The wine sloshes in her goblet as she makes for the window—but when she pokes her head out, there isn't a soul in sight. She takes a large gulp of her wine before setting it back on the table.

Why must her curiosity always get the better of her? Here she is, about to have a relaxing evening she likely won't even remember, when her mind decides to go and play tricks on her. Just to pull her away. Even so, she can't seem to shake the nagging feeling.

After finishing her wine and retrieving her cloak from the White Room, she sneaks out into the garden. It's that perfect pocket of time where it's just dark enough to keep her hidden, but light enough for her to see where she's going. Near the dining hall, just as she'd suspected, are a set of footprints. The rainfall from earlier in the day makes it easy to track the muddy prints all the way through the garden, clear to the other side of the castle. They take her far past the queendom walls and into a part of the forest she's never cared to venture into.

Until now.

She turns her gaze skyward as it grows darker and darker, wondering again if perhaps the shadow was just her imagination running off again. *Wouldn't be the first time.*

The trail of footprints seems to have disappeared, so now she's just wandering aimlessly through an unfamiliar forest. At night.

Just as she's about to give up and turn back, a twig snaps in the distance. She freezes in position, then sidesteps behind a tree, waiting for another sound, another indication of potential life nearby—but there isn't one. She peeks her head around the trunk, scanning the forest for movement, only to find that it's completely still.

With a sigh, she pushes off from the tree and treks back toward the castle. Yes, her imagination has been getting most of her attention as of late. Instead of ignoring it, she's handed over the reins, giving it complete control. Her imagination had run off with Braxton's involvement in the Mallum's appearance, and now with random shadows dancing on the walls. Most days, she'd just chalk it up to the multiple glasses of verdot, but that excuse won't work tonight. She's only had one.

Perhaps this is about something bigger. Whether intentional or not, the Caldari *have* given her the cold shoulder lately. Even Delwynn seems to be playing along. It's been days since she's seen him and, if she remembers correctly, their last conversation ended with her refusing to take his advice . . . so maybe that's why. Perhaps someone will realize she's been missing for—how long has it been? An hour or so? Surely *someone* had noticed.

Her assumption is incorrect. Much to her dismay, she slips back into the castle, undetected.

ARDEN ELIRI

I'M BACK IN our father's den, doing as much research as possible on the springs' alleged restorative abilities. Until Haskell is fully healed, we can't begin our journey across Aeridon. Unfortunately, he'd let me in on a little known fact. He's only been to the base of the Vaekith Mountains once—which means that the *only* place he can transport us to . . . is the base of the Vaekith Mountains. And, according to the map, the jaded spring is near the peak. So that's great.

I finish flipping through the last few pages of yet another book before sliding the next one off the stack. I haven't found anything of use, or perhaps I'm just so anxious to get going that the words and their meanings have all blurred together. Juniper nudges my hand away from the book to get me to scratch her face. I oblige her, and I swear she smiles at me. "Sorry girl," I coo. "I don't have any berries with me."

I reach for my pocket watch, realizing that, once again, I've lost track of time. Haskell's mostly been resting, although he *has* tried to sneak out of the cave every now and again to go for a walk. Much to his chagrin, I've caught him every time.

It dawns on me that we're running low on food—on supplies in general. Being days away from the nearest town has its perks—no people, peaceful nights, and zero disturbances—but it also has its consequences . . . lack of food and supplies being high among them.

I rise from the desk, not bothering to return the books to their shelves. Juniper seems to sense that we're about to leave, so she jumps to the ground and follows me down the many steps that lead into the temple. I do everything exactly as Haskell demonstrated to close up shop, then exit the cavern altogether.

The sun is barely starting its descent as I make my way back to the cave. Perfect. That leaves me plenty of time to check on Haskell, reassess our current food situation, *and* catch some fresh game, if need be.

When I arrive, I'm surprised to find my brother up and moving. He's leaning over a crackling fire, two fish roasting on the spit. Seeing as his back is to me, he doesn't seem to notice my arrival, so I clear my throat to get his attention.

He glances over his shoulder and smiles. "Well, aren't you one for impeccable timing. Hungry?"

I'm starving, but that's beside the point. "What did I say about over-exerting yourself?"

He straightens but keeps that foolish grin on his face. "It's fishing, Arden. It's the least strenuous hunting activity there is."

So he *hadn't* transported. A small sigh of relief escapes me.

He catches on to my line of thought. "If I'd come back with lamb or deer, then I certainly would have had some explaining to do. But not with fish." He rotates the spit for emphasis. "To be honest, it's the most relaxed I've felt in days."

For some reason, the way he says it has me tense up. "Where'd you catch them?" I eye the fish on the spit, instantly recognizing them as yellow bullheads.

Freshwater fish.

"I don't remember exactly. I happened upon this spring I've never seen before. Secluded. Beautiful." He rotates the rod again so that the fish are belly-down. "It was so peaceful I could have fallen asleep and no one would have been the wiser."

My heart nearly leaps out of my chest. As if I need *another* reminder about my encounter with the Mallum—

and the guilt surrounding the fact that I haven't told him about it. *Yet.*

I eye the fish suspiciously. They're almost fully roasted, so I can't tell if there's actually anything wrong with them. Something, albeit I don't know what, tells me not to eat them.

"You know, I'm not really in the mood for fish," I say carefully as I draw closer to the fire. "I wouldn't mind quail. How does that sound?"

"We had quail last night." He studies me with bleak eyes. "I'm good with fish."

"Haskell, we can't eat this fish."

So much for trying to be subtle.

"Why not?"

I know I can't answer him without telling him what had happened at that spring—about seeing him, as a child; our mother, pregnant with me; an unknown person knocking at the door. I don't know how the Mallum had known or how it had shown me any of this. Honestly, I'd blocked it from my mind until now. I'm not at all prepared to talk about this—but I suppose I have to.

"I can't explain why, but I have reason to believe that these fish have been poisoned in some way."

An incredulous look crosses his face. "Arden," he tries to reason with me, "these bullheads came from a freshwater spring just east of here—a spring that's completely untapped, undisturbed." He angles his head toward the fire. "This will probably be the freshest meal we've had since you've been here. And you want to rob us of that?"

I know he's not going to budge on this, so I have to take matters into my own hands. I do something *very* unlike myself. I walk to the side opposite him and grab hold of the spit handle. It nearly burns my skin as I yank it from its place and throw it against the wall. It falls to the ground, a pile of dirt rising up to consume it. And that's when I *know* it's bad because Juniper won't even go near it.

"Arden!" Haskell yells, but I put my arm out to stop him.

"Not but four days ago, I saved your life," I remind him. "We're not about to go down that road again."

RYDAN HELSTROM

RYDAN WAKES TO a petite hand laying over his, fingers interlaced, and a view of Vira's sleeping face. He smiles, watching as her chest rises and falls with each breath. If they were anywhere else, he'd stay and watch her sleep for a while, but after seeing Orihia with his own two eyes for the very first time, there's definitely an urge to explore further—especially since he doesn't know how long they intend to stay.

He holds his breath as he releases his grip, slowly sliding his hand out from underneath hers. As cautiously as he can manage, he rolls over and sits up, gently pushing off from the bed. He glances over his shoulder, just to check and, when she doesn't stir, he finally releases his breath.

After the ceremony last night, Avery had led them through the maze, back to the main area of Orihia. He'd asked Rydan to get a fire started, which he'd had no problem doing, and then had brought over a couple of bottles of aged verdot. Vira had bounced up and down, clapping her hands like a giddy child. Avery had done the honors of pouring the wine, and they'd clinked glasses, chatted, and exchanged childhood stories around the fire.

Rydan had felt unstoppable after those first few glasses. His tolerance was unmatched. Both Avery and Vira had started to slur their words and, soon enough, Rydan couldn't understand anything they were saying. After repeatedly asking Avery what dwelling was his—assuming he even *had* one here—he'd had to use his better judgment and pick a random one to settle his friend into for the night. The poor lad hadn't even made it to the bed when he'd fallen face first onto the floor. If it hadn't been for his snoring, Rydan would have assumed he'd knocked himself unconscious. Like a good friend would do—since that's apparently what they are now—Rydan had scooped him up off the floor and placed him on the bed. He'd even tucked a pillow under his head for good measure.

When he'd returned outside, Vira had been dancing around the fire, stringing together a bunch of sounds and incoherent phrases in an attempt to sing, but it'd sounded more like the warbling of some very loud birds. It'd taken a few minutes for him to catch her—even inebriated she was quick on her feet—but he'd eventually scooped her up, just like he'd done with Avery, and had carried her to yet another random dwelling. She'd been persistent that he stay with her, even going so far as to kiss him on the cheek. When he'd tried to leave, she'd pulled on his arm. He'd obliged her, only intending to stay until she'd fallen asleep, but with their hands intertwined, he'd gotten comfortable and had passed out almost instantly.

Realizing he'd slept fully dressed and with his boots on, Rydan makes for the door, shutting it as quietly as he can manage. A gentle breeze greets him as he climbs down the steps of the house and walks along the gravel pathway. Now that it's daylight, he has a better view of Orihia and what it actually looks like—and it is even more stunning now than it was last night.

Never in his life has he seen such a spectrum of color. Species of animals he never knew existed dart to and fro, and he swears he can feel the energy around him pulsing. It's as if this place is attempting to elevate not only his mood, but his entire state of being.

Whatever it's trying to do . . . it's working.

He jumps off the gravel road onto a larger stone one, following the winding pathway into the depths of the woods. There's something oddly refreshing about this place, something he can't quite put his finger on, but it's as if everything here—the trees, the animals, the plants, the *life*—was put here on purpose. And not merely to exist, but to truly *live* and thrive.

Up ahead, he can see where the forest breaks off into a cliff and dead ends at . . . a waterfall. But not just any waterfall—this one is monstrous, climbing just as high as the ceremony tree he'd gawked at the night prior. The water, which he'd expected to be a deep blue, is actually a range of vibrant colors. Pigments of pinks, purples, greens, and blues gush down the sides of the rocks, whirling into one to form a rippling rainbow. He toes the edge of the cliff, hanging onto one of the branches above him as he leans over and runs his hand through the water. When he pulls it back out, not a trace of color can be seen.

Without a second thought, he releases the branch and plops onto the ground. He yanks his boots off before pulling at his shirt, then shimmies off his trousers. Only his undergarments remain. He steps to the edge of the cliff, watching as a few pebbles slide off the side and splash into the water below. He takes a few steps back to get a running start, then dashes forward until there's no ground left beneath his feet. He tucks his legs into his chest as he plummets toward the water, whooping before he's fully submerged.

When he comes up for air, he glances back up at the cliff and smiles. It was quite a ways down, and he realizes it's been some time since he's felt a surge of adrenaline like that. Ever since abandoning his position in the Cruex and taking off with Vira, things have been, well . . . less than exhilarating. Not that he hasn't enjoyed his time with her—he has—but there's just something about his old lifestyle he can't help but miss.

Miniature fish swarm his feet as he wades over to a small island jutting out from underneath the rocks. He pulls himself up onto a shore of pale pink sand, the grains latching on to every surface of his body. He lays on his back for a few minutes, pausing to catch his breath. In the meantime, his eyes follow a flock of multi-colored doves soaring overhead. They stay in his line of sight for a while, but eventually, they disappear over the cliff and into the thicket beyond.

Rydan scoots back over to the water's edge and sticks his feet in, still mesmerized by the everchanging hues. Every time he lifts his legs, he expects his skin to match the shade of the water—honestly, he's kind of disheartened when he finds that they're not.

He dives into the water once more, swimming until he's back in the center of the spring. Like everything else here, the view above steals his attention. Never has he felt so inclined to just *be*. He floats on his back, eyes fixed on the sky above, completely losing track of time. And, while he'd never admit it out loud, in this moment, he feels incredibly fortunate to be among the illusié ranks.

CERYLIA JARETH

IT KEEPS HAPPENING. Every night since Cerylia had first seen the shadow, another one, or rather, the *same* one, has appeared—and every night she's followed it, only to be led to the same spot over and over again. Surrounded by stillness and silence.

But tonight? She's prepared.

With her cloak already on and her fingers firmly grasping her goblet, she keeps her eyes fixed on the window. She takes a quick sip of verdot before setting it down, then leans forward on her elbows. It should be happening any second now.

Three.

Two.

One.

Like clockwork, a shadow races by.

Without even the slightest hesitation, she jumps from her seat and makes for the courtyard. Her feet carry her to the other end where, like so many nights prior, she slips through the opening that leads to the other side of the castle.

There's movement in the trees.

She's closer than she's ever been.

She takes off down the pathway toward the once unfamiliar forest—which she's now covered almost every inch of—making sure to survey each area she passes. This will be the night she finally discovers who the culprit is. She can feel it.

Her breathing grows heavy as she continues to follow it, her legs burning from the effort. The last time she ran this fast was when she'd found out about . . . Dane.

With a grunt, she forces the memory far from her mind and picks up her stride. It's mere moments later when the movement ahead stops. Her breath hitches as she comes to a screeching halt, using a nearby oak tree to shield her presence. As quietly as she can, she inhales deeply to calm her racing heart, but not before peering around the edge of the tree.

After so many nights of following the unknown, her eyes have grown accustomed to the dark. She starts to scan the area that's just ahead of her when her gaze lands on a clearing—and a familiar figure.

Petite. Cloaked.

It only takes a second to recognize who it is.

Opal.

No one appears to be with her. Cerylia watches with grave intent as Opal begins to walk in small circles, pacing. Waiting.

What is she doing in the forest at dusk . . . alone?

Opal stops pacing and looks up at one of the trees.

Cerylia follows her gaze, unable to see whatever it is that's caught her attention—that is, until a soft yellow glow appears. And just like that, her question is answered.

Opal's been meeting with Xerin.

DARIUS TYMOND

DARIUS FOLLOWS THE guard to the dungeons, winding down the many staircases and darting across multiple corridors. The guard hadn't shared the details as to *why* he's needed, but Darius has a sinking feeling it has something to do with Clive—and his casting.

As always, the dungeons are dank and musty. He's prepared to ignore the grimy hands that usually reach out through the bars, grabbing for him, and the croaked pleas of those he's locked up—but there's none of that today. It's eerily quiet.

An unwelcome shiver creeps down his spine.

When they arrive at the end of the hall, he notices

the guard stops a good ways away from Clive's cell. He turns to face the king. "After you, Your Majesty."

Wanting to get this over with, Darius pushes his way past the burly guard, only to stop dead in his tracks. Every one of his Cruex members, except Cyrus, is sitting on the ground, curled up into a ball like a child would do after being scolded. With their arms locked over their knees, all Darius can see is the tops of their heads.

He approaches with caution.

"Sir Garrick," he whispers, kicking the bottom of the Cruex's boot. Percival doesn't move.

"Sir Garrick," Darius says a little louder. "Answer me."

No response. Instead, his body curls inward even more.

"They can't hear you."

Darius whirls around, seething. If he weren't so livid, Clive's sudden presence would have startled him. Thankfully, his cohort is on the wrong side of the bars— the *inside*. "What have you done to them?"

Clive doesn't break his focus to look at Darius. "Isn't it obvious? I've been practicing."

One of the Cruex yelps in horror.

He's casting on more than two people at a time.

The sickening realization leaves a pit in his stomach.

"I command you to stop."

Clive chuckles. "Oh, is that the game we're playing? Well then, I command you to release me."

Knowing that he could easily be the next target, Darius steps directly in front of the cell, blocking Clive's view of the cowering Cruex. It distracts him enough to stop casting. From behind him, a collective sigh; in front of him, angry eyes.

"Move," Clive hisses. "Or I swear—"

Darius sets his hands on the bars. Clive's gaze immediately falls to the amethyst ring. "I wouldn't if I were you."

Clive takes a step back, clapping his hands loudly as if he's just seen a spectacular show. He walks in a small circle before saying, "Go ahead, Your Majesty. Sic the Mallum on me."

Darius falters. He removes his hands from the bars.

"You and I both know the end game here. You *need* me. You need *this*."

Before Darius can process what's happening, he's suddenly sucked into an abyss far, far from reality. Fragments from his family's past claw at his mind as if they've somehow transformed into tangible, living entities—his Savant's deceit, his undesirable marriage to Aldreda, Braxton's birth, Clive and Aldreda's affair. The images hook him, reeling him in. They fade in and out, some faster than others, until he's left in the same position as the Cruex—breathless on the dungeon floor, coiled into a ball.

Clive's voice is distant, but distinct. "I'm only growing stronger
in here, Darius. At some point, you'll have to release me. Best if it's before I bring this entire kingdom down."

Somehow, Darius finds the strength to lift his head. "I don't need you nearly as much as you think I do."

A bold-faced lie that Clive sees right through. "Then do it," he taunts. "Right here, right now."

Slowly, Darius pushes himself up off the ground. Although they're not visible from beneath his robes, his legs shake violently beneath him. He twists the ring around his finger once. Twice.

Clive smirks, not even bothering to brace himself for the potential impact.

"You may be one of the most powerful Casters out there, but at the end of the day"—his eyes rove the bars— "you're still here. In this cell. *A prisoner.*"

Clive's face falls.

Darius turns away and pulls each Cruex member up from the ground. The guard ushers them toward the exit. He waits until the heavily barred door shuts securely behind the guard.

Darius can't help but relish the defeat as it washes over Clive's face. "I will release you when I am ready—and you can trust when I say that it won't be any time soon."

BRAXTON HORNSBY

IT ISN'T AT all surprising that Darius would choose to leave the very moment they'd started to rebuild their father-son relationship. If that isn't the story of his childhood, he doesn't know what is. At least Aldreda had put in *some* sort of effort—Darius had let her do all the parenting without any qualms.

It's no wonder he's such a poor father.

Braxton spoons the last of the roasted pork into his mouth before pushing the tray to the end of the bed, not bothering to walk it the few steps to the desk. Being locked up for weeks on end does little to combat laziness.

As he scoots back on his hands, the tray teetering on the edge, his fingers graze something cold. How had he forgotten? He pulls the toy from his pocket, raising the small dragon to eye-level, its golden hue nearly blinding.

Who had left this behind? And why?

For reasons he can't explain, Arden's face flashes across his mind. Braxton's stomach drops as he recalls what Darius had confirmed when he'd first been brought back to Trendalath.

Arden killed my mother.

His hand closes around the toy, squeezing it tightly. If it weren't made of metal, it'd surely break. In a huff, he flings it away from him. It clinks against the wooden floor before landing on its side. Helpless.

Just like me.

Try as he might, he can't keep the heart-wrenching images away. Thoughts of his mother and all the ways she could have died—all the ways Arden had *murdered* her—infiltrate his feeble and volatile mind. Suffocation. Decapitation. A stab wound. A chakram-related incident, just like the one he'd had the horror of experiencing.

He presses his hands against his temples as the memory resurfaces. His failure to deviate. The blades slicing the tops of his hands. Raw bone and blood where his skin used to be. And then, when Arden had tried to heal him . . . the pain he'd felt. Like his already frayed bones were being pulled from their joints, slowly and deliberately, one by one. Like salt had just been rubbed into his open wounds, searing into what remained of his ruined flesh.

Had his mother experienced the same fate?

Had she been unable to bear it—the pain?

His eyes flick to the abandoned figurine on the floor. Unexpectedly, his anger softens into grief. *Arden Eliri.* Not only has he lost his mother, he's also lost *her*.

Which one hurts worse remains to be seen.

ARDEN ELIRI

I'VE BEEN READYING the cave in preparation to leave for what feels like weeks now. There's only so many times I can check the cupboards, fold the blankets, and straighten up the benches and tables. I'm ready to go, but Haskell (and his wound) are not.

As the days pass, so does my patience. I can't help but curse myself for losing my abilities, especially knowing that his healing would be further along and we wouldn't have to go on this ridiculous journey in the first place.

I place the blanket back over my brother before venturing to my own room. Juniper has made herself perfectly comfortable atop my knapsack. "Hey," I say, gently swatting at her. She jolts awake and skitters away from the bag to another corner in the room.

I sigh. "Sorry. Didn't mean that." I used to feel funny talking out loud to her, but not anymore. I have a hunch that she understands what I'm saying. Between the knowing looks she gives me and the sounds she makes, I'm almost certain of it.

As I pick my bag up off the floor, something hits the ground. I smile as I realize what it is. A wooden carving of a ship. The one Felix had given me.

I swipe the object from the ground and carry it to my bed. I turn it over in my hands, admiring the intricate craftsmanship. It's nearly an exact replica of the ship he'd captained, the one that had taken us to Lonia. I squeeze it tightly in my hands, feeling a sharp pang in my chest.

I miss him.

It's hard being away, not knowing what's going on. Is he still in Sardoria? Is he safe? Does he even know that I'm gone? And if so, does he miss me too?

If only there was a way to know for sure.

Without taking my eyes off the carving, I stretch myself out on the bed and prop my head up on my elbow. I place the ship in front of me, using the tips of my fingers to twirl it round. So distinguished, so detailed these carvings are. I can't help but examine it closer. The sails, the stern, the bow . . .

As I turn it over, I notice something I hadn't before. A tiny slit in the wood.

Perplexed, I run my finger over it—once, twice—until a wooden compartment reveals itself. With my index finger and my thumb, I reach inside and pull out an object that closely resembles a pearl. I'm not sure what to do with it, but its presence is . . . surprising. A flurry of emotions sweeps through me. My feelings for Felix are suddenly at the forefront of my mind as I face an internal montage of our last few conversations. The way I'd treated him is embarrassing, to say the least. Selfish. Juvenile. Intolerant. The flashbacks make me wonder if he'd even *want* to see me again.

Without warning, the pearl rises from my hand and into the air. It floats before me, glowing a soft indigo, then moves toward the exit of the cave. It reminds me a lot of the orb that had brought me face to face with my father— but somehow, this one is different.

Nonetheless, my interest is piqued.

I keep my focus on the glowing object, reaching behind me to grab both the wooden carving and my knapsack. I follow it out of the cave and into the forest, its glow the only thing illuminating the way. I'm so mesmerized that I hardly realize where it's taken me until I'm standing right in front of it. My breath hitches.

The freshwater spring.

ARDEN ELIRI

I SHOULD TURN back, should run for my life, but I can't seem to shift my gaze from the glowing orb in front of me. It hovers over the water.

Watching.

Waiting.

As if it expects me to do something—to give a signal of some sort.

I'm at a loss for what to do, so I approach the spring, even though my mind is screaming at me to run back to the cave—back to safety. But the ship, the wooden carving, is something Felix had given me. He would never *willingly* give me something that could cause me harm.

Willingly being the key word.

Daft or not, I choose to trust his intentions.

I remove my knapsack and kneel before the spring. The orb mimics my movement. I slide my hands into the water, cringing a little at the slimy moss that greets my skin. It envelopes me, nearly pulling me under. I'm on my knees, leaning on my hands, staring directly into the water's surface. I don't know what I expect to see, but my reflection is the only thing staring back at me.

Confused, I lift my gaze. The orb lingers in the air until, suddenly, it dives straight into the water. A flash of purple follows. Small waves ripple toward me, distorting my reflection. I'm about to take my hands out of the water, strip down, and go after the pearl myself, but suddenly, an image appears beneath me—one of Felix.

In Sardoria.

I blink a few times, not sure if what I'm seeing is real, but it's him—the russet hair, the slender curve of his jaw, the bold glimmer in his eyes. He looks different somehow, almost older—but that's probably just my mind playing tricks on me. It's only been a few months since we've seen each other. How much could have changed?

I keep my eyes fixed on the image, watching the scene play out before me. Felix is standing in front of Queen Jareth, alone. My view is somewhat limited, but I'm almost certain that it's just the two of them—there's no sign of Delwynn, Opal, Estelle, nor Braxton. Xerin's whereabouts briefly cross my mind, but I dismiss the thought as soon as I hear Felix's voice.

His head is bowed, but his plea isn't muffled in the slightest. "Please, Your Greatness, if you'll just let me roam the Roviel Woods, I promise to return. I may not possess Braxton's particular advantages, but I can retrieve what you seek."

Cerylia's tone is flat. "Braxton managed to fail me, and now he's gone."

My chest tightens. *Braxton's no longer in Sardoria?*

"I won't have you leave as well, especially since you Caldari have a way of leaving and never returning."

"You don't know that," Felix counters. "As we speak, Rydan and Vira could very well be on their way back."

"Doubtful."

"Or Braxton."

The queen scoffs. "Definitely not."

"Arden . . . "

My name lingers in the air like an unwanted guest.

Cerylia purses her lips.

"My point is," Felix says, raking a hand through his tousled hair, "you can't possibly know whether or not any of them plan to return because they *could* be on their way back. They could show up here, unannounced, any minute."

The queen blatantly ignores his optimism. "Did you come here to ask for something, Sir Barlow?"

He stands a little taller. "Your Greatness, I can retrieve the ring from Trendalath. And I will return it to you, its rightful owner—"

"I am not," she snaps, rising from her throne, "nor will I ever be, its *rightful* owner."

Felix raises both hands in surrender. "May I take that as express consent?"

"With the Mallum at large, I'm not sure it's the best idea."

"I understand." He pauses before saying, "But will you give me your word that you'll at least consider it? I know your relationship with the Caldari is strained. I hope you can see that I'm just trying to do my part in keeping the peace."

She raises a brow. "By asking for permission?"

He shrugs, then cracks a smile. "I suppose so."

"I will consider it."

"I have your word?"

"You have my word."

He bows in thanks.

The water grows foggy as the image dissipates. "No," I say, splashing my hands in the water, not ready for him to leave—but the fog only grows denser before clearing altogether. My reflection returns.

I hang my head as I slide my arms out of the water. I sit back on my heels and run a hand over my face. The scent of dampened leaves and dirt after a recent rain engulf me. I close my eyes before taking a deep inhale. In my exceptionally vulnerable state, I half expect the Mallum to appear, but the spring remains still—and so does the forest around me.

The pearl's glow grows brighter as it rises from the depths of the spring. It breaks through the surface and, just barely skimming the top of the water, floats toward me. I sit in silence. When it's hovering at eye-level, I reach into my bag and pull out the wooden ship. The compartment is still open. I carefully lift it to the floating object and it glides right in, the wood securing itself back in place. I run my finger over where it's just disappeared, hoping I can coax it back out, but I can't even find the edges of the compartment. It's like it's vanished altogether. Defeated, I throw the wooden ship back in my bag, then take a few minutes to replay in my head what I've just witnessed.

Felix is still in Sardoria—which means he's safe—but possibly not for long since he's offered to leave to retrieve . . . a ring? From Trendalath? I vaguely remember King Tymond wearing a ring that day in the healing ward with Aldreda. Putting two and two together, I'm almost positive it's the ring Cerylia's talking about.

Am I the last person to find out about the Mallum? Everyone seems to already know about this lurking malevolent force except for me. Coincidence?

And Braxton . . . Braxton's no longer in Sardoria. I

can't imagine him fleeing without good reason. *I wonder where he's gone.*

The more I attempt to sort through my thoughts, the more complex they become. Try as I might, I can't seem to clear my head. Perhaps another stroll in nature will help. With a sigh, I secure my knapsack over my shoulders and head in the direction opposite the freshwater spring.

CERYLIA JARETH

CERYLIA REMAINS IN the White Room long after Felix has left. She ruminates over the many implications of her latest discovery regarding Opal and Xerin, now adding Felix's proposal to the list. It seems the Caldari want nothing more than to get away from here— and that they're willing to go to tremendous lengths to do so.

Felix's proposal, although not surprising, has certainly added an interesting layer to her evening. While she appreciates his asking for permission, if she allows him to leave, the others will surely follow.

Perhaps the good fight is over before it's even begun.

Perhaps giving up *is* the way forward.

With signs of an impending headache, she rises from her throne, eyeing the tea cart near the window. Much to her surprise, she doesn't need to call for Delwynn. An eddy of steam escapes from the spout of the teapot. She hadn't even noticed when it'd been brought in. Had it arrived before or *after* her conversation with Felix?

She brushes the thought away as she lifts the lid, the floral scent of jasmine and mint wafting toward her. Not her favorite, but it'll do. She pours herself a cup, adding a few drops of honey before raising it to her lips. The herbal remedy immediately soothes her headache.

At least she knows she's made one right choice in not calling Delwynn. Company is the last thing she wants right now. Sitting alone with her thoughts is just what she needs—any more outside influences and she'll no longer be able to discern which thoughts are hers and which aren't.

Her eyes travel to her throne, but she doesn't feel like sitting. They shift to one of the open windows. She smiles as she glides across the marble floors, taking care to not spill her tea. For some time, she gazes out the window, admiring nature's subtle bloom during a season where everything should still be covered in a blanket of white. She's always preferred the snow, but there's something about this premature spring that awakens a sense of hope in her—that perhaps everything will work out just as it's supposed to.

The pleasant thought stays with her until, out of the corner of her eye, she catches a distant, but discernable glint. Her chest falls as she swivels her head toward the tea cart. She hastily places the cup on the ledge and marches over to it. Fastened on the side is something vaguely familiar. She plucks a small pearl-sized item from the engraving in the metal cart. She examines it closely, mesmerized by the purple and blue refractions in the light.

It takes a moment for her to realize what it is and, when she does, her heart sinks. It's certainly of illusié origin. She would know because she'd found them hidden all over Trendalath castle—when she and Dane had reigned—before it'd been invaded by the Tymonds.

Somehow, the Tymonds had known their every secret, their every plan, their every *move*, often before she and Dane had even figured it out themselves. If history has proven one thing, it's that their bloodline has a knack for playing dirty.

Cerylia raises the object a little higher, just to be sure. Indeed, it is a speculor. Which means someone within her queendom is playing dirty as well . . .

And there's no doubt in her mind as to *who* it is.

RYDAN HELSTROM

AS RYDAN CLIMBS out of the water, he notices a strange silver-blue mist near the cave-like structure. He briefly considers turning back to check in with Vira and Avery first, but his curiosity gets the better of him. Tiptoeing around the edge of the water, he can feel his feet melt into the sand. He hastily reaches for the jutting rocks, then shimmies his way around the formation, taking notice of the colorful fish swimming just beneath his feet. A final step and a small hop brings him to more firm terrain. His eyes lift, mouth dropping at the sheer size of the cave.

It's *enormous*.

The moment he steps inside, a shiver creeps down his spine. The air around him is thick with moisture, making it simultaneously chilly and damp. His wet clothes don't help the situation either. With narrowed eyes, he tries to discern just how far back the cave goes. Even with the bright sunlight pouring into the entrance, it's hard to tell. He glances at the walls with what he knows is an irrational expectation: to see a torch—or any light source, for that matter.

This isn't Haskell's cave, he reminds himself.

It's then his gaze falls to his hands.

The perfect source of light.

He recalls what Avery had told him—about how he needs to *feel* in order to summon his abilities—but he isn't angry. Far from it, actually.

Perhaps a relaxing swim wasn't the best precursor.

Venturing even farther into the cave, he reaches a point where the sunlight from the entrance is no longer visible. Standing in complete darkness, he closes his eyes, trying to bring forth feelings of rage. He pulls and pulls and pulls, but, at the moment, even feelings of irritation are hard to come by. Refusing defeat, he begins to envision the faces of those who have wronged him.

Arden's face is the first to pop into his mind.

King Tymond's is next.

Focusing on the two of them should do it.

He opens his eyes as a faint warmth rises to his cheeks, but when he lifts his hands, he's still engulfed in darkness. With a sigh, he turns toward the cave exit when he suddenly knocks into something firm and immobile. Confused, he stretches his arms out in front of him, his palms making contact with what feels like a wall. Since he can't see anything, he figures he must have gotten turned around somewhere—but as he sidesteps along the wall, he comes to find that it's fully enclosed.

His chest constricts as panic overtakes him. Without so much as a second thought, he begins to pound on the wall, hoping he'll somehow break through the solid membrane. In his flummoxed state, his foot catches on the edge of what feels like a rock. Tripping over it would send him flying even deeper into the darkness, but he catches himself just in time. He bends down to pick up the rock and, just as he's hoisting it into position to hurl it at the wall, a faint red glow stops him. His eyes travel to the source of the light—the stone he's currently holding. At first, he assumes he's somehow set the stone on fire, but his fingertips haven't ignited.

It takes a few moments for his eyes to adjust. With a renewed sense of sight, he slowly brings the stone, which is no bigger than his head, in front of him before walking along the enclosure. Indeed, the entrance to the cave seems to have disappeared. But when he turns away from the wall, he notices another glimmer in the distance—this one also red. Seeing no choice, he uses the stone as a guiding light. The terrain gets rockier and rockier, and the walls seem to close in on him, narrowing with each step, until he finally reaches the source of the glimmer. The darkness begins to fade as a curtain of crimson takes its place.

The first thing his eyes land on is a column made of black onyx. It sits in the center of the vast expanse, adjacent to hundreds of jagged stairs that appear to be made of the same material. As he takes another step, he realizes that what was once a narrow cave is now a massive chamber—one that stretches immeasurable lengths left and right, up and down. His gaze follows the top of the column, which points upward at a cone-shaped opening. An orange light shines from above, illuminating every inch of the enclosure. Just as he's about to take another step, the glow from the stone reveals the drop-off he's about to plunge into. He shifts all of his weight onto his heels to keep from falling. *That was close.*

With a shake of his head, he curses under his breath before holding the stone out in front of him. His eyes skim the staircase, following the trail that leads to just below where he's currently standing. Black stones surrounded by ruby-tinted liquid make up the long pathway. It's not thick enough to be blood, but not thin enough to be water.

Rydan realizes that in order to get to the column, he'll have to climb down from the ledge, then onto the seemingly stable platform below. How stable, he isn't sure, but there's only one way to find out. The stone resumes its natural, non-glowing state as it leaves his hand and plummets to the platform below. It lands with a loud thud but doesn't crack or break.

Carefully inching forward, he presses his back against the wall, leaning to his left to see what, if anything, he can use to make it down safely. Small grooves in the formation are an option, but not with the heavy boots he's currently wearing. Seeing no other choice, he slips them off and carefully drops them over the ledge, watching with satisfaction as they land just inches away from the stone. His eyes follow the indentations, and he realizes there *should* be just enough of them for him to make his way down without cracking his skull open.

With his right hand, he places the tips of his fingers inside one of the grooves, and does the same with his left. He scoots closer to the lower grooves before placing his right foot in one. A lengthy inhale follows as he pushes off with his left foot. If not for the orange light casting its reflection on the liquid below, he'd blindly be swinging from groove to groove.

After a few labored minutes of scaling down the wall, he peeks over his shoulder to find that he can now easily jump and make it to the ground safely. Counting to three in his head, he pushes off from the wall, twists in the air, and lands flat on his feet. The platform moves slightly, but not enough to throw him off balance. He has his Cruex days to thank for that.

He gingerly picks up the stone, its crimson glow appearing as soon as it touches his hands. The pathway before him stretches on and on. There's enough light shooting down from the uppermost chasm to guide the way, but something tells him not to leave the stone behind. He takes the first step, wishing that he'd brought his bag with him. The stone is heavy in his hands but, even so, he makes progress along the pathway much faster than he'd thought. He's careful to avoid any areas where the reddish fluid has pooled, skipping and hopping over them.

As he draws closer to the central column, he can't help but notice the scent of something rancid. Tightness pulls at his chest as his eyes begin to water. He picks up the pace, desperate to get away from the smell, but it only grows stronger. He's a few steps away from the onyx staircase when he braves a look at his feet. On either side, the liquid has started bubbling violently, as if preparing to erupt. One look down the pathway tells him that he's too far away to make it in time—but that he's close enough to throw the stone and have it land safely ashore. A split second decision renders the stone catapulting through the air. It lands at the foot of the staircase before rolling onto its side. Barefoot, arms pumping at his sides, he sprints as fast as his legs will take him until he reaches the edge of the platform.

Much to his relief, the moment his feet leave the pathway, the bubbling ceases. He waits, eyes fixed on the now-still liquid, waiting for it to start up again—but it remains eerily still. He lugs the stone from the ground and cradles it in his arms before ascending the first of many onyx steps. Only when he's halfway to the top does he realize that the putrid scent from earlier has almost completely dissipated. Remnants linger in the air, but it isn't enough to cause a physically adverse reaction like before.

He's panting when he finally reaches the top of the stairs. He sets the stone down before keeling over and drawing in large, hindered breaths. Leaving the stone behind, he walks along the narrow pathway until he reaches a large rectangular dais. The reflection of the light above gives the black surface a mirror-like quality, and he carefully steps onto it. Surrounding the center column in a circle are eight smaller pillars, each made of a different type of stone. As he approaches the first one, he notices that, on the sides, there's an engraving of a crest. It's placed directly in the middle. Upon further inspection, each of the eight pillars contains a unique crest.

He swipes his hand along the top, his fingers grazing a raised area. It's a metal insert of the corresponding crest—and it appears to be locked into place. He examines the others to find the exact same thing . . .

Except for one.

One of the pillars is missing its metal insert.

Puzzled, Rydan crouches to take a closer look at the crest. He traces his index finger along the swirling inner lines, noticing that not only do they form a backwards C; they also seem to make the shape of a flame—lots of them, actually. The crest is vaguely familiar, although where he's seen it before stubbornly refuses to spring to mind.

As he continues to trace the shape over and over again, a memory surfaces. In Lonia. Waking up with a bruised skull. Eyes focused on the fabric swaying from the rafters above. The Soames's residence.

His hand stops moving entirely.

It can't be.

But it would make sense. The Soames were illusié. They'd been on King Tymond's—and subsequently the Cruex's—hit list. Before revealing their secret, the woman, Radelle, had insisted that he'd had the wrong house. Arden had clearly been in agreement, seeing as she'd knocked him—*her partner*—over the head with a lantern. But he'd refused to listen.

He'd taken their lives anyway.

A final look at the crest tells him exactly what he needs to do—and where he needs to go next.

DARIUS TYMOND

IT'S BEEN DAYS since Darius last visited Clive in the dungeons. Nevertheless, their last encounter has played on repeat in his head. Even though he'd gotten the last word, something about their interaction had left him with a sense of unease. It's since crossed his mind to go back down there yet again, but every time he begins to descend the steps, he thinks better of it and goes about his day.

What he *should* do is pay Braxton a visit—seeing as they'd left things less than cordial—but Darius has other things to attend to. Like initiating four new members into the Cruex.

His numbers have dwindled ever since Rydan and Arden had failed him and gone rogue. And then there'd been the snapping of Elias Kent's neck after he'd disobeyed orders—something that still hasn't been revealed to the group. Especially not to his cousin, Hugh Darby. No matter though. For as long as he can remember, he's been covering his own tracks, not to mention the transgressions of those around him.

This won't be any different.

He turns the corridor that leads to the Great Room, passing the King's Guard on his way.

"They've arrived," one grunts.

"Just outside the drawbridge," says another.

"Gather the rest of the Cruex," Darius orders. He doesn't utter another word as he slams the doors to the Great Room shut behind him. He's halfway to his throne when another idea comes to him. "Guards!"

As if waiting for that very call, the doors open.

"Bring Braxton along, too."

"Certainly, Your Majesty."

"And close the doors on your way out," he snaps.

The King's Guard retreats, doing exactly as commanded, while Darius huffily continues onward to his throne. The familiar jewel-encrusted armrests do little to calm his nerves, but after looking at his amethyst ring perched atop his right ring finger, everything falls into its proper place. He lifts his gaze to the double doors and waits.

Percival is the first to enter the room, followed by Ezra, Hugh, and Cyrus—and finally, Braxton. He motions for the guards to bring his son forward, but Braxton remains rooted to his spot in the back, leveling a steely gaze directly at him. Darius pretends not to notice as he shifts his attention to another guard standing by the doors, who gives a swift nod to indicate that the new assassins are waiting just outside.

Darius rises from his throne before greeting the Cruex. "As you well know, with the Caldari and rogue Cruex at large, it's high time we increased our numbers." He pauses, scanning each of their faces. No one looks surprised—if anything, they look weary . . . like they're just waiting to be dismissed so they can carry on with their training. The sheer absence of expression—what can only be described as overwhelming *indifference*—is oddly infuriating. Even though all eyes are on him, the attention of the room seems to be elsewhere.

Emphatically, he clears his throat. "I've sought out four of the best assassins from all over Aeridon to induct into the Cruex. And," he says, pointing at each one of them, "since there are also four of you, you'll each be responsible for training and initiating a new member." The disdain on Ezra's face is undeniable. "Sir Denholm, is there anything you'd like to say before we proceed?"

Ezra opens his mouth to respond, but Percival nudges him in the side, answering for him, "Looking forward to it, Your Majesty."

Darius narrows his eyes before giving the order to the guard stationed at the double doors. "Bring them in."

One by one, his new assassins enter the room, falling in line beside the original Cruex members. From the interior pocket of his robes, Darius produces a scroll. He unfurls the parchment, eyeing each new recruit as he reads their names aloud.

"Sir Jedrek Easton." A towering brute with gold-flecked russet hair and soft gray eyes steps forward. "You will train with Hugh Darby."

Darius settles on the next assassin in line, a stalwart man with flaxen hair and deep hazel irises. "Sir Hamill Debney, you are assigned to Percival Garrick."

"Sir Lyle Cauley." A man of average height steps forward, sweeping chin-length auburn hair from the front of his face to reveal bushy eyebrows, brown eyes, and an overtly square jaw. "You will join Ezra Denholm."

"And lastly, Sir Lane Devall." As the figure steps forward and removes an oversized hood, Darius realizes he's misspoken. Ebony ringlets cascade over petite shoulders, mirroring the woman's skin tone. Hazel eyes bore into his own. "Pardon me. *Lady* Lane Devall will work with our most senior Cruex member, Sir Alston."

From the look on Cyrus's face, it's apparent that he

wasn't expecting an assignment, but he nods at Lane before stepping forward. "May I approach, Your Majesty?"

Darius waves for him to proceed. Once at the top of the dais, Cyrus leans over, just inches from the king's ear, and whispers, "Perhaps the boy should work with Lady Devall."

It takes a moment for Darius to register to whom Cyrus is referring. "You mean Braxton?"

"Yes, Your Majesty. Think about it. It could be a worthwhile reintegration into Trendalath. He's been absent for quite some time. Perhaps working with the Cruex will provide an incentive to stick around."

"What makes you think he doesn't want to stay?"

Cyrus sighs. "Just look at him."

Darius angles his head as discreetly as possible so that he can see just past the side of Cyrus's body. Sure enough, Braxton's standing in between two guards with crossed arms and a hostile expression. Darius leans back into his seat and nods his head. "Very well."

He waits for Cyrus to fully descend the steps and fall back into line before instructing the guards to bring Braxton forward. His son flinches as they each lay a hand on his shoulders, but he doesn't struggle against them. Only when Braxton stands before him, directly in front of Hugh Darby, does he get an idea. "Sir Darby, please come forward." Hugh steps in line with Braxton. "Sir Easton and Lady Devall." He tilts his head, signaling for them to follow suit. "The four of you will work together."

Confusion clouds Braxton's face as he turns to look down the line of assassins. His mouth opens in protest, but before he can say a single word, Darius turns his back to them. "Welcome to the Cruex."

BRAXTON HORNSBY

USHERED INTO THE hall with the rest of the Cruex, Braxton tries to work his way back to the double doors, but the effort is futile. It wouldn't matter anyway, seeing as the guards have stationed themselves right in front, blocking any chance of entry. Looks like he'll have to speak with Darius at a later time.

"Any word from him?"

"No. Still nothing."

"I'm sure he'll turn up soon, mate."

Braxton follows the conversation, not even aware he's eavesdropping, until one of the Cruex turns to look

at him with piercing russet eyes. "You're the king's son—
Prince Tymond."

"I prefer to be called Braxton."

A wordless exchange passes between him and his
fellow blonde-haired Cruex. "Looks like we'll be working
together. I'm Hugh." He sticks his hand out. "Happy to
make your acquaintance."

Not wanting to be rude, Braxton meets his grip.
"Likewise." He looks to the other Cruex.

"Percival," he says, his amber eyes gleaming. "Seems
Ezra's already called a meeting in the courtyard. Probably
to go over our training schedule." He and Hugh both roll
their eyes at the same time. "Come on," he says, jogging
down the hall. "The others have already left."

"We'll catch up with you," Hugh says with a wave of
his hand. Percival grins before rounding a corner and
disappearing from sight. "So," he says, turning his
attention back on Braxton, "after a decade of being away,
what made you decide to come back?"

"You know about that?"

"Of course I do. I'd be surprised if anyone in Aeridon
didn't know."

Braxton continues walking, but doesn't respond.

Hugh shoots him a sideways glance. "Based on your
silence, I'm guessing you were brought back here against
your will."

"Something like that."

"I thought your being back had something to do with your mother." He sucks in a sharp breath, realizing how inconsiderate he sounds. "What I mean to say is that I was sorry to hear about your mother. She was a remarkable woman."

"I wouldn't know," Braxton replies glumly. "The only memories I have of her are from when I was a child."

"Well listen, if there's anything you want to know, just ask me. Queen Tymond was very involved in our Cruex training sessions—as much as your father would allow, anyway. She certainly acted as a maternal figure for most of us."

The way he says it sends a spark of jealousy straight through him. He'd fled when he was just ten years old— still just a boy. All Aldreda had wanted was to raise a child. To have something to nurture. To protect.

He'd taken that from her.

Wanting to change the subject as quickly as possible, he says, "I didn't mean to eavesdrop back there, but I couldn't help but hear Percival ask you about hearing from someone—"

"He was referring to my cousin, Elias," Hugh says, finishing the thought. "A couple of months ago, King Tymond assigned each Cruex to a specific region in Aeridon. To look for you and to look for"—he lowers his voice—"Arden. Elias went to the Isle of Lonia, just like he'd been instructed, but he never returned. At least, not to my knowledge."

"Everyone else returned safely?"

A quiet nod.

"Have you asked Darius about it?"

"Haven't had a chance to. It hasn't been addressed in any of our gatherings either. He's been so preoccupied with recruiting new Cruex members, it seems he's forgotten all about the old ones."

A long, uncomfortable silence stretches between them as they approach the courtyard, save for Ezra's incessant shouting for them to hurry up. It can be heard from clear across the grounds.

"Well, like Percival said, I'm sure he'll turn up soon."

"Thanks. I hope you're right."

Braxton offers his new friend a small smile before following his lead and jogging over to catch up with the others. There, he finds himself unintentionally standing next to Lane Devall. She regards him with wide eyes, the specks of gold dotting her irises glimmering in the afternoon sun.

"Sorry I'm late," he mumbles. "I didn't know I was doing this until, well . . . now."

"For a moment I thought you'd opted out."

How I wish I had that choice.

"We haven't formally met. I'm Lane."

"Braxton," he says with a nod.

Ezra claps his hands three times, commanding the attention of everyone in the courtyard. The assassins line up in a neat row, making sure to stand next to their assigned trainer. "If you weren't already aware, King Tymond has appointed me as your weapons advisor. We'll train from dawn until dusk every day for the foreseeable future." He gestures to a nearby table. "As you can see, we have plenty of weapons for you to choose from— however, as a member of the Cruex, it's expected that you know how to handle each and every weapon on this table. You can choose your primary later, if you don't have one already, but becoming an assassin for King Tymond requires that you have sufficient knowledge of all required weaponry, not only in wielding, but also in defensive situations. Are there any questions?"

More than I can count. As tempted as Braxton is to blurt out the many thoughts currently circulating his mind, he keeps his mouth shut.

"Good. Our new assassins will defend first. Cruex, choose your weapons."

Braxton doesn't know *what* he's considered to be, but before he can give it a second thought, he finds himself being dragged to the table by Hugh. "Whether you like it or not, you're one of us now," he whispers while handling an iron mace. "Best choose a weapon."

"I haven't so much as had even an *hour* of weapons training," Braxton counters under his breath. He can't help but notice a blade similar to Arden's chakrams at the far end of the table. His gaze falls to his hands as he's reminded, yet again, that he can no longer deviate—that he's no longer illusié. He reaches across the table and picks up the curved blade. It seems enlisting in the Cruex has come at a most opportune time. Who thought he'd ever be one to think that?

"That's what you've decided to go with?" Hugh asks pointedly. "Are you sure? Chakrams are one of the more advanced weapons, difficult to get the hang of. Might I suggest—?"

"That won't be necessary," Braxton interrupts as he runs his hand along the blade. "This one I've had more experience with than I care to admit."

ARDEN ELIRI

IT'S FINALLY HERE. The day I begin my journey to get my abilities back. Haskell seems to be fully healed—he's up and moving about the cave with more strength (and less grunting). I've held off as long as possible, trying my best not to rush him or make him feel like he's holding me back . . . but I've been packed and ready to leave since the day he told me about the jaded spring and its alleged restorative abilities.

"How much longer will you need?" I ask Haskell as I poke my head into his room for what's likely the third time within the hour. I don't mean for my excitement to come off as impatience, but given the expression on my brother's face, that's exactly how it's being perceived.

"Like I said twenty minutes ago, I'm not sure yet," he responds, wiping the sweat from his brow. "You have to remember, you've had weeks to get ready. But I—well, today is the first day I've really been able to be on my feet for more than an hour."

A faint warmth blooms in my neck, traveling upward to my cheeks, but I turn away before he can see it. "I packed some extra turmeric in case the wound reopens or becomes infected."

He stops what he's doing. "Why would you say something like that?"

The warmth returns. "I just—I don't know, want to be prepared." I tilt my head, watching him as he resumes packing.

With a sigh, he throws his head back, his gaze pointed at the ceiling. "Perhaps if you leave me be so I can finish up here, we'll be able to leave sooner."

In true sibling nature, I stick my tongue out at him before stalking away from his room. I make it back to the kitchen in a huff. Juniper is sitting right next to my overstuffed bag. Apparently, I'm not the only one who's ready to get out of here. As I scratch her behind the ears, she regards me with inquisitive eyes. I almost start talking to her, since Haskell clearly doesn't want company at the moment. It's not that I don't trust my brother—I do—but being holed up in solitude, completely isolated from civilization, can really warp the mind. I would know—I used to visit the prisoners in Trendalath when I was younger. Didn't understand what they were saying half the time.

My heart flutters. *That's the first childhood memory I've been able to recall.*

It's then I notice, in front of me, a long hallway lined with torches. I've seen it before, but never took the time to venture down it. Using the daylight from the entrance of the cave, I follow the long hall, down, down, down, until I reach a large room. Papers, books, and maps are strewn all over the tables, except for the one in the far back corner. Unlike the others, it's neat and tidy, and there's a large piece of parchment held down by some intricately designed paperweights.

As I draw closer, I realize it's a map. I walk around the table, taking in the beauty of Aeridon when I notice something strange. It hasn't been completed. Rough ink meets my index finger as I trace the semi-crooked lines. It dawns on me that Haskell *drew* this map and must be filling in the blank areas with symbols of mountains, trees, rivers, and towns once he's actually visited them in person.

Both Trendalath and Sardoria are complete, with drawings of their respective castles and neighboring towns—Miraenia, Chialka, and Declorath—and so is Lirath Cave. Much to my dismay, both Drakken Isle and the Vaekith Mountains are blank, waiting to be filled in; and so are the Crostan Islands.

Come to think of it, I've never been to any of these locations either, which has me briefly wondering what to expect. Certainly no civilization, maybe a dwelling or an exceptionally small town every here and there. I'd think it'd be colder almost everywhere, seeing as they're located north, save for the Crostan Islands—then again, Lirath Cave is also north and it's been unseasonably warm for this time of year.

The thought has me wanting to retreat to the kitchen and check my bag to ensure I've packed proper attire, but then Haskell would suddenly be ready to go and *I'd* be the one keeping us behind schedule. Still, I have the urge to venture out of the cave, just for an hour or so, maybe find some wild horses for us to ride. An hour should be plenty of time for Haskell to finish packing . . .

I nearly jump out of my skin as a tall shadow enters the room. My hand flies to my chest. "Don't sneak up on me like that!"

Haskell rolls his eyes. "What are you doing in here?"

I shrug. "I got bored. Maybe if you'd pack a little faster . . ."

His pointed glare shuts me up immediately.

"Looks a lot like our father's place, doesn't it?"

"I hadn't really thought about it, but yeah," I say, looking around again. "It certainly has its similarities."

He sweeps his hand over the parchment, then puts both hands on the table. "I need to show you something."

I watch with interest as he walks to the other side of the room, to one of the messier tables, and begins searching for, well, I don't know *what* exactly. He shuffles through pile after pile of papers, looking more and more irritated with each failed attempt. Finally, he stops and turns to face one of the walls. His eyes scan the hanging scraps of parchment, the fading photographs, the exquisitely detailed drawings. A hum escapes his lips as he begins to murmur to himself.

I remain quiet, a mere bystander to his thoughts.

Finally, he turns to look at me. "They took it."

A blank stare is my only response.

"Why would they take it?"

I open my mouth to speak, but seeing as I have no idea what he's talking about, I'm at a loss for words.

He begins to pace, stroking his beard every few steps. "This is precisely the reason I keep to myself. If I don't allow anyone in, then nothing goes out. Nothing goes missing—"

"Haskell," I intervene, finally finding my voice. "What in lords' name are you talking about?"

"You'd be wise to take caution in who you place your trust in." He shakes his head. "Even our own kind—illusié."

His words snag on something in my mind. "Do you mean to say that you've housed other illusié *here*?"

My question is met with the shuffling of more papers. I march over to him and yank the stack from his hands before throwing it onto the floor. I grab him by the shoulders, essentially forcing him to focus on me and nothing else. "Haskell," I say, nearly out of breath from our minor tussle, "did you have other illusié stay here with you or not?"

He lowers his head. "Yes."

My voice falters. "When?"

He presses his lips together in a firm line. I get the feeling he knows something, but doesn't want to tell me, which makes me even more frustrated. "When?" I press.

"A few months ago." He rips away from my grip and faces the wall again.

I try to think back over the past few months, but so much has happened that I need more information. I *need* to know who was here—but something deep in my gut tells me that I already know.

"But why *wouldn't* I trust them?" Haskell goes on, even though I haven't been listening. "I thought that if they were like me—*my kind*—that they would respect me, my home . . . " I cringe as a scrap of parchment crinkles underneath his hand. "Not taking things that don't belong to you, for instance. Is that so much to ask?"

I don't respond because I want him to keep talking—and thankfully, he does.

"They'd looked so helpless out in the snow. I mean, when I'd found them, I was certain the girl was in hypothermic shock, already petite as it were." He shakes his head at the memory. "Looking back, I'm disappointed in myself. I fell for their act. So damn foolish." He heaves a long sigh. "It just makes me wonder what else they may have taken."

I'm not even the slightest bit curious about whatever it is he wants to show me. I can only focus on four words.

They. Helpless. Snow. Petite.

I suck in a sharp breath. I don't even have to ask who he's talking about. I just *know*.

Rydan and Elvira were here, in Lirath Cave.

With my brother.

RYDAN HELSTROM

MAKING IT OUT of the cave had been less challenging than the situation Rydan currently finds himself in. And that's saying something.

After discovering the crest in the temple and its probable link to the Soames family, Rydan had trekked back into Orihia to where he, Vira, and Avery had set up camp. His first instinct had been to pack his things without a word and start his journey through the Thering Forest toward the Soames's place, but Vira certainly has a knack for making such plans difficult.

The moment he'd set foot back in the dwelling, the interrogation had begun. Question after question about where he'd been and why he'd been gone so long circulated the small space between them. He'd been able to dodge most of her questions—or at least provide a somewhat satisfactory response—but knowing Vira, she'll get to the bottom of it eventually.

Luckily, he isn't planning on being here for that.

"I'm gonna go wash up," he says, breezing past her before she can get another word in edgewise. Just as he's rounding the corner, the hinges on the front door creak. Rydan pokes his head back around. It's just Avery.

Instead of heading to the washroom, Rydan makes for the bedroom. He grabs a few items from the armoire before kneeling and pulling the partially packed knapsack out from under the bed. He tosses the final few items into the bag and, just as he's pulling himself upright, footsteps sound right outside the room. He doesn't have to think twice before tugging on the edge of the blanket, pretending to straighten it.

"Food's ready." Avery's voice is flat.

Rydan doesn't turn to face him. He runs his hands along the bed and proceeds to fluff one of the pillows. "I'll be there in a minute."

Instead of retreating, Avery draws closer and closer until he's standing directly next to Rydan. "What are you doing?"

Rydan turns to face him before shrugging. "I thought I saw something."

Avery's eyes flick to the bed. "Saw what?"

"A bug—a spider maybe." The lie sits heavy on his tongue. "Vira hates spiders."

Avery slaps him on the shoulder. "I won't tell her if you don't."

Rydan forces a faux smile. "Your discretion is appreciated."

Avery angles his head at the door. "Come on, wouldn't want our food to get cold."

After a very filling dinner and an entire bottle of verdot, Rydan would be surprised if Vira makes it another minute. Eyes drooping and on the verge of drifting into a heavy sleep, he bids Avery adieu before scooping her from the leather armchair. Feeling a little hazy himself, he tries to steady his wobbling legs as he carries her into the bedroom. With one hand, he pulls back the blanket he'd straightened earlier, and gently lays her underneath the sheets. She doesn't even open her eyes before curling up and turning onto her side. Faint snores indicate that she's completely out—and likely will be late into the morning.

Carefully, Rydan slides the knapsack out from underneath the bed and loops the straps over his shoulders. He presses two fingers to his lips before setting them lightly on Vira's pillow, next to her head.

Before he turns to leave, his eyes travel to the window at the brightly lit night sky. He's never been one to travel long distances at night—he'd much rather wait until morning—but he feels obligated to confirm what he'd discovered in that cave.

That the crest belongs to the Soames.

That it belongs to the innocent family he'd murdered.

Gravel crunches underneath his sturdy boots as he takes the winding path that leads to the invisible wall between Orihia and the Thering Forest. By some stroke of good fortune, a full moon hangs overhead, casting its sultry glow through the leafy canopy. Even so, he can't help but notice the shadows darting between the trees— at least, he *thinks* they're shadows.

Shaking the thought from his mind, he trudges onward, the temperature dropping with each step. To keep his mind preoccupied, he reviews his working plan. Once he makes it to the Soames's house, he'll search the premises for potential intruders. Seeing as the house has been abandoned—save for the young boy—it should be empty . . .

A twig snaps nearby, causing him to freeze. He turns over his right shoulder, then his left, but the forest is completely still. He tightens the straps of his knapsack and continues onward, picking up the pace. It shouldn't be too much farther. It's then he happens upon a small clearing, which is . . . *strange* for a place that's supposed to be deserted.

The moment the house comes into view, a shiver works its way down his spine. He tries to block out his last failed Cruex mission—the abhorrent look on Arden's face as he'd wielded his longsword—but the memories stick in his mind like sap on a tree. He waits a few moments—for movement, for a flickering light—but there's nothing. Against his better judgment, he draws closer.

The first thing he notices is that the front door is wide open. He swings his knapsack around to retrieve his throwing axe. It's not much in the way of weaponry, but it's all he'd managed to fit in his bag. Blade in hand, he creeps up the wooden steps, then presses his back against the outer wall. He readies the axe, raising it to chin level, before peering around the corner. The only source of light comes from a lone lantern in the living room.

Putting his Cruex skills to use, he slinks along the side to investigate the backyard. No sign of anyone. The ladder he and Arden had climbed sits idly against the house, untouched, and he decides to check the roof and the skylight for any potential sign of entry. He secures the handle of the throwing axe in his back left pocket before climbing the rungs. No sign of anyone up here either.

Confident that he truly *is* alone, Rydan descends the ladder and circles the other side of the house until he's resumed his position at the front door, throwing axe in hand once again. There's no one here.

He enters the house, picking up the lone lantern with his free hand as he surveys his surroundings. It only takes one look to realize that there's another major difference. The bodies of Radelle and Erle Soames . . .

They're gone.

He sucks in a sharp breath, his confidence from before rapidly fading. He decides to check the rest of the rooms for good measure. The kitchen is empty. So are the two bedrooms. He even checks the washroom. As he returns to the living room, he realizes that, even with the moonlight pouring in through the skylight, it's still too dark to make out the rafters—and anything that might or might not be hanging from them. Looks like his plan to leave and return in one night isn't feasible after all. He assures himself that he can stay the night here. Vira and Avery shouldn't suspect anything. They'll probably just assume he's ventured off again, gone exploring.

Here's hoping.

With his mind made up, he closes the front door before securing the lock. Next, he shuts the windows and slides the bolts into place. Hungry from his travels, he raids the cabinets, discouraged to find only stale bread and mealy apples. He can always go hunting in the morning, if he's even here long enough to do so.

Now to find a place to sleep—normally he'd take the master bedroom, but in this particular situation, that just feels . . . *wrong.* He eyes the young boy's bedroom just across the hall. He makes it to the doorway, then stops, contemplating. Even though he hadn't killed the child, he'd been *about* to—if it hadn't been for Arden and her decision to knock him unconscious with the very lantern he's currently holding. Indeed, sleeping in there would feel just as wrong.

With a sigh, he trudges back into the main room before settling on an armchair that faces the front door. He places the lantern on the ground, then drops his knapsack at his feet. The throwing axe lands on top of it with a soft thud. He swings his legs over one of the armrests before folding his body into the worn leather. A long breath escapes him as he relaxes his jaw, shifting back and forth until he finds a comfortable position.

As he's crossing his arms and about to close his eyes, he can't help but feel particularly exposed. His prior assassin-self would be undeniably disappointed—come to think of it, so would the rest of the Cruex. With a grunt, he flings his arm over the side and snatches the axe, bringing it close to his chest.

That should do for tonight.

CERYLIA JARETH

IF CERYLIA HAD to choose one word to describe the past couple of weeks, it'd be *unease.* Her castle no longer feels safe, especially after discovering the speculor attached to the tea cart. In fact, her entire queendom feels littered with harmful intentions. Day after day, with each winding corridor she takes, she half expects to come across yet another betrayal, another deceitful act. Felix's proposal to retrieve the amethyst ring from Trendalath has no doubt lingered in her mind, but how can she trust him after what she's witnessed between Opal and Xerin? Their undisclosed meetings?

The past few nights, she's forced herself to visit that

very spot—but neither culprit had shown up. Either they'd moved locations, or they'd finished up their discussion. She prefers to think it's the former because the latter would mean they've finalized something . . . and she hasn't the slightest inkling as to what that might be.

Opal's not one to give anything away easily. Her expression at breakfast this morning is proof of that.

"More hash?"

A plate of diced potatoes enters Cerylia's line of sight, interrupting her thoughts. "No thank you."

"I'll take some," Opal says.

"Seconded," Delwynn chimes in.

Cerylia lifts a steaming mug to her lips, her eyes fixed on Opal the entire time. She must have a tell— something to indicate she's up to no good—but if she does, she's certainly good at hiding it. *I could just out her right now and ask about Xerin. Catch her completely off guard.*

Opal thanks the servant before digging into her breakfast, completely oblivious to the thoughts churning in the queen's head.

"Any word from Xerin?"

Cerylia immediately perks up as she shifts her gaze to Delwynn. Realizing the question is directed at her, she sets her cup down on the saucer and shakes her head. "Unfortunately, no. Have either of you heard anything?"

Opal stops chewing, eyes now cast toward her lap.

"Nothing to report here," Delwynn responds, but Cerylia's hardly paying attention. Her focus is entirely on Opal.

The girl lifts her gaze. "I did see Xerin, but it was some time ago." She quickly adds, "Our conversation was brief."

"Oh?" Cerylia feigns knowledge of the situation. "This is the first I'm hearing of this."

"Please accept my apologies, Your Greatness. He asked that I keep it between us."

A small flicker of hope ignites in the queen's chest. *Perhaps she can be trusted after all.* "Can you at least tell me if he's found the others?"

She merely shakes her head.

"No he hasn't found them, or no you can't say?"

"He hasn't found them," she says quietly.

"Is there anything else I should know?"

Opal rises abruptly from the table, clutching her stomach. "Yes. Don't eat the hash." And with that, she flees to the nearest washroom.

Delwynn turns back in his seat. "That was strange."

Cerylia taps her fingers against the table.

Strange doesn't even begin to cover it.

DARIUS TYMOND

DARIUS RAISES HIS hand to knock on the door that leads to Braxton's chambers. Given their last interaction—or lack thereof—when he'd abruptly assigned Braxton to train with the Cruex, he wouldn't be surprised if his son chooses not to open the door. He's about to raise his hand to knock a second time when, much to his surprise, it swings open.

"Wasn't expecting you." His hair tousled, clothes unkempt, it's obvious his son's had trouble assimilating into his . . . *new role*.

Darius follows him into the room, noticing the slight limp in his right leg. "Chakrams?" he asks as he closes the door behind him.

Braxton turns to face him. "How did you know?"

"When throwing chakrams with your left hand, you step into a firm stance with the opposite leg. Carries all the weight." Braxton regards him with a shocked expression. "What? Did you think I'd forget my own son is left-handed?"

He shrugs before taking a seat on the edge of the bed. "Honestly, I'm not sure what to think."

"You're confused about the Cruex assignment."

"That's just one of many things."

Darius sighs as he scoots an armchair away from the hearth to face him. He sits, resting his elbows on his knees. "Training with the Cruex where you're free to roam outside is better than sitting in here all day, alone—"

"I'd hardly call it free when I have guards escorting me to every event, every *room* in this castle."

Darius presses his mouth into a firm line. "That's to be expected. You were brought here against your will, Braxton. I didn't know how you'd react, if you'd want to leave, even though . . . well, this is your home."

The lines in Braxton's forehead soften. His voice lowers to just above a whisper. "I was hoping to say a proper good-bye to my mother. To get closure."

Darius studies him for a moment before sitting back in his chair. "I'm afraid the ceremony has already taken place. She's adrift at sea."

"She would have wanted her burial to be here, in Trendalath. In the castle."

Although Darius is fully aware of this, he knows keeping Braxton in the dark is in his best interest. "How would you know that? You fled ten years ago with no intention to return."

Braxton narrows his eyes. "She was my mother."

"I'm not arguing with that. If we'd had the space, I would have accommodated her request." A bold-faced lie.

He seems to relax at this. "May I see her chambers some time?"

"Later, perhaps. It's been difficult knowing that, eventually, I'll have to part with her belongings." Then, with an exaggerated crack of his voice, "They're all I have left of her."

Braxton nods in understanding.

"I know I may not show it but"—he pauses, debating his choice of words—"I'm glad that you're back. Your mother would have wanted it this way, even if she's not here to say so herself."

Braxton lowers his gaze, fidgeting with the corners of a blanket. The sight of him so timid, so vulnerable, instantly reminds Darius of when he'd been a child—the petrified look on his face whenever he'd scolded him, and the instant relief that had followed whenever Aldreda had come to the rescue. If only he knew what a traitorous snake his mother had been. But that knowledge wouldn't serve him now.

Everything in due time.

Before they can continue their conversation, there's a quiet rap on the door. They both turn their attention to the dark head of curls that's just made an appearance in the entryway.

"My apologies, Your Majesty." Lane bends at the waist, bowing her head. "Your Royal Highness."

"Braxton," he murmurs in a futile attempt to correct her.

"Is it that time again already?" Darius asks.

"It would appear so. Ezra's waiting in the courtyard."

Darius pushes himself up from the chair and makes for the door. "I'll let you get to it then." He glances over his shoulder. "Until next time, son."

He doesn't wait for Braxton to respond before breezing past Lane and exiting through the chamber door.

BRAXTON HORNSBY

"I DIDN'T MEAN to interrupt." Lane stands awkwardly in the entryway to Braxton's chambers, a soft blush slowly crawling up her cheeks.

"Don't worry about it. I doubt that'll be the last of our conversations." He leans forward before pushing off his knees to stand.

"Looked serious."

He shrugs. "I suppose it was. We were discussing my late mother."

Lane bows her head. "Forgive me. I didn't mean to pry. I'm sure that's a sensitive subject."

"For me it is, but for him"—he angles his head at the

door—"it's far from it."

"We all experience grief differently. Give him time."

Put off by her response, Braxton gives her a curt nod, then heads to the armoire to retrieve his chakrams. When he closes the door, Lane is standing on the other side, directly in front of him. Startled, he jumps back, his weapons clattering to the ground. "Mind announcing yourself next time?"

"Sorry," Lane murmurs as she bends down to pick up the blades. "Old habits die hard. Once an assassin, always an assassin."

"How'd you get started in all of this anyways?"

"I grew up in Lonia. My father worked at the docks, and my mother collected wares to sell to nearby merchants. We barely scraped by." A shadow falls over her face. "It wasn't an easy childhood."

Braxton softens at her tone. "Doesn't sound like it."

"I told myself I could have something different—that I could have more—but I knew I couldn't follow in their footsteps. I didn't want to." She sighs. "So I fled."

There's a faraway look in her eyes, one that indicates there's more to the story than she's letting on, but he doesn't press further. "You and I have that in common."

She shoots him a sidelong glance. "But you're back now."

"Yeah," he scoffs. "Against my will."

She stifles a laugh. "Sure doesn't seem that way."

"How do you mean?"

Her eyes roam the chambers. "Looks to me like you're doing just fine, *Your Royal Highness*."

"I told you not to call me that."

"Whether you like it or not, you *are* a prince You're living in Trendalath Kingdom. Your father is the king. No matter which way you spin it, you're royalty."

He can't argue with her there.

"Come on," she says, pulling on the sleeve of his tunic. "Ezra will have our heads if we're late again. And maybe this time, you can give me some warning before flinging those things at my head."

Braxton follows her out the door, fingers tightly gripping the chakrams. "Correct me if I'm wrong, but assassins are usually so well-trained that they don't *need* a warning."

"When we're training, it's different."

"Your target isn't going to give you a warning."

She stops and turns to face him, the gold specks in her eyes blazing like hot coals. "They never need to— that's just how quick I am."

The way she says it, like she's done it countless times with no remorse, sends a shiver down his spine. It reminds him a lot of someone he knows . . .

Arden.

He breaks away from her stare before continuing down the corridor. "It'll make you better, having no warning. You'll just have to act."

A laugh sounds from behind him. "Ouch. Have you always been this harsh or can I assume I'm getting special treatment?"

She catches up with him, walking in stride. He doesn't bother to look at her before saying, "It's just like you said . . . old habits die hard."

ARDEN ELIRI

I ASK HIM again. "Rydan and Vira were here? With you?" Haskell nods, but before he can respond I ask, "When did this happen? Where are they now?"

Raising his hands so that his palms are facing me, he says, "Slow down. No need to get all worked up."

I regard him with wide eyes. "Rydan and Vira *fled* Sardoria without so much as a farewell. We've been searching for them—"

"*We*?"

I clamp my mouth shut.

"I hate that you're keeping something from me."

"That makes two of us," I retort.

An uncomfortable silence ensues before Haskell finally shakes his head and sighs. "Yes, Rydan and Vira were here with me—for quite some time, actually. They were so weak when they arrived. I was certain Vira would suffer immensely from hypothermia, being out in the woods and all with such heavy snowfall."

I don't press further, but stay silent in the hopes that he'll continue.

"I gave them shelter, food, and a place to sleep so that they could gather their strength again. When they discovered I was illusié, things changed."

"How did they find out?"

A smirk. "Rydan caught me in a lie. I'd claimed to be out hunting and ice-fishing in the middle of a blizzard."

I smile. "Did they reveal themselves to you?"

He nods. "It took some coaxing but, eventually, yes."

His answer catches me by surprise, especially with the way Rydan had reacted when he'd first discovered his igniting abilities—a shocking secret we'd both been there for. I don't know Vira well enough, but if I had to guess, she'd gotten it out of him—persuaded him in some way in order to gain Haskell's trust.

"Vira was hell-bent on heading back to her childhood home in Chialka. It's a shame, really. Not knowing what happened to her family . . . "

I don't think he realizes the irony of his statement.

"Anyway, I helped them along. Transported the two

of them to Chialka, then left. Left my pocket watch with Rydan, too."

"The one from our father? With the Eliri inscription?"

He raises a brow. "That's the one."

So Rydan knows that Haskell is my brother.

"When did you transport to Chialka?"

"Wasn't but a month or so ago."

My stomach drops. I turn away from him, pretending to rummage through my bag so I can think. Rydan's known about Haskell—about my *family*—for this long and hasn't even tried to reach me? To come find me? Tears of betrayal prick the corners of my eyes. Sure, there's hostility between us—*that* I'm completely aware of—but what's hard to believe is that it would run this deep . . . that he would keep something *this* monumental from me.

"Arden?"

Realizing I've had my back to him this entire time, I finish shuffling through my bag, grabbing hold of the nearest item within reach, before turning back around to face him. The pocket watch dangles from my fingers. "Do you think they'd still be there?"

His eyes shift from the watch to my face. "In Chialka? Lords, I don't know. They could be anywhere by now."

"Did they give any indication as to where else they might go?" A solemn shake of his head sends my mind reeling. "We need to go there. Immediately."

"What about your abilities?"

Oh right.

"Arden, what aren't you telling me? I did my part. I told you about Rydan and Vira. It's your turn."

I reluctantly swallow my pride. "Rydan and I—well, we were . . . " The words escape me. I take a steadying breath. "We were both in the Cruex."

"Were you close?"

My response catches in my throat. "Yes."

"What happened?"

I cast my gaze toward the ground and shrug. "We were assigned to a joint mission in Lonia. Things didn't quite go as planned—and by that, I mean to say that they went horribly, *horribly* wrong. I, uh . . . I left him behind with no proof of the assassination." My cheeks burn at the memory. "He returned to Trendalath and Tymond locked him up."

"And where did you go?"

"The Thering Forest. That's where I was introduced to the Caldari. They helped me save Rydan—as if he were one of their own." My eyes flick to his. "I healed his injuries so that he, *we*, could escape. We ventured to Sardoria where Queen Jareth offered us asylum. And that's where . . . " My voice trails off, the intensity of my brother's stare rendering me speechless.

"Go on," he whispers.

I close my eyes. "That's where Rydan discovered he was illusié. He fled, and Vira went with him."

Haskell eyes me knowingly. "Do I sense a bit of remorse?"

I recoil at his presumptuous tone. "I went back for him. I saved him from Tymond." I shake my head adamantly. "No remorse here."

"Jealousy then?"

I stifle a laugh of disbelief. "Hardly."

"And yet, what I'm hearing is that you want to go wherever he is?"

He's made his point, but I don't dare affirm it. "We better get moving," I say quickly, gathering my bag. I begin to walk past him, but he gently grabs my arm.

"What is it that you need, Arden?"

I turn my head to look at him, studying his face. I don't want to answer, mostly because I haven't had enough time to think about how I want to handle this—how I *should* handle this—but the anger I feel right now is all-consuming. There's only one word resting on my lips.

"Closure."

RYDAN HELSTROM

RYDAN WAKES TO heavy streams of sunlight breaking through the many rips in the curtains. He shoots to his feet, forgetting for a brief moment where he is. The axe falls from his lap and clangs to the floor, just barely missing his big toe. He sidesteps around it, then makes for the kitchen.

Famished, he begins raiding the cupboards until, from out the window, he spots a well. Only then does he realize just how dry his mouth is. He heads back into the living room to retrieve his canteen from his knapsack, then exits through the front door and circles around the house. With his free hand, he shields his eyes from the blazing sun as he stumbles across the grounds.

There's a bucket already attached to the rope, so he lowers it into the well, the sound of sloshing water making him even keener on quenching his thirst. He pulls on the rope impatiently until the bucket reaches the top of the well. He maneuvers it over onto the side, throwing his canteen to the wind as he cups his hands into the half-full bucket and brings them to his mouth to drink. The water is crisp and refreshing, and more relief follows as he splashes some onto his face. Shaking the remnants from his hair, he leans against the well, hands gripping the cool stone. He turns his face toward the rising sun and closes his eyes.

A few minutes later, he recalls what he's doing here. He swipes the canteen from the ground before reentering the abandoned household. The first thing he does when he walks through the front door is look up at the ceiling. Sure enough, hanging from the rafters is a torn piece of fabric. There seems to be an emblem stitched into it, but with the way it's violently swaying back and forth from the current draft makes it hard to tell.

Skylight it is.

A quick scan of the house tells him that the only way to get to the skylight is from outside. His stomach growling, he pulls on his boots, tugging on them to make sure they're secure, then trudges out the back door. He locates the ladder and starts climbing, his déjà vu growing stronger with each rung. One look into the skylight tells him that it might just be easier to *move* the ladder indoors. With a sigh, he climbs back down before hoisting the ladder over his shoulder and tipping it sideways to get it through the door. He clambers through the kitchen, nearly knocking into every piece of furniture along the way, until he finally reaches the living room. He positions himself underneath the rafter, takes two steps back, and heaves the ladder off of his shoulder so that it's leaning against the wooden beam. He shakes it a few times to ensure it's stable before climbing it once again.

After what feels like a long-awaited victory, he snatches the cloth from the rafter, waiting to look at it until his feet are firmly planted on the ground. He loosens his grip on the wad of cloth before gingerly unfolding the delicate material. Sure enough, there's the crescent shape—the same swirling outline of flames on the crest he'd seen in Orihia—but the pillar had been missing a metal insert, not a cloth one. *If I can find that metal insert, I can activate whatever's in that cave.*

He hurries over to his knapsack and pulls out the pocket watch Haskell had given him. His eyes nearly bulge at the time. Speaking of Vira . . . there isn't a doubt in his mind that, by now, she's probably realized he'd left, and if he doesn't get back soon, both her and Avery could show up here unannounced.

He glances back down at the Soames crest. It'd be foolish of him to leave without at least searching for its metal companion. It could very well be the key to unlocking something that might help illusié . . .

The irony of that thought isn't lost on him.

He's spent the majority of his life assassinating illusié targets and now he's trying to help them? But after what he'd seen just outside of Orihia . . . all those dead bodies . . . and learning about the Mallum . . .

It's clear that something *much* larger is at stake.

So Vira and Avery will just have to wait.

DARIUS TYMOND

THE STENCH OF rotting flesh is the first thing Darius smells as he enters the underground tunnel below the dungeons. "Torch," he demands, sticking his arm out in the darkness behind him.

"It was only lit a few moments ago . . . " Cyrus's voice trails off as he fumbles with two torches, handing one of them to the king. "Wouldn't you rather send the King's Guard to perform such duties?"

"Had this been taken care of in a timely manner *by* the King's Guard, like I'd requested, then yes." He kicks the underside of Elias's boot. "How far gone is he?"

Cyrus walks up and down the side of the decaying

body, pinching his nose as he bends down to examine the boy's remains further. "There's no point in staging his death. By the time we do, what's left of him will be picked off by the buzzards."

Darius sighs. "I'm shocked Sir Darby hasn't approached me yet. Elias *is* his cousin."

"*Was* his cousin," Cyrus corrects.

A pointed stare. "It's too bad I didn't get to make an example out of him—"

"You snapped his neck the moment the opportunity to do so presented itself."

Every muscle in his body stiffens at his consort's unwarranted tone. "Is there anything we need to discuss, Sir Alston?"

Even in the dim lighting, his face is ashen. "No, Your Majesty."

"With the way you're countering my every statement, I would assume otherwise."

He casts his eyes toward the ground. "The Cruex numbers are dwindling significantly. We could have at least given him a chance. He *did* reveal Arden's location, after all."

Darius's gaze flicks to the decomposing corpse before him. Perhaps Cyrus does have a point. Perhaps he *could* have spared the boy's life, somehow found a use for him—even if it was no longer as an active member of the Cruex. But, if he's learned anything during his reign, it's

305

that nothing ever stops after the first. One lie turns into two, two turns into three, and soon you have such an intricate web of betrayal and deceit that even the spider that wove it would find itself tangled and pleading for mercy.

"It's too late for him," Darius says without even the slightest hint of remorse. "Burn him." Just as he's about to turn on his heel to leave, Cyrus stops him.

"What will you tell Hugh—er, Sir Darby?"

There's an intentional edge to his voice. "I trust you'll come up with a reasonable explanation."

"And what about the others?"

Darius extends the torch out in front of him, moving it slowly from one side to the other. Body after body lay atop one another, creating mounds of human blockades along the tunnel. "You know as well as I do that they're not dead."

Cyrus rises from his place next to Elias. "I'm well aware. What I *don't* know is what you're planning to do with them."

"No need to concern yourself with such matters."

"No need?" Cyrus whirls around, his torch sending shadows dancing on the tunnel walls. "You've been stockpiling bodies for years—and what's worse, I've been the one helping you."

At first, Darius doesn't respond. He just raises his hand so that his ring is clearly visible. "I'd watch your tone, Sir Alston, unless you want to end up down here like the rest of them. Understood?"

He succumbs. "Yes, Your Majesty."

Satisfied with the outcome of their conversation, Darius turns to leave, his robes collecting dirt as they sway back and forth across the tunnel floor.

"What should I do with the body?" Cyrus calls out.

"Like I said before," Darius calls back, "burn it."

CERYLIA JARETH

THE CLOCK IN the bell tower chimes. Cerylia stands in front of a gold-plated mirror, cloaked in navy. She fashions her hair into a loose braid that falls down her back before pulling the hood over her head. She opens one of the drawers to her vanity, the speculor rolling to the front. With her thumb and forefinger, she gingerly lifts it from the tray and drops it in her inner breast pocket. With her cloak secured and lantern in hand, she makes for the chamber door.

The silence throughout the corridors is deafening. She climbs her way up the castle stairs, checking around each corner to ensure that she is indeed alone. When she reaches the floor just below the bell tower, she makes a swift left, hurrying along until she reaches the end of the hall. Placing her right hand on the stone wall, she slides it up and down, side to side, until she finds what she's looking for—a slight gap that's indiscernible to the naked eye. "*Revela*," she whispers, placing more pressure on the indented area. A rectangular section of the wall begins to move in and back, farther and farther, until it slides all the way open. She steps inside, eyeing a sconce covered in cobwebs, before turning to face the opening. "*Retras*." The wall appears to shift back into place, but she places a firm hand on it to be sure.

Even with the lantern extended out in front of her, it's hard to see, but she descends the winding staircase with grace. She's almost reached the bottom when she nearly trips and tumbles the rest of the way down, but the sturdy iron railing catches her.

The first thing she does when she reaches the bottom is locate the many candles that are scattered around the hidden chamber. She takes her time lighting each one, patiently waiting until the room comes into view. It's exactly how she'd left it. The walls are lined with a special barrier—by illusié design, of course—to keep any noise in. Papers are strewn all over the limestone flooring and, at the back of the room, sits an array of tables and cabinets, all pushed up against one another.

Her failed shield.

She can't help but shudder at the thought of her last attempt.

Her illusié abilities are far from honed. But, in order to refine them, she must have a magickal *living* target in which to direct them at—something she's been lacking for many years. Her ability is not one that can be regularly practiced, and it certainly isn't one she prefers to use often. She'd never exercise something like this on the Caldari. The Savant, maybe. But not her allies.

Even if they aren't acting like it at the moment.

Setting the lantern down on a nearby table, she removes the speculor from her cloak before flinging it over a wooden chair. She approaches the small oval stand in the middle of the room, takes a deep breath, and gently sets the speculor on top of it. She backs away, making sure it doesn't roll off, before heading for the back of the room. Once she's positioned herself next to the cabinet—having chosen one of the taller, more robust ones—she swings the top cupboard open, followed by the middle and lower ones to create a makeshift shield.

Bending at the knees, she peers through the narrow gap between the top and middle doors. She stares at the speculor, willing her eyes not to blink, focusing on it until everything else fades into the background. Her eyes close. With the image seared into the backs of her eyelids, she imagines taking from it—grasping, pulling—until the speculor is nothing more than a void of non-memories and departed visions.

Her knees begin to shake. She tries to hold on for just a while longer, feeling the surge of energy as it rises within her. Violent hissing and screeching ensnares her auditory senses, but she remains still, unbothered by the deafening noise. The shaking has moved up her knees to her thighs, her hips, and now her stomach. In her mind, she can see the speculor exploding into dozens of tiny fragments, shattering at the very word she's about to speak. When the shaking takes over her chest, she knows it's time.

"*Extragé.*"

But the word is spoken a split second too soon.

The familiar feeling she's waited for doesn't wash over her, nor do the speculor's memories or visions. She opens her eyes just as a blinding orange light disperses throughout the room. Realizing that she's failed yet again, she flings herself behind the cabinet and collapses onto her knees, covering her head with both arms. A thunderous roar reverberates throughout the walls, the entire chamber quaking in its midst. Cerylia moves her arms closer to her ears, determined to wait until the obscure energy passes and diminishes to nothing more than air itself. She's gotten a glimpse of this before, survived it before. It's possible to do it again.

She lets it run its course, refusing to open her eyes or uncover her ears until the ground beneath her stops quaking. At one point, it gets so close that she can feel it pressing against the top of her head—it's then she decides that if she's going to attempt this again, she must invest in a better shield.

Finally, the ground stills. The noises cease. The orange light fades. Cerylia drops her arms from the sides of her head and pulls herself upright, using the cabinet doors for support. Slowly, she peers around the still-open door, her eyes landing on the speculor. It sits idly on the table, as if it didn't just release its vengeful wrath on her.

Her legs still trembling, she slides out from behind the wooden structure and sidesteps to the center of the room. She pulls a cloth from her pocket and gently tosses it over the speculor. She gathers her cloak, throwing it around her shoulders, before retrieving the wrapped speculor and securing it back where it belongs. Lantern in hand, she begins the arduous climb to the concealed door.

Each failed attempt lowers her spirits, but she knows they're not in vain. It may not happen tomorrow. It may not happen the next day. But eventually, she *will* try again . . . and succeed.

BRAXTON HORNSBY

BRAXTON HONESTLY NEVER thought he'd be one to enjoy hand-to-hand combat, but working with Lane has pleasantly surprised him. Ezra has a tendency to switch back and forth between weapons and non-weapons training, and today appears to be a non-weapons day.

"Approach your partners."

Braxton finishes lacing his boots before standing in front of Lane. A coy smile tugs at the side of her mouth. "I don't think you're ready for this."

"If it's anything like last time, or the time before that, I'm more than ready."

Lane chuckles as she shakes her head. "You caught me on an off day—"

"According to Ezra, assassins can't have 'off days'. Especially not the Cruex."

She checks to make sure their trainer isn't looking before hitting him in the shoulder. Hard.

"Devall!" Ezra shouts. "Did I say you could begin?"

"No, sir," Lane says, completely composed, but the moment Ezra turns away, she puts a hand over her mouth to stifle a laugh.

Braxton can't help but do the same.

"Would you two pay attention?" Hugh scolds from behind them. "We don't need Ezra flying off the handle again."

"Okay, okay," Lane whispers as she waves her hand in the air.

"Question, Devall?"

Her face falls. "Nope, just . . . stretching."

"Right." He levels a steely look at her before addressing the rest of the group. "*Now* you may begin."

Lane assumes her stance, slightly bending her knees, arms raised at an angle from her chest. Braxton mirrors her, bouncing on the balls of his feet. Her first attack is swift and direct—a straight punch to the throat—but Braxton sees it coming. He slides to the left and parries the attack with his front hand. Instantly, she attempts to cross-attack with another punch, but he redirects it away from his face, using the force of her own attack against her. With one hand on her elbow, he places the other on the back of her neck and applies just enough pressure to cause her arm to lock and her body to keel over. She taps the side of his leg to indicate she's had enough. He releases her, stepping backward to give her some space. "Perhaps you should stick with weapons training," he teases.

She shakes her arm out before rolling her neck, readying herself once again in her fighting stance. "Hate to break it to you, *Prince*, but I'm taking it easy on you, what with you being a first-timer and all."

Braxton drops his arms. "Don't. If I'm going to train, I want to do it right."

A shadow flickers in her eyes. "Duly noted."

The sudden shift in her demeanor tells him that perhaps he shouldn't have said anything. He raises his arms, resuming his stance, but quickly realizes that Lane isn't going to attack him. Instead of facing him, she turns around.

Waiting.

"It's almost too easy," he murmurs to himself as he darts toward her at full speed. He's about to jump and bring an elbow down on the space between her neck and left shoulder when she suddenly whirls around and wraps him in a rear chokehold. With his right arm free, he attempts to elbow her in the side, but she swiftly knees him in the back of the leg, causing it to give out completely and throw him off balance. Realizing she has the upper hand, she swings her arm underneath his collapsed leg, lifting him sideways off the ground. Braxton tries to tap her arm, but finds he's gone entirely limp in her stronghold. Within seconds, she's slamming him into the ground, the right side of his body landing with a loud thud, immediately aching from the impact.

"Nice one, Devall!" Braxton hears Ezra shout from across the courtyard. He groans as he tries to sit upright, but his shoulder's throbbing with such intensity that both of his arms feel like they're heading into a state of paralysis.

"You okay?"

Lane's voice is far away as black dots speckle his vision. "I'm fine," he croaks as he curls into a ball on the ground.

"You don't look fine to me." She steps over him and kneels, gently lifting his chin. "Your face. You've lost all color."

"He's in shock." A strong voice approaches and within moments, Ezra's kneeling next to Lane. "Should take him a few minutes to recover. In the meantime, you can train with me."

Lane's face falls. It's the first time Braxton's seen her look even slightly distraught. "No, that's quite all right," he says, clenching his jaw at the immense pain shooting through his arm. "I'm good to go. Really." Ezra couldn't look more disappointed if he tried and, for some reason, Braxton finds solace in that.

"You sure?" His final attempt.

"Sure as I can be."

Without another word, Ezra turns and stalks away from them, surely off to torment one of the other trainees.

"Thanks for that," Lane says, offering her arm for support. "Of all the Cruex, he's the one I try to stay away from."

Braxton winces as he takes one step, followed by another. He's hardly able to focus on what she's saying and has to replay her words in his head. "Why's that?"

"One look at him told me that he plays dirty."

His mind flits to Arden. "All of the Cruex play dirty. And seeing as you're now one of them, you might as well get used to it."

ARDEN ELIRI

I DON'T KNOW where Haskell's transported us to, but it certainly isn't Chialka. I'm currently facing a forest, the tall trees and shrubbery making it difficult to determine exactly where I am, but as I turn around, an enormous mountain range comes into view. The Vaekith Mountains.

Which means we're in the Roviel Woods.

Before I can say anything, Haskell takes off in a full-blown sprint. I curse under my breath as I dart after him, Juniper nipping at my heels. It's clear he has no intention of slowing down, but when he finally does, I'm winded and panting, unable to catch my breath. I plop down onto the ground, my hand resting just above my thumping heart. "What. The. Hell?" I manage through labored breaths.

"I'm surprised you were able to keep up." I roll my eyes, but he doesn't seem to notice. "We'll go to Chialka, I promise. But we may as well start here."

I shoot him a confused glance.

"Seeing as we were already up north, I figured we may as well take advantage and come here first and at least look for the alleged spring."

"Since you can transport," I counter, attempting to stand on my still-trembling legs, "it doesn't really matter, now does it?"

"I wouldn't expect you to know this, but the farther the distance, the worse the after-effects of the transport." He throws me a smug look. "In actuality, you should be thanking me."

Juniper circles my feet before prancing over to him. "Even you're siding with him?" I blow a stray hair out of my face. "Unbelievable."

"I'm telling you, this makes the most sense. Not to mention—"

"Let me stop you right there. We don't need to do this right now. What we *need* to do is go to Chialka."

"We don't *need*—"

"Haskell." My tone is flat as I desperately try to recall our last conversation in Lirath Cave. "You mentioned that

Rydan and Vira took something. Don't you want that back? And what about your pocket watch?"

A hint of guilt flashes across his eyes, as if he's hiding something. But then, with an adamant shake of his head, he says, "No. This is more important. Plus, we're already here."

It's clear I'm not going to win this one, so I shut my mouth and begrudgingly follow him out of the woods and up the winding pathway. Even though the mountains are capped with snow, the trail we're currently walking along isn't icy in the slightest. On the contrary, the dirt is dry as bone. The terrain shifts from smooth and dusty to coarse and bumpy. At this point, we're only about halfway up the mountain, but I call out to him to stop anyway. "Are we going all the way to the top?"

He tightens the straps of his knapsack as he turns to look at me. "Do you have a better idea?"

I angle my head to the left. "Well, we could give this ominous-looking entrance a whirl." He climbs back down the trail a few paces until he's standing right next to me. "What do you think?"

"You're the one looking for shortcuts. We'll give it a shot, but if anything happens, it's on you."

"It wasn't my idea to come here in the first place."

"Oh, but it was. Before I told you about Rydan and Vira. Remember?"

Touché.

"Fine, I'll lead the way. Did you happen to pack a

torch?" I ask, but Haskell's not looking at me. His gaze is fixed on something ahead. I follow his stare until I see it.

A flickering in the distance.

"Seems we're not the only ones here," he whispers.

My first thought is that maybe a fellow Caldari is here—Braxton, maybe? Rydan and Vira? *Felix?* My heart drops into my stomach. "Come on," I say, pulling on the sleeve of his tunic, but he stops me.

"It could be the Savant."

"Or it could be the Caldari."

He releases my wrist from his grip. "Arden," he says with lethal calm, "it's not safe."

"Sure it is." I pat my holsters as a reminder. "I can't leave here knowing that someone's been here or currently is here right now, at this very moment." Before he can say another word, I jog down the narrow cave corridor and grab the torch from the wall sconce. "Come on!" I yell, my voice echoing.

Haskell heaves a loud sigh before trudging down the path. He grabs the additional torch from the other bracket. "I want it on the record that I said this was a bad idea."

"Yeah, yeah," I say waving my hand dismissively in the air. My gaze falls on a rather short, half-circular opening. "This way." I walk over to it and crouch down, sticking my head inside. "I can't see anything."

"If you think I'm crawling into that death trap, you've

lost your damn mind."

Before I can register what's happening, Juniper's at my side, jumping straight into the dark abyss. "No!" I yell, dropping the torch as I reach for her, but it's too late. I fumble for it, but it's been snuffed out from landing in the dirt.

Meanwhile, Haskell's taken my place, peering into the dark space. "I can't see her," he grunts. "It looks like a giant black hole.

"I have to go after her."

"Arden," he says softly, trying to reason with me, "we don't know what's down there."

"Yes we do. Juniper's down there."

He pinches the bridge of his nose before drawing a long breath. "You know what I mean."

"I can't just leave her, Haskell."

"Listen to me, okay? It's too dangerous. We may as well just turn around now before anything else happens."

"Best of luck with that." Before he can process what's happening, I reach for his torch, prying it from his fingers, then slide into the void.

"Arden!"

The echo of my name is the last thing I hear as I travel down an obscure tunnel, heading straight into the unknown.

RYDAN HELSTROM

"MORE WATER?"

Rydan doesn't realize Vira's talking to him until she shakes a pitcher in front of his face. The liquid sloshes around, breaking his concentration. He shakes his head.

She shoots a sidelong glance at Avery, who's busy devouring his second plate of food, before setting the pitcher down and taking a seat on the bench next to Rydan. "What's going on with you?"

He's tempted to pull out the ripped fabric containing the Soames family crest he'd discovered the other day, but thinks better of it. "Just tired."

"Hmm." She brushes a stray hair from her face, the

golden color glistening in the moonlight. "If I didn't know any better, I'd think you were hiding something."

He stiffens slightly. "What makes you say that?"

"I know you better than you might think."

He forces a smile. "Nope. Just tired."

"If you say so." She shrugs before picking up the pitcher and heading back inside the house. Rydan watches as the door swings shut behind her, then averts his attention to Avery. It crosses his mind to show *him* the crest, seeing as they're both Ignitors—but Avery's nose-deep in yet another glass of verdot.

Maybe not tonight.

After he'd searched the Soames's house for a few hours—with no luck finding a matching metal crest of any sort—he'd rushed back to Orihia, hoping his absence hadn't been noticed. He hadn't been so much concerned about Avery as Vira, given how observant she is. Turns out he'd been right to be concerned because even two days later, she's still giving him a hard time about it. He has plans to go back to the Soames's eventually, but not before coming up with a valid excuse—one Vira will believe without question.

Rydan's about to call it a night when a loud wail sounds from inside the dwelling. He shoots up from his seat just as Avery lifts his head off the table. Rydan sprints across the terrace toward the house, pulling on the back door with so much force that he nearly yanks it off its hinges.

324

The sight before him is gruesome.

Xerin's on the floor, chest bare, writhing in pain.

Vira kneels at his side, frantically trying to stop the flow of blood from the long sporadic gashes covering his body. Rydan rushes to the washroom, searching the cabinets in a frenzy. He emerges with a dozen or so clean rags, tossing a handful to Vira as he kneels on the other side of Xerin. He hardly notices the hinges creak as the door swings open again for Avery to walk in.

"Would you get over here and help us?" Vira snaps.

In his drunken stupor, he stumbles over, knocking into nearly everything he passes by.

Rydan shakes his head. "Hold this," he says to Vira before standing and leading Avery to a chair. Teeth gritted, he whispers, "You're not coming anywhere near him in your current state. You'll do more harm than good. That's the last thing we need right now."

Avery doesn't so much as protest. He sits back in the chair, clearly more than content just watching everything unfold.

Rydan rushes back over to Vira, resuming his place at Xerin's side. "What happened?"

"I . . . I don't know," she says, on the verge of tears.

Rydan leans past her to look at her brother's face. Eyes shut. Shallow breathing. "Did he fall unconscious when he got here?"

"I was in the kitchen," Vira recalls, voice shaking.

"I heard the door open, then some heavy breathing and a loud thud. When I came into the living room, that's when I saw him." Her eyes rove her brother's marred body. "Like this."

Rydan removes one of the cloths, taking a closer look at the gashes. They don't seem to be from a weapon nor an animal bite. In fact, they're entirely unfamiliar. He briefly recalls an injury he'd sustained while training in the Cruex . . . how Arden had been there. A lump forms in his throat. "When you were cooking earlier, did you happen to notice any turmeric in the kitchen?"

Vira considers this before nodding. "I think so."

"Bring it here and then go search the other dwellings," Rydan instructs. "I'll stay here and tend to your brother."

She rises on trembling legs. "How much do you need?"

Rydan gives Xerin another once-over. "As much as you can find."

Hours pass until Xerin finally stirs. Rydan looks across the room to find Avery still in the same chair, fast asleep—or possibly unconscious—and Vira leaning up against the wall, also asleep. He crawls backward and gently nudges her in the shoulder. She wakes instantly, eyes wide with alarm. "It's okay, it's just me," Rydan soothes. "Xerin's waking."

Her eyes flick to her brother. She straightens against the wall, stretching her arms overhead, before pushing herself to her feet and walking over to Xerin. She kneels just past his head, lightly resting her fingertips on his temples. He stirs again, eyelids fluttering. "Xerin?" she whispers.

There's an indiscernible slur of words.

"You're okay," she tells him. "You're safe."

He seems to float in and out of consciousness until, suddenly, he's thrashing against her grip. Vira's hands fly away from his temples as she hurriedly scoots back on her heels. Rydan intervenes just in time, pinning him down by the shoulders. "No one here is going to hurt you," he says. But the feral look in Xerin's eyes indicates otherwise.

Slowly, Rydan releases him.

Xerin sits upright, hands grazing the many bandages covering his body. Seeing that he's calmed some, Vira approaches, although cautiously. "What happened?"

He looks at her, eyes softening. "I . . . I don't know."

"You don't know?"

He shakes his head. "I don't remember."

"When you arrived, you looked like this—with cuts and scrapes all over your body," she says, trying to jog his memory. "You fell unconscious almost immediately."

She angles her head at Rydan. "We found some turmeric to help speed up the healing."

Xerin furrows his brows, but doesn't respond.

Rydan keeps his distance, standing a few paces away as he observes the interaction. Xerin's curt responses and lack of *wanting* to remember strikes Rydan as odd— suspicious, even. If someone had sliced him up, leaving him with multiple gashes all over his body, he'd certainly remember every detail of the encounter. Unless . . .

"Was it the Mallum?"

A shadow darts across Xerin's crimson eyes. His tone is unsettling, his answer even more frustrating. "Like I said, I don't recall."

"Well, whatever attacked you must have been of illusié origin," Vira says. "These marks"—she runs a hand over one of the bandages—"I've never seen anything like them."

"Nor have I."

Xerin looks between the two of them. "I don't know how many more times I can say it. I don't remember." He shoots a harsh look at Rydan. "Now, if you don't mind, I need to get some rest."

"You're welcome to stay here—"

Xerin cuts her off. "I'll be sleeping in my own house."

Vira's face hardens.

Rydan can sense that the mounting tension between them is about to reach its breaking point, so he quickly interjects, "We'll be here if you need anything." He offers

Xerin a hand to help him up, but he doesn't take it. His stubbornness causes him to grunt and wince as he slowly stands all the way up. Vira steps out of the way, but not before crossing her arms. Not another word is spoken as he walks through the door and out into the night.

DARIUS TYMOND

WHILE BRAXTON HADN'T seen Darius watching from the courtyard, it'd been a disgrace to witness his training with Lady Devall. She'd won more rounds than he could count. And while he knew the fight hadn't exactly been fair—what with Lane having been an assassin for *years*—he also knew the outcome would have been completely different if Braxton had been able to fully access his abilities. To deviate.

The Mallum wasn't supposed to attack him.

I suppose I have only myself to blame for that.

He dabs the corners of his lips with his napkin as he finishes the last of his supper, deciding that perhaps he should pay Braxton a visit. Every time they sit down to talk, though, their conversation seems to be cut short. Even so, he rises from his chair, flinging the napkin on the table, before making for the doors. He rounds the corridor that leads to the first set of stairs, but not before running directly into the King's Guard . . . and Hugh Darby. He does his best to appear calm, but with the way Hugh is looking at him, it's hard not to feel rattled.

"Excuse us, Your Majesty. We were just on our way to the Great Room to see you."

"Unfortunately," Darius says as he pushes past them, "I have rather important business to attend to—"

"Like finding my cousin?"

Darius turns, slowly, then sets his menacing gaze on Hugh. "As an esteemed member of the Cruex, Sir Darby, you, better than anyone, understand the risks of being an assassin. You understand the risks of each mission you are assigned to—"

"I'm not doubting that," he interrupts. "But not speaking of it, not *informing* the Cruex of any information you might have—well, that makes it seem like you're hiding something."

"I assure you I am not. And to assume your King of such treachery is deplorable. Punishable by death "

Hugh's mouth presses into a firm line.

"Guards, need I remind you to only bring *pertinent* matters to my attention." He turns his back to them, waving his hand dismissively in the air. "I'm retiring to my chambers for the evening."

"I had a word with Sir Alston."

Although the statement throws him, he continues to climb the stairs. "Good for you, boy."

"He told me that you sent Elias to Lonia."

"That is indeed true."

"*After* he'd already returned."

Darius stops at the top of the staircase and turns, his expression lethal in every sense of the word. "And did Sir Alston mention that I sent *the both* of them back to Lonia on an undisclosed mission?"

"No," Hugh falters. "No, he failed to mention that."

"Hmm," Darius sneers. "Seems you might want to get your facts straight. Perhaps Sir Alston is the one you should be talking to. After all, isn't he the one who last saw your cousin alive?"

Hugh's face pales. "I . . ."

"If I didn't need you to train our newest Cruex members, I'd lock you in the dungeons myself."

"Your Majesty, please forgive me—"

"Consider yourself one of the fortunate ones, Sir Darby. Many aren't so lucky. Just go down there and see for yourself." Darius grabs hold of the banister before rounding the corner and disappearing from sight. It seems his plans for a relaxing evening have been derailed, yet again.

Instead of opening the door to his chambers, he breezes past it, heading for Cyrus's. Their last interaction in the underground tunnel had been anything but cordial. He just wants to confirm that they're still on the same page and that his instructions from the other day had indeed been carried out—especially before Hugh starts another round of interrogations.

He reaches Cyrus's door, knocking twice before announcing himself. He knocks again, but the door remains shut. Darius grunts before heading down the corridor to where one of the guards is stationed.

"The key to Sir Alston's chambers." It isn't so much a request as it is an order. The guard nods. Darius follows him as he retrieves the key, then returns to the door and jams it into the lock. He swings it open to find . . .

Nothing.

"Your Majesty?" the guard prompts.

"Search the grounds for Sir Alston and bring him to me at once," Darius says through gritted teeth. "And do not stop until you find him. That's an order."

CERYLIA JARETH

THE SPECULOR SURE is burning a hole in her pocket. Ever since her failed attempt to bring forth her illusié abilities, Cerylia hasn't let it out of her sight. She's also made it a point to check every nook and cranny of the castle—every wing, every room, even the alcoves in the courtyard—but to no avail. Seems only one speculor had been planted . . . in the White Room.

She has yet to approach Opal about the indiscretion, nor has Xerin deigned to return with any news on the whereabouts of Rydan, Elvira, or Arden . . .

Is he even aware that Braxton is also missing?

The thought enrages her. That he'd been the one to

ask for asylum for the Caldari. That she'd stuck her neck out for him and this seemingly deceitful group. She'd only offered up Sardoria as a safe haven *after* she'd discovered that Arden was among them. Had it not been for her, where would the Caldari be? Locked up in Trendalath, or worse, killed by the Mallum.

Perhaps they're all too deserving of such cruel fates.

She's strolling the grounds when she realizes just how quiet the castle has become. What was once a place full of merriment and rapport is now nothing more than living quarters. It's been days, possibly even weeks, since she's seen Felix or had him approach her about his proposal. Opal has kept to herself and so has Estelle. Come to think of it, she's hardly seen Delwynn either.

She takes a seat on a nearby bench and raises her face to the sky. Rays of sunlight cascade across her face, warming her from the inside. She takes a deep breath before checking the surrounding area, then pulls the speculor from her pocket. Where it was once a soft gray, it's now completely clear, refractions of light darting across the gravel. As she lowers it, she notices someone approaching at a rather quick pace.

Delwynn.

As discreetly as she can manage, she buries the speculor back in her pocket, pretending to be occupied with the rosebush adjacent to the bench. From it, she plucks a single ivory rose, pulls the head from its stem, and nestles it in her hair, just above her ear.

"That looks lovely, Your Greatness," Delwynn says as he bends into a low bow.

She dips her head, a pleasant smile gracing her face.

"There's someone here to see you."

Cerylia stiffens the moment she sees her old friend.

"Queen Jareth," Cyrus says as he approaches.

Cerylia rises to her feet but not before dismissing her advisor. He opens his mouth in protest, but she shoos him away before he can utter another word. Once she's sure he's out of earshot, she turns to face Cyrus. "Well this is unexpected."

"And from your tone, slightly off-putting."

She bristles at the presumption, but keeps her voice level. "Not here. Someone might see." She leads him to the edge of the grounds, just beyond the courtyard, but not far enough to be on the outskirts of the castle. A large fir tree and a few small shrubs are the only things blocking them from view. "You should have come sooner."

He chuckles. "That's mixed messaging if I've ever heard it."

"You took Arden as a prisoner of Trendalath." She narrows her eyes. "Why? That wasn't part of the deal."

"I was in a bind, Your Greatness. I would have informed you—"

"But you didn't. So I've been in the dark, waiting—wondering if my oldest friend had finally fallen prey to the Tymond reign."

"I had to see it for myself—his intentions . . . "

"They've never been pure. You know that as well as I do—hell, *better* than I do." An undeniable warmth crawls up her neck, spreading to her cheeks. "Where is Arden now?"

A solemn shake of his head. "I wish I knew. I was hoping she'd be here. With you."

The words send a spike straight through her chest.

"I found her in the Isle of Lonia, in Orihia, before taking her to Trendalath."

"Then you were the last one to see her. Arden fled Sardoria long before then. I've had no idea where she ran off to."

"It seems her brother has found her."

Cerylia can hardly find the words. "Haskell is *alive*?"

"My guess is that they're together as we speak. If we find Haskell, we'll surely find Arden."

Cerylia's jaw goes slack. "But how is he—?"

"Alive? Honestly," Cyrus says with a long sigh, "I was hoping you'd have the answer to that."

BRAXTON HORNSBY

"THANKS FOR WALKING me back. You didn't have to do that."

Braxton shrugs. "Don't mention it."

Lane shoots him a sidelong glance. "Is there a reason?"

Braxton stops in his tracks. "Does there have to be? I walked you back because I wanted to."

Lane wags her finger at him as she approaches her chamber door. "You're a Tymond. Tymonds always have ulterior motives."

Braxton throws his head back and sighs. "How many times do I have to tell you? I'm not—"

"I know, I know. You're not a Tymond." A coy smile tugs at her lips. "Lighten up."

"I'll lighten up when you stop calling me *Prince Tymond.*"

"Didn't do it this time."

"I'm sure you wanted to."

She glances down at her feet. "Hey, that was a good session today."

"That's a nice left hook you have there," he says, rubbing his jaw for emphasis. "I'll be feeling this for weeks."

"Right. Sorry about that." Her cheeks bloom with color. "I got a little . . . overzealous."

"I suppose you could say that." He winks. "See you tomorrow?"

She smiles. "Where else would I be?"

"Goodnight, Lane." He returns her warm smile, watching as she disappears behind the chamber door. He turns away and puts his hands in his pockets, feeling the odd urge to whistle as he walks back to his room. There's something about Lane he can't quite put his finger on. She's intimidating, yet soft; blunt, yet sweet; ruthless, yet forgiving. A walking contradiction that is, dare he say, *wildly* attractive.

His thoughts scatter when he absentmindedly bumps into Hugh. He's about to greet him with the usual slap on the back, but then he notices the less-than-pleasant look on his face. Without so much as a hello, Hugh pushes past him and marches down the corridor.

Braxton has no idea what's got him so worked up, but he'll be damned if he doesn't find out. "Hey, slow down," he calls out as he jogs to catch up. Hugh might be short, but he's quick. He only picks up the pace, forcing Braxton to run faster. When he finally reaches Hugh's side, he grabs his shoulder and says, "Hey, tell me what's going on."

Hugh's weary eyes meet his. "Just had a run-in with your father."

Why does everyone insist on reminding me that I'm a Tymond? Braxton is about to correct him, like he has with Lane dozens of times, but decides against it. Hugh's certainly in no condition to be reprimanded—that much is clear. "What happened?"

"I finally confronted him about Elias."

"Your cousin?"

Hugh nods. "I know he's hiding something."

Braxton doesn't want to add to his misery by telling him that he's probably right, so he just keeps his mouth shut.

"Elias is too well-trained to have something happen to him. I found out he made it back before any of us— something the king conveniently forgot to mention."

"Who told you that?"

"Sir Alston."

"Have you talked to him since?"

Hugh shakes his head. "Said he didn't know what happened to Elias after they went back to Lonia. Suppose they split up or something. It's just so unlike him." He shifts uncomfortably between his feet, then rakes a hand through his russet hair.

It's then Braxton notices he's carrying a large burlap sack. "What's in there?"

"Oh, this?" He angles his head. "Instead of throwing me in the dungeons for accusing him, the king's assigned me to handmaiden duties. Humiliating."

Braxton shakes his head. "Not at all. Let me guess— potatoes?"

"How did you—?"

"When I was a child, I used to sneak meals down to the prisoners." He smiles at the memory. "I couldn't understand why they'd been locked up in the first place. I wanted to help. Make things a little better for them."

"Well, if you want to help, I won't stop you."

Braxton takes the burlap sack from him. "Lead the way."

Braxton can hardly believe how much worse things have gotten in a mere decade—the filth, the stench, the begging and groaning. After visiting just the third cell, throwing loaves of bread at the many prisoners crammed into the space, he'd considered running back to the mess hall to fill up as many canteens of water as his arms could carry—but it wouldn't be enough.

It would *never* be enough.

"It's tragic, really," Hugh says, carrying on a conversation that Braxton hadn't realized they were having. "All these people—probably down here just for saying the wrong thing or being in the wrong place at the wrong time. For all I know, Elias could be down here."

"Don't say that," Braxton says, trying to keep the mood light. "He's not down here."

"Elias Kent?" A gruff voice echoes.

Wide-eyed, Hugh turns to look at Braxton before rushing to the cells in the very back. "Who said that?"

"Hugh!" Braxton calls, dropping the bag in front of a cell of desperate hands. He runs along the dimly lit dirt path, realizing he'd never made it this far when he was younger. He'd had no idea the dungeons even went back this far. How many people had Darius locked up in here over the years? The thought makes his stomach turn.

When he finally reaches Hugh, his face is pressed against the iron bars. "Who's in there? What do you know about my cousin?"

A demented chuckle sounds from the farthest reaches of the cell. "Apparently more than you."

Hugh bangs against the door with his fist. "Tell me what you know!"

Braxton grabs his friend's wrist before he can do any

more damage to himself. "Hugh, listen to me. The people down here—they'll say anything if it means they might be able to escape."

Hugh breaks free from Braxton's grip. "He said Elias's last name. How do you explain *that*?"

Braxton searches for a logical response, but he can't find one. "Let's just forget about this and head back upstairs."

An adamant shake of Hugh's head tells him that they're not going anywhere anytime soon.

"Prince Braxton Tymond, is that really you?"

Braxton freezes in place as a wave of confusion washes over him. He moves closer to the cell, placing his hands on the iron bars to peer inside. "Who are you?"

A lanky figure emerges from the shadows. As he approaches, Braxton can clearly see the prominent circles under his eyes. Paired with his unkempt, wiry copper hair, disheveled doesn't even begin to describe his appearance. Although Braxton can't place from where, he knows he's seen this man before—*talked* to him before.

The man stands just a few steps away from the cell door. "You don't remember me?" He lowers his head and shakes it, clicking his tongue in disapproval. "I expected more from you."

"Tell me how you know me."

The man's smile turns lupine. "I'll do you one better."

Braxton's about to ask how when, suddenly, he's

plunged into a familiar setting—as a young boy, on the side of the castle, fishing. *A memory.* A woman's voice, that he recognizes to be Phillippa's, calls him inside. As he's running to the castle doors, he's stopped by a spritely man who stoops down and opens his arms wide.

"Uncle Clive!"

"There he is! My, how you've grown."

Braxton watches as the child version of himself, no older than six or seven, steps back and puffs his chest out. "I'm stronger, too."

The man laughs. "I can see that. Where are your parents?"

The boy shrugs. "Probably in the big room."

He smiles. "The Great Room it is, then."

The memory falls further and further away until Braxton finds himself back in the dimly lit dungeons, fingers still gripped tightly around the metal bars. He narrows his eyes, trying to get a better look at the man.

"It's true," he croaks.

"What's he talking about?" Hugh looks to Braxton, completely and utterly confused. "What just happened?"

Braxton ignores him. He wets his lips, his mouth suddenly dry. "You're my . . . uncle?"

"Well, from a hereditary perspective, no," he replies, nearly choking on the words. "But I was around for most of your childhood. You saw so yourself."

"You saw *what*?" Hugh asks, desperate to be included in the conversation.

Irritated, Braxton whirls away from the bars to face his friend. "This is Sir Clive Ridley. He's a member of the Savant."

Hugh snorts. "If that's true, what are you doing locked in the dungeons?"

His eyes go frank and cold. "Darius and I have . . . well, we've had our differences."

"That much is clear."

Braxton elbows Hugh in the side. "You mentioned something about Elias. Do you know what happened to him? Where he might be?"

"Before we go any further, I have a request." Clive looks to the guard stationed at the end of the chamber. "I assume you're a member of the Cruex?" The question is directed at Hugh, who nods feverishly. "Bring me the key and I'll show you what you seek."

"*Show*?" Hugh looks to Braxton.

"I don't know how, but he was able to take me back to the past."

A soft chuckle. "Close. You weren't actually taken back in time. I simply cast a past memory around you."

"Caster," Hugh whispers in recognition. He snaps out of whatever daze he seems to be in. "So if I bring you the key, how do I know you won't just disappear?"

"If I show you what happened to your cousin, how do I know you won't just leave me locked in here?"

Braxton keeps his eyes on Clive but his words are

directed at Hugh. "Seems like you have less to lose."

"Do you want to know what happened or not?"

Hugh looks back and forth between them before pulling away from the cell. "Fine. I'll do it."

"Make it swift," Clive murmurs. "That guard's certainly seen better days."

Braxton tucks himself in a shadowed corner, but not enough to lose sight of Hugh. Although he's been training with the Cruex, he never thought he'd actually see them in action—and on Trendalath grounds, no less.

Hugh sweeps his hand across the top of a barrel, the faint clink of chains echoing off the walls. Braxton's eyes flick to the guard, but he's sitting against the chamber wall, eyes focused straight ahead. When he goes to look at Hugh again, he realizes just how stealthy his friend is.

"What the—?"

A figure leaps from the shadows, chains rattling in the air. They loop around the guard's neck in one deft movement. In mere seconds, Hugh's managed to get behind the guard, grunting as he pulls the chains down and back with tremendous force. The brute twists and turns, trying to unsheathe his sword, but his gasping indicates that he can hardly breathe. Hugh lets out one final grunt before yanking the chains to the side so that the guard falls to his knees. He draws closer, tightening the chains with each step until finally, the guard's head lolls to the side, his body crumpling to the ground.

There's rustling as Hugh searches for the keys and shortly after, the sound of jangling metal. The other prisoners grab for him as he walks by. Undoubtedly full of adrenaline, he dashes up to each door like a crazed lunatic, threatening that they'll be next if they don't keep it down. The chambers fall eerily silent as he gets closer, his soft footsteps the only audible sound.

Hugh doesn't even look at Braxton as he approaches Clive's cell. His chest is moving so rapidly that it looks like it's about to explode. "Show me what you know."

"Bravo," Clive commends him. "I couldn't have done it better myself."

"Show me what you know," Hugh says again, jaw clenched. "*Now.*"

Clive raises his hands in the air. "As promised."

Just as Braxton's about to pull Hugh to the side, the scenery around him changes to that of a small oval room. He lowers his gaze to find none other than Arden Eliri, unconscious and bound in metal chains. He turns his head to the left, realizing that Hugh is also in the room. He rushes over and pulls him to the very back, into the shadows, right before multiple masked men begin to enter through the doors. Darius is the last to arrive.

"What's going on?" Hugh whispers.

Braxton brings his index finger to his lips.

Hugh nods.

They both bring their attention back to the room.

"You will heal my wife."

It takes a moment for Braxton to process. *My mother isn't dead yet.*

Arden refuses. Darius calls forth one of his Savant.

Braxton winces as she's hit with bolt after bolt of pure, unhinged energy. Each time Darius asks her to heal Aldreda, she refuses, and each time he uses another member of his Savant to inflict pain. He knows her hatred for Darius runs deep, but what had Aldreda ever done to her to deserve such a cruel death?

Braxton watches once again as Arden declines, the weakness building in her eyes. "I don't know if I can watch anymore of this," Braxton murmurs. But when he turns to look at Hugh, his attention is fixed elsewhere. He follows his friend's gaze until he sees a young man—with a striking resemblance to Hugh—kneeling at Darius's hand.

They watch in horror as Arden approaches Elias with a longsword, her focus wholly fixed on her target. Braxton can see the conflict in her eyes, the way her mouth twitches in earnest. *She's trying to speak.*

"Elias!" Hugh lunges forward, but Braxton grips his arm and pulls him back.

"It's a memory. We can't change it. We need to see what happens."

The blade is now resting against Elias's neck. A drop of crimson trickles from a fresh wound. Just as Arden lifts the sword to deliver the fatal blow, the word Braxton had hoped to hear leaves her lips.

I'll heal her.

The sword clatters to the ground. Arden falls to her knees before losing consciousness. The guards take her by the arms to drag her out of the room . . .

But not before Darius snaps Elias's neck.

ARDEN ELIRI

WHEN I COME back to, I'm belly-down and I can't see a damn thing. I dig my palms into the ground and push myself onto my knees, frantically searching the area around me with only my hands to guide me. My fingers brush the strap of my knapsack and I pull it closer, blindly rummaging through it to find some source of light. There isn't one. I curse myself for not having my healing abilities—that soft white glow would do a whole lot of good right now. Not only for my pounding head, but also for my limited eyesight.

I rub the back of my head, wincing at the bump that's already forming on my scalp. It takes a moment to remember where I am and why I'm here. I spring to my feet. "Juniper!" I call out, feeling around in the darkness. It only takes me so far. I bump straight into something solid. I curse again, foolishly kicking at whatever's in front of me. Pain courses through every inch of my body—so now I not only have an aching head, I also have a throbbing foot.

Perfect.

In an effort to distract myself, I call out Juniper's name again, but I'm met with silence. I yell Haskell's name for good measure, but still, nothing. I turn and slide down the sturdy formation, feeling defeated. I let my head fall into my hands and squeeze my eyes shut. By the grace of the lords that be, I hear a faint voice call out my name.

I quickly push myself back up and inch along the wall. "Haskell!"

I hear my name again.

I follow the quiet but distinct echo that's reverberating off the walls, somehow managing not to walk straight into another one. I call out my brother's name again. He says mine and it's much louder this time.

"I'm okay!" I yell up to him, hoping that he can hear me. "But I can't see anything!"

A gurgled response.

"I can't understand you. If you come down here, you'll slide along a chute." I try to recall how far I'd fallen, how long it'd taken, but my recollection is fuzzy. "Make sure to bring something to re-light the torch. It's pitch black down here!"

No response.

One isn't needed, though, because mere moments later, I hear a long string of shouting to my left. I shuffle against the wall back over in that direction, keeping my eyes peeled for any sign of light. Something suddenly flickers above me, and I dive out of the way right as Haskell comes flying through the chute. He flails in the air, the lit torch leaving his grasp, before crashing to the ground in a heap of limbs. I leap over his body, slamming into the ground face-first as I make a miraculous catch.

Haskell groans at the same time I do. "That was *not* enjoyable."

I laugh, wincing at the pain in my side as I roll onto my back. I make sure to keep the torch raised in the air, spitting dirt and pebbles from my mouth. "At least you managed to keep the torch lit."

He pushes himself up onto his elbows. "To be honest, I don't know how I did that."

I bring the flame closer to the ground, searching the area for my own torch. I find it scattered against one of the cave walls, buried slightly underneath the silt. I shake the dirt away before attempting to light it. I wait for my flame to grow in size before passing Haskell's back to him.

"Where are we?" he says groggily.

"I must admit, I'm surprised you're even conscious. That fall completely knocked me out."

"I know. I was calling your name for over twenty minutes."

"You waited that long before jumping in after me?"

"I wanted to know that you were alive before risking my life, too—especially since I told you not to do it in the first place."

Blunt, honest words. I have to fight against my somewhat rational urge to slap him. "Some brother you are."

"Hey," he says, rubbing the back of his head, "I've risked my life for you once already."

"And you'll never let me forget it, either."

We both seem to realize at the same time that we've reached an impasse, so I extend my arm and help him to his feet. "Did you find Juniper?"

I shake my head. "I couldn't see a damn thing."

As if on cue, he lifts his torch so that it's just above my head. "I think I found her."

I whirl around, following the light from the flame. I'm about to dash over to where she's sitting when Haskell's grip on my upper arm stops me. "Something's not right."

"What are you talking about? She's right there."

"Arden," he whispers. "Look closer."

He releases my arm. I turn away from him, holding the torch out in front of me. The first thing I notice is her fur. It still has its marble texture, but it's no longer a crisp dual-tone of black and white. Instead, it's a deep gray—as if she's somehow aged the way a human would.

"Juniper," I whisper, taking a step closer.

At my movement, she retreats.

"Juniper, it's me!" I rush over to her, hoping that she'll recognize me, that I'll be able to fix whatever's wrong with her, but just as I'm about to reach her, I'm jolted backward with such force that it knocks the wind out of me. I mutter a string of incomprehensible sounds as I try to catch my breath. As if that isn't enough to deal with, Juniper's eyes suddenly begin to glow a sickly yellow. Her mouth opens to reveal jagged, sharp fangs. Horrified, I shimmy backwards on my elbows.

In an instant, Haskell's beside me, pulling me to my feet. "We have to go! I can transport us out of here."

"We can't—not without her!"

"Arden," he tries to reason with me, "it isn't safe here. Something's gotten to her and if we stay here any longer, it'll come for us, too."

I shake my head adamantly. "I know what it is and I'm not afraid of it." I wrench myself from his grip. "You hear that? I'm not afraid of you!" I yell. "Show yourself!"

I don't even realize I have tears streaming down my face until I feel Haskell's palms on my cheeks. "Listen to me, okay? We'll come back for her. But we can't stay. If we stay, we die. There will be no escaping."

The reality slices through me like glass. If we stay, the Mallum will eventually come. It'll absorb Haskell's illusié abilities. It'll kill us both.

I run my fingers along my forehead before pressing them against my temples. I shudder as a loud sob breaks free from my chest. I can't bear to look at her, but I know I have to. My gaze lands on her face, bared teeth and all. I can feel my heart shattering with each word I speak. "I'll come back for you. I promise."

The tears continue to fall until I'm whisked away, pulled into yet another obscure oblivion.

RYDAN HELSTROM

USUALLY HE CAN discern whether he's in his waking or sleeping hours, but tonight, Rydan can hardly tell the difference. If it's his sleeping state, it feels just as lucid as his conscious state—but if he's asleep . . . well, he sure hopes he *is* asleep.

It starts with a shadow burrowed in the far depths of his mind. Not wanting to be revealed. Not wanting to be troubled. It just sits there—waiting—but for what, he doesn't know. Looking at it, knowing it's even there, is enough to send signals of discord throughout his entire being. A flicker of movement—invisible to the eye, but sharp and well-defined in the mind.

He calls out to it, to ask what it is, what it wants. But it remains silent. Ever watching. Ever waiting.

There's something familiar about its presence.

Something he's experienced before . . .

A feeling, perhaps?

Disjointed, the shadow moves. It's hard to tell, but it seems to be searching for something. *Take, take, take.* An overwhelming sense of unbelonging. And then . . .

As if a ripcord has been pulled, he's jolted from his dream state. Surrounded by darkness, he frantically pats the area next to him, calming as soon as he feels the softness of the sheets beneath him. When he turns his head, he can hear Vira's light breathing. Asleep.

It had been a dream. Just a dream.

With the thought comforting him, he rolls back over and falls into a deep, uninterrupted slumber.

"He's gone."

Rydan joins Vira at Xerin's house, peeking through one of the windows that doesn't have the curtains drawn.

"The doors are locked, both front and back. I've been standing here for five minutes, knocking. Waiting." She sighs. "He shouldn't have left. Certainly didn't give those wounds proper time to heal."

She moves away from the window, but Rydan stays,

eyes scouring every inch of the dwelling. Sure enough, there's no movement. No windows are cracked. The bed is made. The hearth hasn't been lit. Everything appears to be untouched. He doesn't have the heart to tell Vira that Xerin had left immediately after arriving. He hadn't stayed in Orihia that night—or any night thereafter.

"Come on," he says, pulling her away from the house before she thinks herself into oblivion. "You know your brother—he'll be back at some point."

She sighs. "You're right. I just wish I had some way to know that he's okay." She veers off down a separate trail. "Meet you there in a few? I'm going to wake Avery and let him know it's time for breakfast."

He tips his head in her direction. "How very kind of you."

She rolls her eyes. "If you could fill the pitchers with fresh water . . . I have a feeling he's going to need one to himself."

That's an understatement. Rydan gives her a quick smile before continuing on down the pathway that leads to their place. When he walks in, he finds two empty pitchers sitting on the table. He's about to grab them and head to a nearby stream when he notices something peculiar. The door to their bedroom is cracked.

I know I shut it this morning.

He breezes by the table, nearly knocking over the chairs as he approaches the door. With a gentle nudge, he pushes it the rest of the way open. Like he used to do back in his Cruex days, he does a thorough scan of the room. No visible intruders. Bed still unmade. But the armoire doors are flung open . . . and the drawers appear to have been rifled through.

He tiptoes across the room, inching along the wall, until he reaches the armoire. Someone has definitely been here. He gathers and refolds the scattered items, putting each one back in its proper place. Only when he reaches the last drawer does he realize that something is missing.

A pit forms in his stomach as he recalls his dream.

Perhaps it *had* been real after all . . .

Take, take, take.

He rummages through the items, not caring in the slightest that he's completely undoing all the work and effort he'd just put in to make the drawer tidy again.

It doesn't take long to figure out what's missing, what Xerin took. The fabric with the Soames family crest.

CERYLIA JARETH

CERYLIA MAKES IT a point to usher Cyrus into the White Room with as little commotion as possible. She's informed the Queen's Guard that no one should enter, not even under dire circumstances.

Delwynn included.

Cyrus sits across from her with his hands folded on the table. Although he seems to be bursting at the seams with information, he remains quiet. Suppose she'll have to goad it out of him.

"So you met with Arden in Orihia," she begins, sliding a teacup and saucer over to him. "And from there, you took her captive."

Cyrus shoots her a pointed glare. "I know it sounds bad, but my intentions were in the right place."

Cerylia can't help but shake her head. "He could have killed her." She doesn't have to say the king's name for him to gather who she's referring to. "And *you* would have had Eliri blood on your hands."

Cyrus doesn't refute the statement. Instead, he lowers his gaze. "There's something I haven't mentioned yet. Something Arden told me in Orihia."

She regards him with a solemn expression. "Go on."

His words come out rushed and frazzled. "Arden told me that she may have had contact with her father."

"When?"

It takes him a moment to think about this before he finally answers, "Before she came here. To Sardoria."

A sharp intake of breath. "And she's with her brother now?"

"I can only assume based on the events in the healing ward the day Aldreda died. She disappeared in a flash of green light."

"With a Transporter," Cerylia agrees. "Well, knowing that she's with her brother provides some consolation."

"I'm sorry it's taken this long for me to bring this to you." The earnest look in his eyes is genuine. "I'm afraid we're running out of time."

"The Mallum," Cerylia murmurs.

"Thousands of illusié abilities have already been

taken, as evidenced by the thousands of bodies stockpiled underneath Trendalath castle."

"Any word on Volkharn, on the jaded spring?"

Cyrus shakes his head. "I've been with him on multiple trips, but I still don't know what he does there. I've attempted to follow him, but I can't get close enough to see anything. Not without that damn staff."

His words snag on something in her mind. "Of course! How did I not think of this before?" She reaches into the inner breast pocket of her cloak and sets the circular object between them.

"Where did you—?"

Cerylia waves a hand dismissively in the air. "Never mind that. Do you think we can use it?"

It takes a moment for Cyrus to catch on to her train of thought. "You mean, plant this on his staff?"

"What better way to see for ourselves?" She taps the edge with her finger so that it rolls over to him. "Do you think we can sequence it?"

He picks the object up to examine it further. "It may take some work," he says, rotating it between his fingers, "but I don't see why not."

BRAXTON HORNSBY

PANTING, BRAXTON PULLS the covers over his unconscious friend. By some miracle, he'd made it through Trendalath and up to his chambers without anyone questioning, or even *noticing*, that he had one of the Cruex members thrown over his shoulder like a sack of potatoes.

Ah, the privileges of being royalty.

He lays two fingers on Hugh's neck to confirm there's still a pulse. All good there. Now he just has to wait for him to wake the hell up.

Braxton lets out a sigh before falling into a nearby chair. The events in the dungeons whirl in his mind.

We set Clive free.

The reality hits him like a ton of bricks.

Arden had refused to heal his mother, over and over again. But, eventually, she'd agreed. Had she lied simply to stop the torture from the Savant? Or had she actually had a change of heart?

While Arden's motives are still unclear, Darius's have never been clearer. Both he and Hugh had witnessed the cold-blooded murder of Elias at the king's hands. No mercy had been shown. Not even a flicker of remorse as the body had dropped to the ground.

A shiver snakes its way down his spine. He turns his head to look at Hugh. He may be calm and asleep now, but when he wakes . . . there'll be hell to pay. And for good reason. But if they reveal their hand too soon? The punishment for freeing a prisoner is death by execution, and Braxton's already seen enough of that. They cannot let Elias's death be in vain—which means they'll have to play the king's game, as difficult and as heart-wrenching as it may be.

Consumed by his thoughts, he nearly jumps at the knock on the door.

"It's me. I've brought food."

Braxton sighs with relief at the familiar voice. He looks to Hugh and decides to pull the blankets up even further so that they're fully covering his head. He scurries across the room and opens the door, gesturing for Lane to come in.

She's holding a tray of potato hash, pork, what looks like roast beef, and some grapes. She gives him a sly smile. "I wasn't sure what you wanted, so I grabbed a little bit of everything." Pink blossoms beneath her dark cheeks. "I hope that's okay."

"More than okay," Braxton says, leading her to the chair that *isn't* facing the bed. "And thank you. I'm famished."

She sets the tray down, seeming to notice his hurried actions, then takes a seat. "Is this a bad time? You seem a bit preoccupied."

Because my father killed one of the Cruex and may have killed my mother, too? Nah, not preoccupied at all.

If only it were that easy.

Not knowing *what* to say, Braxton extends one of the pork legs to her. "Hungry?"

She narrows her eyes. "No, thank you. I just came from the mess hall. That's why I've brought you . . . food."

As if on cue to have the worst timing in the world, Hugh stirs in the bed, letting out a soft groan. Braxton drops the pork leg so that it clatters onto the tray, then coughs, hoping it'll cover the sound.

Much to his surprise, Lane doesn't turn around. She keeps her eyes fixed on him. "You're acting strange."

Out of his periphery, he can see the blankets begin to move. *Hugh's starting to wake.* Which means he needs to get Lane out of this room as quickly as possible. "You know, it's just pre-conversation jitters. My father will be arriving at any moment to talk more about"—he lowers his voice—"well, my late mother."

The longer she stares at him, the more he can feel the lie rotting on his tongue. There isn't a single flicker of emotion on her face. Finally, she says, "You know, I came here because I wanted to talk. I thought we'd become friends. But whatever this *lie* is"—she waves her palm at him in a circular motion—"doesn't even come close to that."

Braxton's throat tightens as she hastily brushes by him and makes for the door. "Lane," he says, trying to find the right words, but she's already halfway out the door when she finally acknowledges him.

"You know, you should really reconsider where your loyalty lies. It might be worth having a friend or two in the Cruex." She shrugs her shoulders. "Maybe you really are more of a prince than you thought."

If only for a moment, he meets her raw, aching stare. It's only after she's closed the door that he hangs his head in quiet resignation.

DARIUS TYMOND

DARIUS IS STANDING at the end of the hall when he sees the only female Cruex member, Lady Devall, leaving Braxton's room. Based on the way she storms away from the door and down the corridor, he assumes that the conversation hadn't gone quite as she'd hoped.

Her footsteps trail off and, just like before, he finds himself alone once again. He debates whether or not to visit Braxton, taking a step forward, only to retreat and move back again. It may not be an ideal time to speak with his son, but when is it ever? And when has a foul mood ever kept him from carrying on with his plans?

He moves along the corridor with such stealth that not even his footsteps echo. He's just steps away from Braxton's chambers when a familiar feeling overtakes him. While he's only felt it a few times, it's undoubtedly the work of a Caster—but that's impossible because the only Caster for miles is locked up. In his dungeons. Right beneath his very feet.

His stomach twists into knots as the floor beneath him suddenly turns to dirt and grass, the hall now a vast thicket of greenery. Above, nothing but blue skies dotted with clouds. Based on the size and number of trees, he determines that he's standing at the edge of the Roviel Woods—but it's not present day. No, this is the *past*.

He turns around, knowing exactly what to expect, exactly what memory's being casted around him. His gaze lands on a stunning woman at the far end of the path. Her head is down, russet waves cascading over her shoulders, and looped in her arms is a wicker basket. She moves gracefully along the dirt path, only straying from it to pick from a variety of wildflowers. As if she can sense him watching her, the woman suddenly straightens, her emerald eyes traveling to the very spot in which the king stands. They pierce right through his very soul.

Although she's far away, he extends an arm out, reaching, reaching, reaching. When he attempts to step forward, he finds that he's rooted in place.

"I've brought you another basket."

She breaks her gaze, turning behind her.

Darius follows the voice, his anger sharpening like a blade when he sees who's once again trying to take his place. "I said that," he whispers to himself. "This is *my* memory."

And yet the woman, with the most heartwarming smile, takes the basket from none other than Clive Ridley.

"Thank you," she says, holding up the other one for him to see. "Aren't they just marvelous?"

Clive swipes a purple flower from the basket, plucks the head from its stem, and gently places it behind her ear. "Lady Eliri, you have never looked more stunning than you do in this very moment."

She blushes before dipping into a small curtsy. "That is very kind of you."

"Shall we?" Clive extends his arm, to which she swiftly loops her own in his.

Blood boiling, Darius attempts to take another step forward, but his feet remain rooted. "This is my memory!" he shouts after them, hoping the disturbance will be enough to shake free from the illusion. It only adds to his helplessness as he watches the pair walk merrily into Trendalath castle.

Arms pinned at his sides, fists clenched, Darius shouts into the ethers. "When I find you, I *will* kill you!"

An ominous laugh surrounds him as the once vivid landscape fades from view. "There's a price to pay for every choice we make. You chose power. If you ever hope to win this war you've waged, you cannot kill me. You and I both know that you *need* me."

Darius opens his mouth to respond, but Clive isn't finished talking.

"So what'll it be? Would you really choose vengeance over your precious memories?" He clicks his tongue against the roof of his mouth. "How many times can you possibly fail the ones you love?"

Clive's always known just how far to plunge the knife and how to keep twisting it. What's worse is that he's right. His memories are all that remain.

Darius bows his head in his defeat. "I'm not sure how you managed to pull this off from the confines of your cell, but release me and I shall release you. You have my word."

"Oh, but my *King*," Clive sneers, his voice fading into oblivion, "I'm already long gone."

ARDEN ELIRI

I DON'T KNOW how long we've been walking for, but given the current state of my legs, I'm guessing it's been a while. My mind reels with images of Juniper, making it hard to focus on the blurry figure in front of me. I don't know why we haven't turned back. I don't know why we haven't given up yet.

My absentminded state causes me to run straight into Haskell. "Sorry," I mumble as he turns to face me.

He glances over his shoulder at the long stretch of trail ahead of us before meeting my gaze. "I know you're upset about Juniper—"

"Upset is a severe understatement," I interrupt. "I'm

completely distraught. I can't focus on anything. And I have no idea why we haven't just turned back by now." I don't realize it until I stop talking, but I'm crying.

Full-fledged sobbing, actually.

Haskell wraps me in his arms, holding me tight. I bury my head in his chest and continue to cry. I can feel the steady beat of his heart as he rests his chin on my head. I pull away from him, leaving multiple tear stains on his leather coat. "I just want to go home."

He gently grabs me by the shoulders. "Arden, listen to me. We may not have found what we were looking for, but you can't lose hope. We'll figure this out. We'll find the spring and get your abilities back."

My throat catches. "I'm not concerned about that right now. What we need to do is go to Chialka."

His eyes soften. Much to my surprise, he nods, then pulls me in for another hug. "Just say when."

I squeeze my eyes shut, preparing for the transport. "Now."

❧   ❧   ❧

Chialka is just how I remember it. The Yoshino cherry tree towers over us as we walk along the pier. "Do you remember which house they went to?"

"Didn't make it that far," Haskell says. "I dropped them off away from the docks, then left shortly after."

"After you tossed Rydan your pocket watch."

"You seem to be quite hung up on that detail "

Because I am. When I'd first found out, I'd been downright furious—but now I'm just hurt that Rydan didn't care enough to come find me. To tell me that I have a *brother.*

A living relative.

"Perhaps we can ask someone if they know Vira. This is her hometown after all. I'm sure one of the townspeople would be able to point us to her childhood home." Haskell doesn't seem to notice that I've stopped walking. He turns over his shoulder. "Arden?"

But my gaze is fixed on the harbor—one port in particular, actually—and the lack of a docked ship. I rush past Haskell, flying down the rickety wooden steps, until I reach the pier adjacent to where *The Corsair* should be docked. "Excuse me!" I shout, hoping that someone with useful information is aboard.

A stout man with plump cheeks and a receding hairline appears at the stern. "Who's causing all that racket?"

"Excuse me," I say again, waving one of my arms in the air so he can see me. "Can you tell me when *The Corsair* last left port?"

The man scratches his head. "Are you a friend of the Bancrofts?"

"Yes," I lie—although, technically, Avery and I *had* gotten off on the right foot . . . until the Mallum had shown up and ruined everything. "Avery was supposed to return this morning, but there's been no sign of him." I figure name-dropping will help make my story more believable. It seems to work.

"He's been gone for at least a week, maybe more."

I can't explain it, but something tells me that Rydan and Vira had gotten on that ship. I try to think of a clever way to get more information. "There's been terrible weather in Athia," I start, hoping he'll correct me if I'm wrong. "I worry that perhaps he's crashed or worse, been thrown overboard."

The man narrows his eyes. "Athia? I think you mean Lonia." He looks me up and down before processing his thoughts out loud. "Odd though, seeing as he'd just come back from dropping off a shipment. Short turnaround time, if you ask me." He shakes his head. "Had some passengers onboard. Two, I think."

Definitely Rydan and Vira. "You wouldn't happen to be heading that way, would you?"

The man's about to answer when Haskell finally catches up to me. I throw him a stern look, hoping he'll get the hint to keep quiet and stay in the background until I'm done.

"And who's this?" the man asks.

"My brother," I say flippantly. "So, are you heading that way?"

"To Lonia? It's the only place I sail to."

My heart rises in my chest.

"But I've just returned today. Won't be heading that way again until the day after tomorrow."

This news weighs it back down. "Is there any chance you might be willing to make an exception?"

He hobbles onto the deck, using the rails for support. The way he carries himself reminds me a lot of Delwynn before I'd . . . I don't allow my mind to wander any further than that.

"I'm sorry to say that I can't make an exception. Not this time. I've got appointments with the merchants, and they've been patiently waiting on their supplies. It'd be a waste of a trip—"

"What if we pay you?" I interrupt. "Make it worth your while?"

He seems intrigued enough to consider this, but then shakes his head. "Mine's the only ship running to Lonia for the time being—well, until Avery returns. You must understand, I have a duty to the people of Chialka and Lonia. They're depending on these supplies."

I'm tempted to ask *what* supplies exactly, thinking that perhaps Haskell can transport and fetch some, when he unexpectedly emerges from the shadows and pulls on my arm. "Thank you for your time, sir. We're sorry to have bothered you."

I open my mouth to protest, but he's pulling me back up the steps so quickly that I don't get the chance. We reach the top of the docks and I'm about to let him have it when I notice the peculiar look on his face. "Why did you pull me away? I almost had our trip to Lonia arranged."

"Are you sure about that? Because from what I just heard, that man isn't leaving Chialka again for another two days."

I clench my jaw, doing everything I can to suppress the urge to smack him. "What would you suggest then?"

His eyes shift from my face to just over my shoulder. Even though I'm almost certain I won't like what I'm about to see, I turn around, following his gaze. Way off in the distance, I can see a small speck moving about in the water, thrashing against the most marginal of waves. With a firm shake of my head, I say, "Absolutely not. We are not taking a *rowing boat* to Lonia. Do you even know how long that would take?"

"Are you saying you'd rather just sit here and wait for two days?"

"No." I find myself at a loss for words. Honestly, I don't know what to do—but I *do* know that we're not taking a damn rowing boat across the Great Ocean. "There has to be another option. We can find a different ship."

"You heard the man," Haskell counters. "His is the only ship sailing to Lonia besides *The Corsair*."

"Be that as it may, I happen to be very persuasive."

"And if that doesn't work?"

I shrug. "We can always steal one."

"Arden Eliri," Haskell says under his breath. "We are not, under any circumstances, *stealing* a ship. Especially when there's a perfectly reasonable option staring us in the face."

I stifle a laugh. "I take it you've never sailed the Great Ocean before, have you?"

"Well, no. But—"

"Well I have. *Twice* . . . " As soon as the words leave my mouth, an idea comes to me. I fling my knapsack off of my shoulders, rummaging through it like I won't live to see tomorrow.

"What are you doing?" Haskell asks, the alarm apparent in his voice.

I don't respond as I continue pulling things from my bag. Finally, at the very bottom, my fingers graze what I've been searching for. I retrieve the small wooden ship, then hold it out in front of me.

"I don't get it," Haskell says. "What is that?"

"I know how we'll get to Lonia," I say, my breath catching in my throat, "but you'll need to go get our captain first."

ARDEN ELIRI

HASKELL BETTER RETURN soon before the townspeople start to get suspicious—but it might be too late for that. I'm sitting in a local Chialka tavern, downing what's probably my third or fourth glass of ale.

Seems I've lost count.

Sure, it'd been my idea for Haskell to return up north to get Felix and bring him to Chialka, but that doesn't necessarily mean I'm ready to face him again. In light of what's happened with Juniper, the thought of facing Felix *and* Rydan within such a short span of time is enough to make my heart palpitate. I have no idea what I'll say to either of them—what they'll say to me—

although there's *a lot* that needs to be said from both sides.

At first, I hadn't wanted to involve Felix in this. As much as I miss seeing him and being around him, I never wanted to intervene in his alleged plans to retrieve the ring from Trendalath. I'm not even sure if he knows that *I* know that he's spoken with Cerylia about it. Seems we'll have *plenty* to talk about.

My thoughts scatter as the barkeep sets another frothy beverage in front of me, and it's then I realize just how inebriated I am. I don't want Haskell to see me like this—certainly not Felix. I tap on the edge of the bar, waiting for the woman who served me to finish her conversation with one of the patrons. She eyes me warily as she approaches. "Afraid I can't give you another."

I look down at the full mug. When I lift my gaze, she's already turning away. "That's not what I was going to ask," I say as I reach out and gently grab her by the arm. She shrugs off my grip, but doesn't stray. "I wanted to see if you had an open room in the back—somewhere I could sleep this off."

She looks me up and down, twisting a rag between her hands. She throws it over her shoulder and leans over, motioning for me to come closer. "I do, but I don't normally rent it out—not even for a brief nap."

"Please," I say. "I'm expecting my brother and his friend to arrive sometime this evening. I can't let them see me like this."

She seems to consider my request. "Older brother?"

I nod fervently.

"I understand how that goes." She angles her head toward the other end of the bar where a spritely man is organizing a variety of goblets and mugs. "He gets on my case more than I care to admit."

I smile, hoping that this commonality between us is enough for her to oblige my request.

"How much coin do you have on you?"

"Only enough to pay for these drinks." When she frowns, I quickly add, "My brother didn't leave me much."

She laughs. "Been there before." She steals a glance down the bar to make sure her brother is preoccupied before scurrying to the end nearest us. "Leave your drink and follow me."

I nod, repeating my thanks over and over again, as I slide off the chair and follow her to a discreet door in the very back of the tavern. She ushers me inside, checking one last time to ensure no one saw us before closing it. A narrow cot sits at the back of the room; next to it, a nightstand with a lone lantern, and adjacent to that, a rocking chair. But that's it—there's no other furniture in sight, save for a woven rug.

"It's not much, but the wood is thicker than it looks. Creates a decent sound barrier. You should hardly hear a thing."

"It's great, thank you. What do I owe you?" I begin to

dig through my pockets, only stopping when she raises a hand.

"We'll settle up once your brother gets here."

I give her an appreciative smile.

"Speaking of which, who should I be keeping an eye out for? What does your brother look like?"

I stumble over to the bed, shaking off my boots along the way. "He's tall with dark hair. Has a beard. Same eye color as me."

"His name?"

"Haskell."

"You said he'll most likely be with a friend?"

My heart climbs into my throat as Felix's face floats across my mind. Words escape me, so I just nod.

"Care to give a description of him? Or his name?"

"Felix," I say, just above a whisper. I know I should give her more than that to go off of—and there's certainly no shortage of images of Felix in my mind—but the thought of seeing him again, *in person*, is too much for me to process at the moment.

"Haskell and Felix," she repeats, making for the door.

"If you could wake me first?" I say, hoping I'm not asking too much.

To my delight, she nods.

I'm about to get settled in when I realize something. "I didn't catch your name." Even in my hazy state, I can't help but notice her wavy copper hair, her angular jaw, her jade-colored eyes. She bears a striking resemblance to someone I've met before, but I can't place whom. Terror coils in my stomach at the lupine smile that slowly spreads across her face.

"Sleep well, Arden."

ARDEN ELIRI

THE DOOR SHUTS and I'm surrounded by darkness. An overwhelming memory pays me a visit, taking me back to a place I never want to see again. The Daegrum Chambers. The man in the forest-green mask. Wiry copper hair. Olive-colored eyes. The man who'd appeared with my father in the Roviel Woods. I squeeze my eyes shut, not wanting to relive any of it.

There's no doubt in my mind that the woman I'd just met—the woman who'd led me to this very room—is related to him. The resemblance is uncanny.

She hadn't bothered to light the lantern next to my bed (probably for good reason) and there are no windows in here either, making it so that my surroundings are pitch black. I didn't hear her secure the door when she left, but I'm guessing that it's probably locked. Even so, I know I need to find my way over to it, to at least try.

There's got to be a way out of here.

I slide my hands along the edge of the sheets until I reach the end of the bed. My fingers graze the nightstand. I slowly make my way around the small room, my inebriated state not helping any. When I finally reach the door handle, I turn it for good measure and, as expected, it's locked. I lower myself onto my knees before sprawling out flat on my stomach. There's a gap between the bottom of the door and the floor, but it's so narrow—and the tavern's so dark—that I can't see a damn thing.

I use the door handle to pull myself back up, pressing my ear against the door, hoping that perhaps I'll hear Haskell's voice . . . or Felix's. My spirits lift slightly, until I recall what the woman had said about the walls serving as a sound barrier. Even though I can't physically see them, it feels as if the walls are closing in.

Suffocating me.

A chill sweeps across my neck.

I'm not alone.

I whirl around in the darkness, feeling the Mallum's presence crawling across my skin, the backs of my eyelids, my throat. I attempt to summon the courage I'd felt in the abyss of the Vaekith Mountains, but that time has passed. I *am* afraid. Not so much about what the

Mallum could do to me—it's already taken my abilities—but what it could do to Haskell. To Felix. To the rest of the Caldari.

I can hear my bones rattling with each step I take. Even through my fear, two questions spring to mind. *Why is it the Mallum continues to return only to leave me whole in its wake? Why hasn't it taken my life?*

I don't have time to ponder this further as I back into something eerily familiar. The tips of my fingers graze a ragged cloak, and just as I'm leaning forward to get away, it does something unfathomable.

It wraps its arms around me.

I remain still. For a moment, I consider that perhaps it *isn't* the Mallum. The thought alone makes me want to run, but where would I go? I'm stuck, forced to succumb to the will of whatever has its hold on me.

Arden.

Merely a whisper, but I hear it loud and clear.

Arden.

It's not hurting me. I'm not being attacked. And yet I want to scream at the top of my lungs for someone to come help me. At this point, *not* knowing what's currently in the room with me is worse than knowing.

Arden.

The voice is soft. Gentle. Reminiscent of a woman's.

I bite the inside of my cheek, trying to keep the words locked inside my mouth but, as they always do, they find a way to escape. "You've finally got me right where you want me. Whatever it is you're here to do, just get it over with already."

A hiss and then a snarl. *You didn't kill Aldreda.*

"But I did. I tried to heal her and I failed. Just like I failed Braxton. And Delwynn—"

It was Darius.

I'm certain I've misheard. I think back to my days in the Cruex. The way Darius always catered to Aldreda, how he adored her, how he spoiled her with gifts . . . but then there were the squabbles. The times Aldreda would lock herself on the other side of the castle and not show her face for days. The many affairs . . .

My mind flashes to the healing ward in Trendalath.

Clive mourning the loss of Aldreda—and their baby.

The rage on Darius's face.

"Then why did he ask me to heal her?"

To take what does not belong to him.

Before I can get any sort of clarification, light suddenly floods the room. I shield my eyes as the door flies open, two shadowed figures standing in the entryway. I look behind me, around me—trying to see the entity I'd just been in contact with—when I'm taken by each of my arms. I begin to cough as smoke fills the room, quickly coming to the realization that the tavern is on fire. I turn my head to the left to see my brother. To my right . . . Felix. My heart nearly leaps out of my chest at the sight of him, but I notice he's not looking at me. He's staring straight at my brother.

"Both of you, close your eyes," Haskell commands through labored breaths. "Now."

After being enveloped in darkness, I don't want to go back. I want to stay right here, with my gaze fixed on Felix. As if on cue, he directs those deep russet eyes at me. "Close your eyes, Arden."

I wince as one of the beams just outside the doorway collapses to the ground, leaving only ash in its wake. "I didn't kill Aldreda," I whisper so that only he can hear.

"I know." He takes his free hand and sets it gently against my cheek. "Now close your eyes. I promise I'll be here when you open them again."

I do as he says, a single tear sliding down my cheek.

"Three, two, one . . . "

My world turns upside down.

RYDAN HELSTROM

IT'S BEEN DAYS since Xerin had arrived and disappeared, along with the crest. Rydan's suppressed the urge to share this information because not even *he* knows what to make of it. Keeping it from Vira has weighed heavily on his conscience. Since he can't prove that Xerin took it—or that it even existed in the first place, save for the rough sketch he's just made in his journal—he's at a loss. Not only is he keeping things from Vira, he's also doing the same to Arden.

When she finds out she has a brother . . .

He doesn't allow himself to explore the thought further. Leaning against the trunk of a tree, he points his gaze at the sky, watching as the sun takes the last leg of its descent. Almost immediately, the sky's blend of fuchsia and magenta fades into a light gray with a tinge of blue, and finally into a deep blanket of navy.

He doesn't know quite how long he stands there, staring into the vast nothingness—but his attention is diverted as voices echo from the far end of Orihia. Alarmed, he rushes back to camp, knowing that Vira and Avery may very well have drifted off by now. As he draws closer to the glow of the fire, he realizes that they're both still wide awake.

"Do you hear that?" he asks, swiftly moving to stand next to Vira's side.

She nods, pointing straight ahead. "It's coming from over there, I think."

"Maybe you two should head inside," Rydan says, the voices growing louder. "I'll handle this."

"No need to be concerned," Avery says with a sweep of his hand. "If they were able to get into Orihia, then they're one of us."

He has a point.

Even so, as of this moment, he doesn't know *who's* approaching—they're strangers. Rydan gently guides Vira to stand behind him. Avery follows suit and moves closer to form a small blockade with his and Rydan's bodies.

The figures begin to come into view. They're both tall, although one is slightly taller than the other. The way he moves reminds him a lot of . . .

"Haskell," he whispers, just loud enough for Vira to hear. Rydan's eyes then dart to the figure on the right.

Felix.

But what's even more shocking is *who* they happen to be carrying. Rydan blinks, just to be sure.

It's none other than Arden Eliri.

ARDEN ELIRI

I AWAKEN FEELING submerged. In the midst of drowning. Unable to breathe. When my eyes finally open, I can feel ash-tainted liquid running down my face. I take a deep breath, gasping for air that somehow tastes both smoky and fresh at the same time.

Multiple figures tower over me, canteens of water in hand. It's only after I've sputtered and coughed a few times that my eyes begin to adjust. The first to come into view is Haskell. Then Felix. Then Avery . . . Vira . . .

And Rydan.

The sight of him makes me cough all over again.

My ears are still ringing as I try to recall what the

hell just happened and where the hell I am, but Avery's voice overtakes my own. "I'm telling you, this is *Opal*," he says, clearly still misinformed—which, to his credit, is completely my fault. I'd used Opal's name when I'd first met him and boarded *The Corsair*.

It's then I see Vira pull him aside, and the view above me opens up, albeit slightly. It's dark, but the light of the campfire is enough to tell me exactly where I am. There's no mistaking the distinguished foliage, the multicolored leaves, and the uniquely shaped trees. *I'm in Orihia.*

I circle back in my mind, trying to grab on to any available fragment I can. My chest tightens as the events from earlier come back in short bursts. The tavern. The Mallum. The fire. Haskell returning with . . .

I break from my thoughts, my focus shifting to Felix. He's shaking his head adamantly at my brother, clearly in an argument of some sort. I take a mental snapshot of every detail—every feature—of his perfectly angled face. The windswept auburn hair. The flecks of dirt and ash accompanying his deep-set almond-shaped eyes. The slight curve of his jaw, as if carrying a secret that only he knows.

Lords, I've missed him.

If only I had the strength to lift myself from the ground, I'd be pulling him into my arms and burrowing my face in his chest. I open my mouth to speak, but only more coughing comes out.

"If what you're saying is true," I hear Felix say, "then

there's no way she could possibly be here."

At first, what he's just said doesn't register. It's only when both he and Haskell realize I've stirred and are kneeling at my side that the weight of this truth fully sinks in. *I am in Orihia, right now, allegedly ability-less.*

There's only one way that's possible.

I look between the two of them, a small smile cracking along my ashen face. My voice may be weak, but there's no mistaking the hopefulness in my words. "I'm still illusié."

ACKNOWLEDGEMENTS

This series certainly hasn't come without its challenges. Writing a story with so many plotlines that are so intricately woven together (and from multiple POVs, no less) is new territory for me as a writer. That being said, it's been a joy to stretch myself and my creative side as I've worked to get to know each one of these characters on a deeper level. Thank you for sharing in that journey.

First and foremost, I'd like to thank Source, God, the Universe, the Divine. I call you by many names. I am so grateful for the soul whisper to *write* at such an early age. What a privilege and a gift it is to share my voice this way. Thank you, thank you, thank you.

To my parentals (lol)—Mom, Dad, Paul, Rachel—I am so blessed to have such a supportive family. Thank you for reading my words, showing up at my events, and loving me for exactly who I am.

To my sister, Erin, for always brightening my day, starting a book club with me during the pandemic, and holding space for my emotional and creative ramblings. I know I can be *a lot* at times. It's been neat to see how our love of books has deepened our relationship even further the older we get. I love you, sister-frand!

To Anna Vera, my Taurean soulsister starseed. I cannot even begin to imagine what this journey would look like without you! Thank you for being there when it felt like no one else was, for offering your heart, wisdom, and a listening ear when I needed it most and felt like no one could possibly understand. You've always understood, and I know you always will. Eternally grateful for you!

To Sammi Davidson, for being one of the most dependable, caring, and supportive people I've ever met. From Bali to Canmore to Banff to North Carolina, we've experienced a whole lot together! I'm so incredibly lucky to have someone like you in my life.

To Lisa Siefert, for always being a cheerleader and a sounding board. You champion the works and platforms of others so fiercely, and your dedication to your friendships does not go unnoticed. I am so proud to know you, and am blessed to call you a friend!

To the incredibly talented cartographer, Deven Rue, for bringing The Lands of Aeridon to life. Although the map was completed a few years ago, it's one of my most prized possessions and has a special place on my shelf. Looking at it every day certainly helps keep the magic alive when my creative well is zapped. Thank you!

To my cover designers over at Damonza. You guys rock. I'm so honored to work with you and can't tell you enough how pleased I am with every single one of my book covers. Your talent, professionalism, and overall awesomeness is truly appreciated!

To my furbabies—I know you can't read this, but thank you for always intervening at just the right time. Whenever I need to take a break and won't seem to grant myself one, your sweet, happy faces remind me to be present and close the dang laptop for once!

To Jonathon, for understanding my soul on a level that I'm not sure anyone else can. Life works in such mysterious ways and I'm honored to be such an integral part of your journey, and you mine. Thank you for being a reminder to choose play over work, spontaneity over security, and forgiveness and love above all.

To my clients and Soulflow Collective sisters—I didn't know it was possible to feel so close to people I've only ever met online. The tight-knit community we've built is something I will never take for granted. It is one of the greatest joys of my life. I truly mean that. Thank you for always lifting me up. I love you all!

And finally, to my readers and Instagram/YouTube fam—what a time it is to be alive. It dawns on me every day that we're all over the globe and somehow still able to connect. That is WILD. This journey certainly isn't easy, but I wouldn't trade it for anything. Thank you for supporting my work, watching my videos, reading my books, listening to my podcast… Please know that each of you makes my day that much brighter. It is an absolute privilege and an honor to do this alongside you. #KMCommunity is where it's at!

Don't miss the fourth installment in
the *Shadow Crown* series:

CRESCENT

FIRE

TURN THE PAGE FOR A SNEAK
PEEK OF CHAPTER ONE

COMING 2021

ARDEN ELIRI

FAMILIAR VOICES CARRY from just outside my window. I groan, my head still throbbing from the aftereffects of the tavern fire, then throw the blankets over my legs. A cough climbs up my throat just as my eyes are adjusting to the room, my attention shifting between the door and the rustling curtains. I take a shaky breath, hoping to push it down, but the effort is futile. Even though my breathing is shallow, and I feel the worst I've ever felt, I can't help but crack a smile. I'd be lying if I said I wasn't happy to be back here, in Orihia. I just wish it were under different circumstances . . .

From what I can remember—which is hazy, at best— Haskell had returned to the tavern with Felix in the nick of time. A moment longer and it would have been too late.

After the incident there—with the Savant, with the Mallum—I'd fallen unconscious in the fire. But, thanks to the two of them, we'd transported out of there before any real harm could be done. I don't remember much after that. The last thing I recall is seeing Felix's face again for the first time in months . . . and somehow ending up in Orihia even though I can no longer access my healing abilities.

Oh, and seeing Rydan.

A spike of rage hits me right in the stomach, but before it can settle for good, a knock sounds at my door.

"Arden?"

I breathe a sigh of relief at the familiar voice. "You can come in—" Before I can finish my sentence, Felix comes into view.

"Morning," he says with a grin.

The sound of his voice sends a shiver down my spine—the good kind. "Did I oversleep again?"

"I was just about to wake you." He takes a seat in one of the armchairs before angling his head toward the window to indicate the time. "How'd you sleep?"

I shrug before lowering my gaze, hoping he won't see right through my lie. "Better than the night before, I suppose."

The truth of the matter is I've hardly slept since my last encounter with the Mallum. Everyone here—Rydan, Vira, Avery, Haskell, Felix . . . they're all convinced that my abilities were never absorbed because if they *were*, my being here, in Orihia, wouldn't be possible. Only illusié are capable of seeing and entering this place.

While the argument is convincing, it still doesn't explain why, despite my best efforts, I can't seem to heal anything or anyone I come into contact with. The whole thing has kept me up for days. I'm certain it's starting to show—and if it's not, it will soon enough.

"Vira's made us all breakfast."

I break from my thoughts, giving him an appreciative smile. "Afraid I don't have much of an appetite, but maybe later."

He sits still for a moment, studying me, then rises from the armchair and makes his way to the bed. Without meaning to, I pull at the blankets until they meet my chin. Gently, he picks Juniper up and sets her on the ground before sitting in her place. For that alone, I owe him a debt I can never repay.

Haskell and I had left Juniper in the Vaekith Mountains after . . . well, after *I-don't-know-what* got to her. Haskell had transported Felix back to that lords-forsaken pit and from what they'd told me, Felix had somehow been able to use his amplification abilities to round up Juniper and bring her back without any issues. Upon their return to Orihia, we've all been keeping a close eye on her. She's been acting completely normal . . . or so we've observed.

Flecked with bits of red, Felix's russet eyes blaze like hot coals as they settle on mine. I loosen my grip on the blanket, letting it fall past my chin and shoulders. A small smile tugs at the corner of his mouth as his attention shifts to my bedside table. I follow his gaze.

"Nice to see you kept it," he says, referring to the

wooden carving he'd given me.

I'm reminded then of what I'd seen at the spring—the interaction between him and Cerylia, played out right before me as if I'd been in the White Room myself. I want to ask him about it, but with the way he's looking at me, I can't seem to find the words.

"You know," he says, his voice just above a whisper, "I wasn't sure I'd see you again after everything that happened in Trendalath. When I learned of Aldreda's death, I was certain Darius had sentenced you to . . . " He falters, unable to finish the thought.

"Don't," I whisper. I reach for his hand, lacing my fingers with his. "It's in the past. Let's leave it there."

A muscle feathers in his cheek. "Not for me it isn't."

I blatantly search his eyes for his meaning but come up short. My throat tightens. "Felix," I plead, "you know I didn't do it, right? I was trying to heal her." I can feel the weight of my words before I speak them. "I didn't kill her."

"I know." I wait for him to say more, but with the way he's looking at me, he doesn't need to. It's the same look he gave me after our first dreadful encounter in the Thering Forest—what he was able to sense in me that no one else could.

My darkness.

My shadows.

His grip on my hand tightens before he pulls away.

"Felix," I croak, sheer desperation in my voice, "you can trust me. All I ask is that you let me in on whatever's going on. I might be able to help."

There's an edge to his tone as he says, "Even if you could, it wouldn't change anything."

I try to process the words but before I know it, he's standing by the door with his back facing me, ready to leave. I want so badly to get up, to close the distance between us, but my legs won't budge.

The silence that lingers between us is deafening.

Finally, he turns over his shoulder. He stares at me, not a flicker of emotion on his face. "See you out there."

There's no opportunity to respond as the door swiftly opens and shuts behind him. I ball my hands into fists, fighting against the perfectly rational urge to bury myself in the heap of blankets surrounding me. Try as I might, I can't come to a logical explanation for his hot and cold behavior towards me. One minute, he's the Felix I *think* I know—the one I *want* to know; the next, he's cold, callous . . . a complete stranger.

Even so, I get the sense that he's not telling me something. Whether it's out of concern for me or something else entirely, I don't know—but if I don't get some answers soon, whatever *this* is will be forced to end.

Maybe it already has.

The thought almost has me spiraling even further when I suddenly sense a flash of movement from across the room. My eyes flick to the window where a shadow is lurking just outside.

My breath catches. I blink in the hopes that I'm just seeing things, but the shadow remains. I narrow my eyes, trying to discern who or what it is, but I'm too far away.

One at a time, I throw my legs over the bed, slowly rising until I'm steady on my feet. I take a step forward. The shadow doesn't move. I take another step, followed by another, and another, until I'm clear across the room.

Standing at the side of the window, I grab the edge of the curtain and take a deep breath. I count to three in my head before flinging it open, hoping to reveal the perpetrator. I'm simultaneously relieved and dismayed to find that it's only a tree.

Kristen Martin is the International Amazon Bestselling Indie Author of the YA science fiction trilogy, THE ALPHA DRIVE, the YA dark fantasy series, SHADOW CROWN, and personal development books, BE YOUR OWN #GOALS and SOULFLOW. A writing coach and creative entrepreneur, Kristen is also an avid YouTuber with hundreds of videos offering advice and inspiration for writers and creatives alike. She currently lives in North Houston, Texas.

STAY CONNECTED:
www.kristenmartinbooks.com
www.youtube.com/authorkristenmartinbooks
www.facebook.com/authorkristenmartin
Instagram @authorkristenmartin
www.thatsmarthustle.com